GRÜNWALD

BIG BEN BOOKS
800 S. VALLEJO
DENVER, CO 80223

GRÜNWALD

by

Stanley W. Zamonski

BIG BEN BOOKS
8008 VALLEJO
DENVER, CO 80221

This is only a small part of the immense GRÜNWALD painting by the master artist Jan Matejko. It was a symbol of unity for the Polish people in World War II; a rallying point for a united defiance of Hitler's invasion forces into Poland in 1939.

Its power over the people of Poland so infuriated Hitler, he offered a $750,000 reward to destroy the painting.

"GRÜNWALD" is the true story of the heroic efforts to save this painting. Never before told in its entirety, it is now a story never to be forgotten.

Library of Congress Card Catalog No. 81 - 52087

ISBN 0-937050-22-9

Typesetting and design consultant: Douglas Anderson.

Made in U.S.A.

DEDICATION

*To my mother, Linda
and to Billie and Barbara
whose encouragement and assistance
made this book possible.*

HISTORICAL NOTE

The hero of this documentary novel is the painting "The Battle of Grünwald." It may be of some help to the reader to know some of the historical facts. This story began at the end of the Crusades in the 12th Century and ended with the beginning of World War Two. This book is entirely a work of fact. Only the character description and dialogue are a product of the author's imagination.

On July 15th, 1410, on the broad fields between Grünwald and Tannenburg, Prussian Poland, two Christian forces opposed each other. There were many battles in those centuries, but never in Christian times did two armies fight each other so mightily and defeat so dreadfully. Before that day was over, the greatest knighthood of all Europe lay on the blood-stained field.

More than five hundred years later, "Grünwald" was the rallying cry that inspired the Poles to be the first to resist Nazi Germany. By the summer of 1939, Germany had already moved into the Rhineland, followed by the bloodless conquest of Austria and Czechoslovakia. Again, as did the Teutonic Knights, Germany threatened to take on the whole world. On the morning of September 1, 1939, the Nazis showed their true character. With a ferocity and barbarism unmatched in modern times, they advanced their brutal forces against Poland and World War Two opened.

1

This September day for Ceila Rozek was no ordinary day. It was the sixth day of the war and the streets of Warsaw smoldered after the horrible bombardment. A few men scurried along. She too hurried. So much to be done and so little time left.

She ran up the stairs and entered the Art Museum where she was employed and hurried along its corridors and vast exhibition rooms until she reached the main hall. She stopped in front of the partially suspended Grünwald painting. She watched the men lower the huge canvas from its place of honor on the longest wall in the building. The painting's size required the labor of six employees.

The priceless Jan Matejko painting had hung there for many years, but these last few months it had drawn a special interest. Ceila had passed this way many times and looked at the painting, but never with the intense concern with which she now stared at it.

The faces on the canvas, their fierce, piercing eyes -- the necromancy evoked a faint cry within her. So incredibly awesome, so genuine, so compelling was the battle that she could hear the cries of man and beast, the clashing armor, the clang of steel against steel.

And so it came about that day, July 15, 1410, that the greatest knighthood of all of Europe clashed on the fields of Grünwald -- only the bravest and the boldest; only the young and the proven in battle. Such a proud array of nobility, ability and servitude had never before gathered in the history of Christendom, not even in the recent Crusades.

Sixty thousand hearts beat like hammers when the trumpets hurled the steel-clad avalanche into the battle that vowed to crush everything before it. Even at its worst, nature could not be as devastating as this man-made holocaust with sixty thousand swords, spears and battleaxes flashing under the July sun. With every blow, helmets and breastplates burst like over-ripe melons. Men dropped from saddles and died before their bodies touched the ground.

Knight and beast rushed on, trampling ever closer until the entire conflict crowded Ceila. It was difficult to tell friend from enemy. She felt the bodies surge around her. She smelled the furor of war. Her ears began to hurt from the clamor. She tried to block it out. She turned from the swishing swords aimed at her head. She saw the glare in horses' eyes and the wild fixed eyes behind the nosepieces of the knights' helmets.

Above the sounds of that battle came the drone of aircraft engines. Then the whine of falling bombs, louder and louder. Then the combatants froze on the canvas. This was September 1939. The clang of ancient armor was gone. In its place sounds of modern aircraft, the shrill of falling bombs, explosions.

Ceila sucked in her breath, let out a scream.

"Ceila! Ceila!" a voice cried, reaching out to her. "Ceila, what is the matter?" That was Kordian's voice. He held her trembling body. His voice was gentle, his arms like granite. "Ceila, Ceila, what's wrong?" Kordian asked.

The din of falling bombs and explosions, shrill screams. Any instant the ground would open up and swallow her.

"Everybody, down the basement!"

It was a familiar voice. It came closer. "Everybody down the basement, hurry, hurry!"

She opened her eyes to find herself clinging desperately to Kordian, his broad face looming over her.

They stood breast to breast. Then she saw the familiar scenes of the museum. She looked up at Kordian, thinking he was about to kiss her. She broke from his grasp and stood back.

"Don't, don't," she murmured. "People could get ideas."

Kordian grinned, his eyes mocking her slightly. "What else should I do when you throw yourself at me?"

His intense black eyes swept over her, hesitating at certain points. She was the right age, twenty-five. He was thirty-two.

She pushed away from him. She should be angry.

"Don't take yourself seriously," she smiled. "I only work here, remember. I'm immune."

His face tightened, the dark brows arching downward as he reached out to her, "Don't be so harsh," he said, "people are apt to think we're arguing."

She didn't mind being put in her place. Her popularity had made her too assertive. It seemed so unfeminine, and she was glad when someone could tell her off.

3

He was so different. His male intensity had always attracted her. Now, for some reason, it frightened her a little. She did not pull back as he gripped her arm. "What scared you so . . . so . . . much you even threw yourself at me?" His teeth flashed a grin. "Here all the time I thought it was me." He inclined his head towards her. "Anything I could do to help you?" he asked, his eyes matching his tone.

He had the body of a prize fighter and sported a brown sweater pulled under his shirt collar – an excuse for not having to wear a tie. He wasn't exactly handsome. A perpetual suntan accentuated his maleness and the deep laugh lines around his dark eyes gave him an attraction that brought women to his arms.

She turned again to the Grünwald painting when Curator Bozinski stepped up. "Hurry! Hurry! Everybody down to the basement . . . What seems to be the difficulty here?" The curator smiled.

"God! I just had the scare of my life." Ceila looked at him wide eyed. "I just experienced the most frightening illusion that the painting suddenly came to life and I was caught in the middle of it all. Honestly, it was so horribly real, so positively hypnotic and frightening, I thought this was the end, when Kordian came to my rescue."

"If I hadn't just come along, she might have hurt herself."

"Who knows, she might have been hacked to pieces by those terrible Teutonic Knights." The curator laughed. The exploding bombs round them shook the building.

Curator Bozinski placed a comforting arm around Ceila and started to lead her away. "Come," he said, "We all had better start for the basement." He led her across the large exhibition hall, through the maze of corridors and down the stone stairway. Kordian followed and kept an eye out for stragglers.

4

As Ceila moved down the dark corridors of the basement she could not remove the image of the Grünwald painting from her mind. Strange that this priceless art work should undergo such a vicissitude. She was well aware of the history behind the painting, portraying the crushing defeat of the Teutonic Knights. She knew how much the painting was valued by the Poles in their victory.

She also knew that as popular as the Grünwald had been in Poland, it had the reverse effect on the Germans. Grünwald was associated with their worst humiliation. But even then it came as a total surprise when the Nazis invaded Poland and Hitler offered three quarters of a million dollars reward, plus other considerations, for the surrender of the painting. And so the weird and challenging circumstances of the painting ensued – the end of an honored place in the museum and the beginning of its flight for life.

Ceila moved quickly down the underground chambers, picking her way carefully in the poor light until she entered one of the small rooms.

It was cool and damp. There were others, old men, women and weeping children. She moved toward the dark corner. Once seated she leaned against the stone wall. A ray of dull gray light spirited through the high, small window. Her head bent low with weariness.

She closed her eyes. Her thoughts drifted to the world outside where a city burned and people died.

She sat there, thinking how atrocious and horrible war can be against unarmed and unprotected civilians. She bore traces of the ordeal. How could all this have happened so quickly, when only a few weeks before the world was at peace and one woke up with the morning sun amidst the splashing colors of summer's blossoms? Slowly, out of the not-so-distant past, she recalled these past few weeks.

It was mid-August and the world was at peace as the morning sun cast its warmth across the old Warsaw roof tops. It spilled through shadows of the cobbled streets, across flowered parkways and highlighted the historic marble statues and bronzes of mounted kings and heroes charging forever into a thousand years of battle. Graceful swans glowed even whiter under the sun of still another sultry day, for the summer of 1939 was hot, and the driest in years.

That morning Curator Bozinski saw her approaching even before he heard the steady click of her heels against the walkway. Under the arching lindens the curator was having his regular visit with the birds and squirrels. He watched her, enchanted with a graceful dancing shadow that transformed into a silver-edged female silhouette.

Curator Bozinski pried into everything around him as though it were his personal property. This included Ceila Rozek.

He had always been overwhelmed by her beauty − long, light-brown hair, sad eyes and deep voice. When she first came to work at the museum she seemed distant, but it was because she was shy and possessed by that quality of probity that marks a gentlewoman.

It puzzled him that a girl with her charm and intelligence hadn't married. A woman of twenty-five should have at least two, even five children. Though American born, she had that mystic quality of Polish women which, through the centuries, had captivated sophisticated French rulers and barbaric Eastern satraps.

He waved at her and she smiled. The light glittered in her dark eyes. So eager her smile, so glad her feet the closer she came with that strong and free stride of her long limbs. She was tanned, and wore a two-piece pale-blue suit. The white silk ruffled blouse showed above the jacket and made her clean skin even tawnier.

"Good morning. How are your little friends today?" She had long observed his ritual of feeding the birds which he called his own. They waited for him.

"Morning, morning, Ceila, my dear."

"Has your rheumatism eased any?"

"Bah – rheumatism – it's part of old age." He ran off into incoherent mumblings and reached out to kiss her hand. His voice grew vigorous as he asked, "And how is your love life these days?"

Curator Bozinski reminded Ceila of a white-haired lion. In his mid-sixties, trim and barrel-chested, standing a little less than five feet eight, he was a self-made man and an absolute male ruler with the women at home. He asked again. "How is your love life?"

"It all depends on my moods." She laughed with a slight toss of her head.

"Who would believe you work at it night and day?"

She walked away. "There's work to be done." She walked on with a light stride.

Ceila's small corner office was painted charcoal brown and simply furnished with a large desk, a corner table and two chairs. No carpeting covered the marble floor, and wear was beginning to show near the door. The room was not meant for comfort with its high ceilings. The far wall had a large window. A number of paintings were grouped about. A pile of periodicals lay on the table in the corner. In a prominent spot on her desk was a family photo taken in the States. Ceila gave the photo a whisk of her hand as if dusting off a fly, then looked at it almost

7

as though she were conversing with it. She was only five then. Each morning it would be a half hour before she got down to business, typing correspondence, scheduling and mailing program announcements, setting up interviews, arranging individual and traveling exhibits. She did her work as though she ran the museum. She derived a sense of acquisition and enrichment from her duties. An endless interest and pleasure stirred in the works of so many great artists.

She was finishing some correspondence when the mail arrived. She finished her typing then sorted out the mail and was preparing to leave for the curator's office when he appeared silently in the doorway.

"May I come in?" He walked up to her desk. "Busy?" This morning his face was strained and almost tragic.

"Just this." Ceila smiled and held up a handful of mail. "And some letters for you to sign."

"I'll save you a trip." He took the mail but immediately put it down again and reached for the pen. "While I'm here, I'll sign whatever you have ready and we'll be rid of the whole mess all at one time."

He never flaunted his authority. He left her duties very much to her own discretion.

"How is your mother?"

"Fine. She asked about you just the other day. Said something about dinner some day soon."

"And that fine American friend of yours?" He didn't bother to look up until he was finished signing the letters. "There isn't much I don't know about you."

So that's how Curator Bozinski knew about her American background and these last eleven years in Poland. And what else? she wondered. Certainly he had some conclusions about the American she had been dating. He always showed a particular interest in her love adventures.

He asked, "How is your American professor doing these days? He should be finishing at the university, shouldn't he?"

"He has another week. I'm sure he's glad it's almost over. He's been in Europe now for almost a year and a half. First Russia, then Czechoslovakia, and these last seven months in Poland."

"I'm sure you've made his visit a memorable one."

"It's been more than that. It's been pleasant and the best opportunity to practice my English. After all those years I'm surprised that I haven't forgotten the English language. Being born in America always makes me feel like a woman of two countries."

"The world's ever getting smaller and smaller, making any country your own wherever you might choose to live and work, especially whenever you can make it a better place. After all, it was the nations of the world that made America possible. Little wonder that the Americans feel proud to send their people to other countries to serve. Now for your American friend, how does he feel about leaving you?"

She replied, laughing, "At least he hasn't started packing yet."

"That's always a good sign." He clapped his hands and did a fast one-two step. "If – if I were only twenty years younger, I'd show you a time you'd never forget." He leaned forward. "Before I forget, you and your American friend are invited to dinner tonight. Remember Professor Woda? He's in town, and I'm having a little dinner party for him."

"Any particular time?"

"Around seven. Time for a drink or two before dinner."

Once again the curator's face took on that troubled look. "You know . . ." he hesitated as if seeking an answer to a difficult question. "You know, Poland is again in grave difficulty. It's not easy to forget when one considers the rivers of blood and tears that have been shed on her behalf."

The curator went on about Poland's struggle through the centuries, only to disappear from the map of Europe. Her fighting spirit during the First World War and her struggle for freedom after the war, when the rest of the world relaxed in peace. The curator had been part of that fight for freedom. He was part of Pilsudski's regime, but, disappointed in politics, he gave it up completely when appointed curator of the Warsaw Art Museum.

He began to pace the room. His hands grasped the lapel of his English-tailored tweed coat. Then, with a trembling hand, he removed his rimless glasses and fingered the red groove pinched into the heavy bridge of his nose. It had been broken long ago by the fist of a Russian interrogation officer.

His gray hair had receded so that his forehead looked much higher. The deep lines and pale color of his face gave him the look of a man who had worked too hard, worried too much and slept too little. Distinguished looking, he could have been taken for any one of a half-dozen European nationalities, but it was the command of a half dozen languages that captured the attention of others.

Presently he stopped and looked at her. "At my age I have seen too much of the world and wars that settle nothing. But if it comes, I'll be in there fighting."

"Don't be silly, you've gotten too old to fight." She said this in a voice that was calmer than her thoughts.

He watched her pick up the letters and rise to her feet. He nodded in agreement when she said, "I better get this to the mailbox before I miss the morning pickup."

He followed her out of the office, shaking his finger at her.

"Don't forget about tonight or my little woman would never let me live through the night."

He watched her walk down the hall then called after her, "Ha – and Ceila, should you run into Lolek, tell him I'm waiting. He should have been here by now."

Ceila glanced over her shoulder and nodded. "I'll tell him when I see him."

2

Ceila paused under the brilliant sun and glanced at the museum building situated in the midst of formal gardens with dancing fountains.

When she re-entered the building, Kordian was standing in front of the Grünwald painting.

She eased closer, inhaling deeply as she took in the painting.

The impression Kordian made was demanding, even in the dull light – solid figure standing with stocky legs apart, his arms folded across his chest and his fist clenched. Ceila caught a glimpse of the lines of distress across his face.

Kordian Axentowicz, judging from his demeanor, was very much the great artist he was reputed to be and lived up to his first name, a legend in itself. The name Kordian in a literary sense in Poland had come to stand for a type of character – Don Quixote

GRÜNWALD

or Don Juan in Spain and Hamlet in England.

Kordian was a hell-raising Bohemian who talked openly about himself.

"Hi." Ceila's greeting brightened his countenance. It got a bit tiresome doing all the talking himself, since the museum visitors seldom talked back. As part-time porter at the gallery, he supplemented his income and the experience proved invaluable.

"Ceila – the sunshine of my yearning life. You know, Pani Ceilisu, something will have to be done about Matejko's Grünwald. That damp draught from the windows is far worse for the canvas than a fire. Come, I'll show you."

She felt the impact of his presence as though he had pushed up against her. "Kordian," she sighed, her eyes meeting his. "Sometimes I think that you are as passionately fond of these paintings as if they were your very own."

"Yes," he replied. "Yes, and sometimes I feel even more about them than my own. He flung his right hand to signal at the vast collection, raising his bushy brows with rapture. "From ancient Greece and Rome, to Titian, Rembrandt, Rubens, Vermeer, Renoir and so many more. And let's not forget our Matejko."

They moved closer to the huge "Battle of Grünwald" canvas, viewing it silently. No matter how many times Ceila had looked at this painting, there was always that same strange feeling of solemn respect and fearful admiration. Completed in 1878, the painting had long been acknowledged as the greatest battle scene ever depicted on canvas.

Kordian broke the silence. "What we need is another Grünwald."

"Kordian! Hush!" Ceila's eyes grew wide with displeasure. "How could you talk like that?"

"But Ceila, if war does come, we will not sit back and do nothing while those Nazis march in as they did in Austria and Czechoslovakia." His voice grew vehement. "There isn't a man or woman in the country who doesn't feel that what the Germans need is another Grünwald to bring them back to their senses."

Every Pole was familiar with the war against the Teutonic knights. After nearly two hundred years of terror, the power of the German Order was defeated at the battle of Grünwald. This victory remained a symbol of eternal hope.

"Jan Matejko," Kordian began ominously. "His life full of paradoxes – half-blind, with barely an average education. As an artist he became the greatest recorder of our noble past. It's little wonder then that modern historians compare his character with that of Michelangelo in tragedy and Shakespeare in drama." He went on to remind her of the commemorative Grünwald postage stamp issued last spring in the attempt to alert the world to the Nazi menace. Hitler raised such a protest that the stamp had to be withdrawn from circulation.

When Kordian finished he stood silent before asking, "What do you think about all this?"

For weeks now she had noticed the large gatherings around the painting. There was no need for talk. People looked, and from their faces one could see that their hearts and minds were filled with renewed hope.

She shrugged. "I wish I knew how to advise you."

Staring into his deep-set eyes, Ceila felt as though she were being sucked into a whirlpool. "I think I better be getting back to work. I'll call you when I'm ready. We're working on the first definitive catalogue of the museum's collection."

Kordian asked, in an off-hand manner, "Why haven't you ever married?"

15

She replied, "Could be a number of reasons. Perhaps I'm still looking." She burst out laughing. "Maybe I'm waiting for that knight on the white charger. . . . Girls do hold fast to such silly old dreams, you know."

"I don't believe you," he said. "Aren't you afraid of ending up an old spinster?"

"Thank you so much. But at twenty-five? My dear Kordian, sometimes your thinking surprises me." She reached out and mussed his hair, turned and walked away.

Kordian watched her go. He had seen the women of most of Europe's capitals. But as for the women of Warsaw . . . they had a mysterious and indefinable quality. The changing shadows at dusk.

Ceila was clearly the odd link in her circle of friends and shared relationships. There were some awkward moments during her first few years in Poland. But the years passed quickly and the growing acquisition of friends earned her the affection of those from many parts of the country. These last six years she found most pleasant. She was too busy and too happy growing up to let her mind linger on a way of life long past. She had little time to dwell on childhood memories.

Her friends had been raised in the quest of intellect. Although they had amassed the customary attractions of lovers, husbands, children and even careers, they found in Ceila the odd link. She belonged to no one. They had found her dependable but devoid of great passion; she was an authority on clothes, good food, literature, and had a fair knowledge of sculpture, painting and music. She spoke five languages fluently.

Living with her mother and helping run their apartment house, the steady income allowed her greater freedom than most women. From her mother, who was part German, Ceila acquired not only a sense of business but the love of travel. She enjoyed visits to Italy and Spain with regular trips to France and Germany. Here her friends found her somewhat of an enigma, and they even showed some concern. For though they found her intelligent and sensuous, she was a woman with little thought for triumph and adulation, but of simple pleasure, possessing that mysterious feminine trait which only sought out the pleasant and the self-sufficient. She had had more proposals of marriage than she could remember. She loved the attention of men – sometimes a little unwisely. They were a little amiss that she did not tremble at the thought of scandal. Lately they were relieved at her prolonged relationship with the American. Never did they mention that he was Jewish.

Twenty minutes went by as she was filing some correspondence when Lolek Kossack stuck his head in the doorway. "Hi."

Ceila turned, showing her pleasure as she looked at the man in front of her. At thirty-two, Lolek was tall and handsome – blond wavy hair worn down his neck, thin faced, looking like most struggling artists. Even in the best of clothes he seemed in need of grooming. He wore a loose gray sweater over a pair of baggy corduroy slacks. Lolek's sloppy attire tantalized Ceila's imagination. Maybe he was a man who disdained trivia, as was evident in his impressionistic paintings.

There was a masculinity in the firmness of his chin, the full mouth and the singular repose in his deep blue eyes. There was something more Scandinavian than Slavic in his features. Lolek was already acknowledged as one of the most promising painters. Like Kordian, he was teaching morning art classes at the university and lately was hired by the museum to help catalog the vast collection.

"It might surprise you," she said and smiled, "that we have been waiting for you. The curator has had his hounds out on your trail since early this morning."

"Why me?" Lolek's nose wrinkled at Ceila's scent. "Something new, I bet, from that professor friend of yours." He waved. "See you later." He walked away.

When Ceila turned back to her desk it was almost noon. She reached the phone and dialed Victor's number.

"I've been waiting to hear from you. What's on the program for tonight? Not another farewell dinner?"

"That's just it. We're invited to a dinner party."

"Anybody I know?"

"Yes, the curator and some friends from the museum. He's hosting an old friend from Lublin. And in a way the curator doesn't think he'll be seeing much of you anymore."

"What is all that supposed to mean?" he asked.

"With school out and you contemplating deserting us."

"Who's deserting whom?"

"People have been shot for less than desertion, you know," she said. "You can always find some excuse to prolong your stay."

"Well, if it will make you feel any better, I've thought already on the matter."

"Wonderful!"

3

Early that evening, Victor took a *dorozka* and started for Ceila's place. Victor Zabel had put on some weight since his arrival in Warsaw. He had impressive shoulders and a classically rugged head with clean features and thick, black, wavy hair. At twenty-seven he was rather young for a professor in political science. He specialized in Eastern Europe and was part of a teacher-exchange program.

He became lost in thoughts about Ceila. He had been seeing her these last five months and was growing restive and disturbed. Could he have misjudged their affair, thinking it was as ordinary as those he had before? It started as just another romance, then became enriched with the European flare for mystery until gradually it became as quicksand, ready to engulf him. Victor sensed that Ceila found herself as deeply enamored as he was, and he wondered about the wisdom of prolonging his visit. His conscience had awakened as the date for his departure drew closer.

He had reason to worry. He had always been able to free himself of any romance. But all seemed different now. With Ceila, what had begun as merely luke-warm passion now was necessary to him. Being near her was like a revelation, mysteriously beautiful and placidly memorable.

Fortunately these last few days had been rather busy. He laughed off the rumors of war with the remark that he'd leave just as soon as the diplomatic corps itself should see fit to leave. Life these last few weeks had been a round of luncheons, short sight-seeing trips, cocktail parties and dinner dates.

Presently, as the *dorozka* rolled through the parkway, great hot puffs of flower-scented air blew into his face. The trees were in full leaf, offering welcome shade. He found a peculiar charm in this park in the middle of Warsaw. It was rural but gracefully classic.

He glanced at his watch. It was still early and he was only four or five blocks from Ceila's apartment. He had the driver stop, paid and decided to walk the rest of the way.

As he walked down the walkway under the broad-leaf oak trees, he heard a group of veterans arguing politics in loud voices, arms flaying. After more than a hundred and seventy years of bondage, Poland was a relatively new country. For so long the Poles had had no voice in their government. Now they were absorbed in politics. Whenever three or more met – at the market, after church, at tea – they talked politics.

Something stimulating in the vague dull hum of the city street beyond the park caught Victor's attention. There all sounds were drowned by the rumble of an army caravan of heavy trucks loaded with soldiers and supplies. The rumors and press reports became real in Victor's mind. The past weeks he'd become aware of the number of sales clerks, gardeners and workmen disappearing one by one from their jobs. Bloody incidents were reported almost daily. He now realized that the mobilization was "secret" only in the sense that there were no public announcements. All summer long there had been reports of great German activity along the entire Western Polish border and German warships anchored off the "free city" of Danzig.

Victor suddenly felt restless. He started to walk faster when two small boys at play ran into him. The boys picked themselves up from the turf and ran off laughing.

Walking on, Victor found very little to comfort him. He glanced at his watch and hastened his stride as he neared Ceila's place. He halted a *dorozka* and had the driver wait. He took the steps up two at a time. He knocked at the door. "Come on in," she called. "I'll be with you in a moment. Pour yourself a drink."

Her mother probably wasn't home, he thought. He went to the kitchen and poured himself a vodka and water. He took a sip and walked out onto the balcony filled with potted plants. Twilight began to settle in, but it was still too early for any relief from the day's heat. A minute later Ceila joined him on the balcony, refreshingly pretty in red velvet. The neckline was just low enough to reveal the pink cleavage of her bosom. Her hair piled up in curls on her head and with eyes sparkling, she waited. Victor reached for her, brushing his lips up to her ear, mumbling, "Could eat you here and now, but hate to undo that pretty face of yours."

She pressed close to him: "I can always put on a new face, you know."

"Hardly time for that. Besides, I'm hungry and the *dorozka* is waiting."

21

They started out the door and walked rapidly toward the waiting carriage. He gave the driver the curator's address, and they moved out into the traffic.

"You'll be seeing some old friends." Her voice was pleasant as always, but there was a slight hint of sarcasm. He understood. "Friends" always meant more war talk and she hated it.

They rode in silence, Ceila moved closer until their bodies touched. She asked, "Is something the matter? You seem troubled."

"I'm . . . I'm . . . at loose ends . . . just . . . just . . ." He turned away from her.

"You're confusing me, all right."

"You're so right." He reached for her hand and pressed his lips to her fingertips.

They rode down streets between newsstands with newspapers in several languages and illustrated journals. They passed brightly colored soft drink booths with pink and yellow syrups, shiny rolls of chocolate, and piles of breads and baked goods.

Almost all people on the streets seemed to be carrying long rolls of specially prepared black paper under their arms. Everywhere, homeowners, shopkeepers, and caretakers were blocking out windows. The customary easygoing attitude of the pedestrians was noticeably lacking; long chitchats were hurriedly reduced to a few words, even simple nods.

At their destination, the curator greeted them with a cordial "Hello, hello, hello." He shook Victor's hand and smiled at Ceila. "Mama is helping in the kitchen. Please come and meet my friends."

The second-story apartment had two large rooms and a small kitchen. The large living room also served as a dining room and study. The crowded shelves and cupboards were bursting with dishes and other wares, while the other walls were lined with bookcases, filled with classics, art albums and periodicals. On the small piano were sheets of music and family miniatures in silver frames. A longnecked crystal vase held a half dozen long-stemmed red roses. Their fragrance mingled with the odor of cooking food. Every inch of wall space was covered with paintings, including the walls of the bedroom, kitchen and even the bathroom.

Madame Bozinski, always addressed as Pani Curator, appeared smiling in the kitchen doorway. Victor kissed her extended hand. For an American, this gesture never came easily. He watched the others kiss Ceila's hand and hoped some day to imitate them as gracefully.

Pani Curator put her arms around Ceila, her dark brown eyes wide with joy. She kissed her on the cheek. "My darling Ceila," she said, "it seems so long between visits." Her voice was warm and her accent precise and delicate as the finest crystal.

She was extraordinarily frail. Her thin face made her eyes large. The forehead was high, and her black hair, tinged gray at the sides was parted down the center and pulled back severely to a high knot on the back of her head.

She fascinated Victor with her grace, reminding him of a small kitten. She waved her small, delicate hands.

"Ceila, Ceila, my darling," she repeated. "It seems like months since I've seen you last."

"Mama, what are you saying?" said the curator. "It was only last week."

"So – last week or just yesterday, it's always such a pleasure to see her again."

Ceila put her arm around the woman and said to the curator, "We women have our own way of counting time, don't we, Pani?"

23

Pani Curator smiled back. "That we do. To a man, an hour is an hour, but to a woman an hour sometimes could be a whole day." And with that she excused herself and disappeared into the kitchen. As with most Polish gentry women of the pre-World-War generation, she had been brought up to do nothing that would add to their income. Her parents owned a large estate in the Ukraine. They lived there during the summers and wintered in Warsaw or Krakow. When the Bolshevik revolution came, most of the land was taken from them. The Bolshevists burned their home, pouring oil over the rugs and furniture. Her family had been fortunate to escape. The last few years she devoted much of her time to collecting paintings of the better European and Polish artists, most of them personal friends.

The dinner company was small and congenial. It wasn't long before excited discussion filled the room. Besides Ceila and Victor, there were Kordian, Lolek and Professor Jan Woda from the Lublin Art Museum. This was a little send-off dinner to honor the professor before he returned to Lublin after a week's visit in Warsaw. He was a tall, thin man and his dark suit made him appear even slimmer. He was always adjusting his glasses with a nervous hand. The fading gray hairline and the white slip of whiskers above a sardonic smile gave him a certain senatorial elegance.

In his younger days the professor had been involved in revolutionary activities. He had been arrested a number of times before being sentenced to Siberia, and managed to escape to self-imposed exile in Paris. There he joined his many compatriots and continued his studies at the Sorbonne. Over the span of years, he established himself as a painter and writer as well as historian and teacher. After Poland was restored to the map of Europe he found his country in a medieval condition after nearly two centuries of occupation. From all over the world, Poles like himself, with professional training and experience, returned to fill the country's needs. Here every army, German, Russian, Austrian, Lithuanian or Ukranian, was an enemy destroying everything that it couldn't take with it. Everything had to be rebuilt: bridges, railroads, homes, schools, factories. Every detail of a national government had to be reorganized.

In Professor Woda Ceila found the grace of a proud jungle animal, slowed a bit by age but still quick of mind. Listening to him made her feel very young, attracted as a schoolgirl to her teacher. His green eyes softened in color as he turned from Kordian to Ceila. "Have you seen the opera?"

"Not yet. I'm waiting for Victor to ask me."

"Now, how can anyone resist an invitation like that?" Lolek said.

Everyone laughed. Victor blushed.

"Strange, these wonderful women." The professor cleared his throat. "They always have such a subtle way of going after what they want."

"You may ask, you may beg —" Kordian injected. "You may fall on your knees in supplication, but when they don't want to, what can a man do?"

"There's always tomorrow." Ceila laughed.

Victor said, "I better ask or there will be no end to this. Ceila, would you like to go to the opera with me?" He patted Lolek on the back. "If I don't take you, Lolek here will."

Professor Woda turned to Ceila. "You never told me that your father gave up a promising musical career."

"We still hear once in a great while, but he doesn't inquire when we'll be returning the way he used to. We think he's found someone else." She lowered her face and her voice was sad. "The last we heard he was teaching music at a high school."

They started on the third bottle of wine and Pani Curator had to summon the guests twice before they finally took their places at the table. It was a splendid meal, one particularly prepared to please Ceila and her guest. Nothing was too good for an American. Choice pickled herring and mushrooms started the meal. All during the conversations around the table Lolek had not volunteered a single word. He just sat half-smiling, filled like a stuffed hen ready to be popped into an oven. After the main course of roast duck and dumplings with raisins, the conversation drifted to the new seaport of Gdynia on the Baltic and its competition with the Germans at Danzig. By then the women began to put away the dinner dishes. The mention of Germans turned the topic.

"It's another of Hitler's war of nerves," Kordian said while refilling the whiskey glasses before he wiggled back into his place on the couch.

"But for how long?" asked the curator. "Nerves could lead to bullets and then what?"

"The Nazis are bluffing and when they see that we are ready to fight they'll back down like any old hound dog with its tail between its legs," Kordian said.

"England and France, who needs them?" Lolek said dryly. "Where were they when Prague and Vienna fell? History has a way of repeating itself. I wouldn't be surprised if we don't have to start this off alone. This wouldn't be the first time that Poland was laid like a lamb on a sacrificial altar."

Lolek Kossack looked worried. He was usually cheerful and seldom revealed any hint of his unhappy youth.

His father's activities in Warsaw around the turn of the century had been both political and literary. Hopes for the emancipation of Poland from Tzarist rule placed him among those conspiring for an armed uprising against Russia. He was arrested and sentenced to exile in Siberia. Lolek's mother followed her husband into exile with a five-year-old boy. She died a victim of hardship and privation. The broken man, with the little boy, was allowed to leave Russia, but soon died in Poland's ancient capital of Krakow. There, raised by relatives, Lolek continued his schooling and, as a sensitive boy, was aroused by the historical monuments. The Royal Castle of Wawel and its magnificent Renaissance cathedral inspired him most.

After completing the usual training, he entered The Krakow Academy and won a scholarship enabling him to continue studies in Germany and France.

While in Paris he turned from the academic to impressionism.

Since his return, his work had appeared in a number of important art shows, including a few one-man shows. But sales were infrequent, and as a result he had a part-time tutorship at the university and assisted at the museum.

Lolek reiterated, "Like a lamb on the sacrificial altar."

"Altar nothing!" Kordian shouted, his clenched fist rattling the table. "Why, this country could put five million men in the field this very day. Our cavalry is the best in Europe. Tell me, tell me, what can you do here without the cavalry? With the first drop of rain, any motorized army would bog down like a fish out of water. If war comes, it'll be another Grünwald."

"Grünwald! Grünwald!" said the professor. "Stop dreaming of spears and swords. To die is nothing to speak of lightly. Soldiers die, but what about the living? God forbid the day it should ever happen again: it'll be the end of us all." His trembling fingers swept across the room accusingly.

"The newspapers haven't given any cause for alarm." Ceila tried to cool the conversation.

"The press naturally is censored by the government."

GRÜNWALD

Kordian got to his feet and stood like a teacher. "There is no panic in spite of all the rumors. Should war come, it'll be another Grünwald."

"We all must die, sometime." Lolek's voice was meek.

"Yes – die we must," the curator agreed. "But how we die is what's important. I've become accustomed to living like a man again after years of fighting and hiding like a sick rat. Sometimes I wonder if this whole world hasn't gone mad."

It was almost midnight before the dinner party ended. For Ceila and Victor, the hour was still early – the hour the night people stalked the city streets.

Warsaw was in absolute darkness. All cabs and cars had darkened blue paper over the headlights. The night lay thick and Ceila snuggled close to Victor as they waited for a *dorozka*.

It was a heavenly late-summer night, and Ceila could see the stars as clearly as the lines on the palm of her hand. The streets were far from deserted, and the *dorozkas* that passed held cuddling couples. Ceila smiled and looked up at Victor. They remained silent.

4

They headed for the Old Town, once the pride of Warsaw, the haunt of fashion where the fine carved doorways reflected a glorious past – the huge square lined with medieval houses. There in the shadows, secreted from casual gaze, were the winding staircases that once gleamed with white, soft shoulders and brilliant uniforms of Napoleon's time when seventy thousand Poles rushed to his aid and assumed the dashing lancer's uniform which transformed fat tenors into military figures.

Victor asked, "Any particular place in mind?"

"Fukiers – for a start."

They found it and a few other ancient wine cellars packed with rowdy Bohemians. It wasn't until they tried the Golden Lion that they were finally accommodated, with dance music, soft and sensuous.

The club was on the dimly-lit second floor, a place designed for lovers. While they were led to a table they overheard a woman whisper, "Americans."

Ceila remarked, "I've always liked this place. Have you been here before?"

"Never. With such a small door for an entrance how does one ever find these places?"

Victor ordered, then noticed the happy glitter in Ceila's eyes as she took in the place. He reached out for her hands and she bent over and gently brushed her lips over his fingertips. When the waiter came, Victor withdrew his hands so rapidly that she was embarrassed. He made his apologies awkwardly, explaining that he had never experienced a woman kissing his fingers in public. When their drinks arrived they toasted to his success and drank to her sad but beautiful eyes. Then, inspired by the flow of wine and the scent of her perfume, he lifted his glass, "To us."

"To Victor and Ceila." Suddenly the smile left. Her lips drooped and trembled slightly. Her eyes glistened with tears. After a while she managed a feeble, "To us – to hello and goodbye." She reached for her handkerchief and dabbed her eyes. "Liquor has always had the damnedest sentimental effect on me." The smile returned and the music tempo changed from a sad ballad to a tango. "Let's dance."

Victor took her in his arms and whisked her across the dance floor. Happy, she liked being in his arms. He moved with such grace that she thought he could balance a glass of water on his head without spilling a drop.

Maybe it was the wine. Maybe it was just Victor holding her tightly in his arms.

Again the tempo changed and became dreamy and sensuous.

Tomorrow, she wished, would never come.

These last few months, seeing each other almost every day had become a way of life for Ceila. Friends, sweethearts – but marriage never entered her mind. He must eventually depart. Victor was a match for her in warmth, intellect, compassion, even fury. Her friends liked and accepted him. It was an adventure ever since they'd met, discovering mutual interests in the arts and travel. It was fun teaching him a difficult language, stumbling over the impossible combinations of "czys."She found his interest in Eastern Europe deep and sincere. Little was known about the Slavic countries in the States. To capture the true spirit of the people he had to live with them. Poland was nothing like he had expected.

As the hour grew late, the club spilled over and the place boomed with robust laughter. The wines, champagnes and vodka were dispensed with growing rapidity. There were songs and more songs and dancing, and there was fire and reckless-ness in the music. The drummer tossed his sticks in the air while the pianist beat the keys in a series of American favorites. Victor laughed, raising his voice above the uproar.

Ceila's eyes were on three young officers looking in their direction. They finally joined them.

"You two Americans?" one of them asked.

Ceila winked at Victor. "How did you know?"

"Simple," replied the captain. "From the way you dress and from the American habit of having your money ready every time you order. May we buy you a drink?"

"We'd be happy to have you join us," Victor said.

The captain ordered a round. The youngest of the three nudged his superior and remarked, *"Zgrabna babka."*

Ceila laughed. "I know enough Polish to understand. You just called me a 'cute chick.' You are very kind." She clinked glasses with the young blond lieutenant and made room so they could all be seated.

The captain took out a silver cigarette case and passed it around. Victor was ready with his lighter. The captain asked, " I don't wish to be impertinent, but we were debating whether you were a businessman or a tourist. Which is correct?"

Ceila hurriedly volunteered a reply. "You are quite right, Captain. We're from the American Embassy. This is my husband, Jack Brown, and I'm Florence Brown."

The three scrambled to their feet, almost dumping the drinks. The captain introduced himself and his two lieutenant friends. Each clicked his heels and bowed as they kissed Ceila's hand. The young lieutenant still muttered, *"Zgrabna babka."* Blushing, Ceila looked off to one side. She thought he was rather young for an officer, blond with pale blue eyes. He appeared more Teutonic than Slavic. But then Poles came in all variations of appearance, an aftermath of centuries of transgressing armies.

The captain asked, "Have you been in Poland long?"

"Six months," Victor replied.

"Where are you from? I've been twice to America, always had a warm feeling for Americans."

"Did you like it?" Ceila asked.

"As a visit, yes, but to live, no! Americans are a beehive, busy making money which they don't have time to really enjoy. They tend toward a vulgar display of their wealth, with doctors and lawyers always ready to bleed them out of everything. Beer, hot dogs and baseball is the only American culture."

"I hear you, captain," Ceila answered coldly. True as it might seem, it had the effect of a slap across the face.

"But, I've always had that warm spot." The captain beat himself on the chest. "A generous people but not always too wise whom they support. But then," he started to laugh, "when did Poles do likewise? They could go scot free like Austria and the Czechs and let the French and English worry about Hitler."

Ceila withdrew sharply. This was hardly what she would expect to hear from a captain in the Polish uniform. In fact, it was treasonous. Before she could voice her disgust, the young lieutenant asked, "Where are you from in America?"

Victor, noticing Ceila's reaction, hurriedly answered, "Denver – Denver, Colorado. And you, captain, what do you call home?"

"Danzig. And my silent friend here is from Opiel."

"And you, lieutenant?" Ceila eyed the young blond with an upturned nose.

"Lublin. I attended the college there."

"Do you know Professor Woda?"

"I do, madame," said the lieutenant, pleased he had at last arrested Ceila's attention. "He's with the museum and from time to time teaches at the college." All this interest brought out the bravado in him as he questioned Victor.

"Do you think America could be drawn in if there is another war?"

"There are alliances, you understand?"

Victor saw the color leave Ceila's face. He had never seen her eyes take on such anger. Still, she restrained herself until the captain barked, "Alliances to whom? Capitalists and Jews?"

"Now that's enough of this talk!" Ceila brought down her glass on the table. With dammed-up fury she burst out in fluent Polish, pouring out a deluge of sarcastic innuendos, accusing them of behaving like pigs and vowing to report them to the ministry the first thing in the morning.

Ceila's tirade had struck a nerve, and the officers all stood up as one, growing white with alarm that she was a Pole. A deep silence swept the place. The captain started to apologize.

"Madam, Madam. We beg your pardon, we beg your pardon."

"Get out!" she screamed. "Get out of my sight before I– I– I–!" Her dark eyes narrowed as she looked about in search of something she could hit him with. Suddenly she threw herself upon the officer. Before the astonished man could gather his wits, she gave him a forceful shove.

"You poor excuse for a man! If I were a man I'd blacken that face of yours."

Victor and the officers stood amazed. The officers backed off.

It lasted hardly a minute. Her eyes were still wide with rage when Victor helped her back to her seat. All eyes in the place were focused on them and someone remarked, "There's no hell like the wrath of an angry woman."

Victor nodded. He put his arm around her. She took a large swallow from her glass.

"That Polish temper will be the death of me yet," she said softly. "I hope I didn't embarrass you, darling. But I just couldn't take any more of that arrogant, stupid talk."

It was some time before she was herself again, but not really the same.

"Take it easy, honey." Victor pushed her glass into her hand. "Let's get out of here."

There was still the hint of anger in her voice. "Oh Victor, we were having such a wonderful time."

He brought her hand up to his lips and kissed her fingers curled about his hand.

Later, walking along the silent and deserted Przedmiescie Boulevard, they side-stepped other pairs of lovers. It was a long walk.

5

Victor had received three telegrams from home and friends, concerned for his safety because of the threats of war. He decided to start making preparations for his departure. Europe would become a thing of the past. He did not tell Ceila. He had no intention of telling her until the day he left for the port of Gdynia.

Their little world had become immensely complicated. The slightest action could lead to changes, passions, incredibly complex derangements. Everything seethed with theatrical fervor. Here everything was extravagantly poetic, everything was history and romance, love and war – a living history from day to day.Warsaw's every street had its own history.

Victor reflected. What is happening to me is heavily weighted on the fantastic side. All because of a madman in

Berlin, a simple enchantment has become melodramatic, has reduced all my other experiences to a simple encounter. There is definitely a sudden change in the rhythm of my life.

This evening they were to attend a concert, but he'd changed his mind by the time he arrived at her apartment.

"We'll go another time, if you don't mind," he told her, wrapping the fur piece about her shoulders. "You're as beautiful as ever." His lips brushed against her cheek.

"Is something the matter, darling?"

"No – no – nothing." He smiled and started to crowd her toward the door. "Just plain old American selfishness, I suppose." They started down the narrow, winding stairway. "The *dorozka* is waiting. Too nice a night to hole up in a concert hall. I've been thinking about a secluded spot with dinner by candlelight and maybe some Gypsy music."

"Victor, is something the matter? Are you trying to hide something from me?"

"If it's the concert you insist upon, we'll go."

"Who is insisting on anything?" Ceila snuggled up close. She took him by the arm and led him to the waiting *dorozka*. "I'm hungry enough to eat a horse. Where did you say we're going?"

When he did not reply, she looked him in the eye with her own particular kind of mischievous glint. "There is an old Polish proverb," she said, "that tells us that you'll eat a barrel of salt before you'll know a man thoroughly."

Ceila was pleasantly chatty. He was happy and content with his secret. Then he realized the firmness with which he held her in his arms, as though she might suddenly take flight.

They arrived early at the small restaurant under the White Eagle, just off Nowy Swiat Street. It was too soon for the theater crowd, and the early drinkers had already left for home.

Fewer than a dozen people were in the place. They were directed through the dark, candlelit interior by an elderly, gray-moustached headwaiter dressed in a dinner jacket which had seen better days. He kept bowing politely and muttering, "Please, please," as he guided them to a table. Three Gypsy musicians dressed in white shirts, their trousers tucked into high polished leather boots, struck up a tune. Their huge, dangling brass earrings danced in rhythm to the mazurka. The headwaiter, still bowing, rubbed his hands together. "What would madam and the kind gentleman desire?"

"A bottle of your best white wine, please."

"Will you be staying for dinner?"

"Yes," Victor replied, reaching for a cigarette.

The waiter bowed reverently, "As you wish, as you wish." He backed away.

There was a long silence. Victor excused himself and started for the men's room. On the way he stopped at the bar and had a double whiskey.

When he got back he was hardly seated when he asked, "Do you care if we leave this place?" He tried to be casual.

She took his hand and stroked it gently, "No, no. You'll feel better after a while."

"This goddamn life can be so complicated when you least expect it."

"It's complicated mine, too, Mister Zabel."

"You're talking in riddles."

"What hurts most teaches soonest," she went on. "My mother always told me that ill luck and misadventure are the ways to wisdom."

"And my father always told me that a horse had a bigger head, so let him worry."

"Beautiful, beautiful." She laughed, pushing her hair from

her face. The waiter appeared with the wine.

Victor regained his self-composure as they waited to be served. They touched wine glasses and he told her how enchanting she was. She wore a black dress, a favorite with her on evenings such as this. It was silk and clinging, her arms soft and warm and white like sunlit marble against the black. Beneath those long eyelashes her eyes were dancing.

Soon the wine bottle was almost empty. The bowing waiter returned and they ordered dinner.

Victor changed to whiskey. Ceila said she'd wait. "In these troublesome times, someone has to keep a sober head."

"Troubles?" said Victor, taking a deep swallow from his glass. "Things are quite different back in the States, you know."

"Yes – but the fact remains that we are here and not in the States. Strange how people meet; back there our paths would never have crossed."

"You needn't be here." He was serious. "Ceila, marry me."

He watched the change come over her face; she was completely unprepared. She looked down at her hands. There was a long silence.

"I love you, Victor. But I don't feel that this is the time or the place to be thinking of wedding bells – what will it prove?"

"I don't understand you." He didn't want to believe that her answer could possibly be no. She reached across the table for his hand and with unashamed feminine sensitivity lowered her face until her lips moved across his fingers. He withdrew his hand and, reaching for his whiskey glass, emptied it in one large swallow.

The whiskey felt good and warm in the pit of his stomach. He moved closer. "I don't understand. I just don't understand. I'm serious."

"I know you're serious."

"Ceila, I don't understand."

"Maybe not now, but in time you will."

He lifted his whiskey glass high. "I'll drink to that." His glass was empty. He ordered another, then turned to Ceila.

"You know, as my wife, you can leave this place any time. Good old U.S.A., home sweet home."

There was a faint smile on her lips: "I love you, Victor, and you're sweet – and–" she halted. "No, I'll take that sweet back, and just say you're all man. But, but, how could we . . . the way things are?"

"Why not? I promise that I'll make you the best husband ever. Marry me, Ceila." He moved closer, his warm breath against her cheek, whispering, "I don't think I could live without you."

"Darling, I just don't think it would be fair to all those wonderful people back home, your school, your entire future."

"You seem to forget, they would like to see me settled. It's only proper for a professor to take unto himself a wife and have children, maybe–," he held up two fingers, then three, "and become an integral member of the community."

He kissed her on the ear and she noticed that the whiskey had begun to have its effect on him. "Perhaps." She wasn't smiling anymore. "That's all right for the States, but this is Poland in a world gone mad."

Victor blinked, his mind crowded with all the facts he knew about this woman. Ceila could never be just another housewife – daily trivia of cleaning and cooking and sewing.

He sat there without moving, his eyes on her but unseeing; she was like a crystalline ghost against the blackness. She was a woman whose freedom was something very deep and absolute. By earning her own living she made a rewarding gesture toward this freedom. The last thing she might wish for would be to have her world transformed into a domestic trap.

Victor had another drink. He wasn't happy when he spoke. "All this damn talk. America – Poland – Jew – Catholic! What in the hell gives? People are people – north, south, east or west." He crowded her a little. "You were born in the States, and if you may recall, and pardon the old adage, the melting pot of the world where the Lewandowskis became Levens and Greenbergs became Green."

Ceila reared back, her Polish temper very much in evidence. Her words shot out like pellets. "Victor, how could you! If it made any difference to me that you were a Jew, I'd never have gone out with you in the first place. You – you – you just don't understand!" She stuttered and slowly began to choke up inside. "What – I – have been trying to tell you is that if this were another time, another place, you wouldn't have to try so hard. But – but, it seems you just do not understand. We are here."

A mask-like expression covered her face. "You just don't understand. I'm here because I want to be here, and I could never, never, never leave, as long as there is the threat of war. I have an obligation not only to this country, but to my mother and all my wonderful friends, and all my hopes and dreams."

With abandon, Ceila's face twisted with sorrow. Tears flooded. Her handkerchief was soon wet through.

Victor felt sorry for her. A helplessness grew inside him. He drew her close and held her. She wasn't crying just for herself, but for the whole world. He pressed her even closer. "What makes you so nationalistic?" She didn't answer. "After all, you're American born. What makes you so strongly pro-Polish? You act like you're ready to die for this country."

"Who knows?" She leaned away and blew her nose.

Victor drew her face to his and kissed her. Her face was warm with the taste of tears.

Dinner was served. She appeared to have no desire for food. She asked, "Would you like to know how I came to be as I am? Nationalistic, pro-Polish and all that?"

"Yes, I would like to know; it's a part of your life you seldom speak of."

She straightened to face him. Her eyes narrowed. She wet her lips, then started talking about her family. They lived in a Pennsylvania coal town with a population of nearly thirty thousand, of whom more than half were immigrants from Eastern Europe.

"Father was a musician." She came alive. "He could play a piano like a master. He came to America first, and once located there sent for my mother and the baby – who soon died in an epidemic."

She went on to explain how they spoke only Polish at home until her folks learned a little English. Mama always sent her off to school in prim starched cotton dresses, and she imitated the Americans, hating to be referred to as "Polak." She never could forget the time the geography teacher asked each of the children to walk up to the front of the class and point to the country and capital city from which their parents came. She could not find Poland. The teacher told her to take her seat. On the *pre-war* map, Poland was not shown. She felt cheated. She never liked that teacher again. The idea of being American-born and treated like some foreigner! The textbooks were so biased and distorted that it was not until high school that she learned that Copernicus was not a German but a Pole.

She went on to relate how the Poles, like other immigrants, formed their little ghettos. Everywhere in these communities one saw the emblems of Poland's old glory: the sad countenance of General Kosciuszko, one of the founders of West Point; the painting of the dashing Count Pulaski, the father of the

American cavalry who was killed in the Revolution.

In her childhood years Ceila attended the patriotic rallies. She learned to sing the patriotic songs and ballads. When she first attended public school she found English somewhat difficult.

In 1928, Ceila's mother inherited some property in Poland. With Ceila and her brother in tow, she left for Europe. They had been here ever since. This summer, when the Nazis marched into Czechoslovakia, her brother, to escape conscription into the Polish army, returned to his father in the States.

"What made your mother decide to remain in Poland?" Victor asked.

"Mama has always been independent. So much so, in fact, that I often found it difficult to decide who was the real head of our family. With the money from the estate, she invested in a small apartment house, with the idea of remaining for a short time. There was a great housing shortage and a lack of capital. Mother was fortunate. The money from the inheritance and what little father sent all went into income property. And so my mother and I are still here."

"But why Poland?"

"You might be surprised. These people here are my mother's people. She did not exactly hate it in America, but it makes a lot of difference when you don't speak the language. My mother's parents weren't too happy when she married. Her family had long been in the leather tanning business, and she was sent to school in Paris. When she returned, she met my father, a pianist with the Warsaw Symphony. But he was at the age when the Russians were rounding up Poles for military service, so the two got married and fled to America. She missed the things that meant the real life to her. The gay and colorful restaurants after the theater. She always complained about the lack of parks and cultural pursuits in America. Only labor difficulties, strikes and terrible depression."

Victor had had another drink. The glow grew warmer until the world about him fuzzed. The glow, like a brief sunrise, was followed by gloom.

Ceila paid the bill and with the waiter's aid they got Victor to his feet and started toward the door.

"We'll be home soon," she told him.

The waiter summoned a *dorozka* and opened the door. The heavy, gray-whiskered driver, flashing a ready smile, helped push Victor in. Ceila gave the driver Victor's address. He signaled the team of black horses with the snap of the reins.

It was four in the morning and the chilled air felt fresh, a relief from the midday heat. A flicker of light glowed on the eastern horizon. The blackness of the night and the shadows still enveloped the tree-hemmed boulevard. The songs of birds started to greet the new day.

When they arrived, Victor lifted his head unsteadily, but he was too drunk to move by himself.

The driver again had to assist, much to Ceila's embarrassment. He laid Victor on the bed with the comment, "Madame's husband must have had one too many . . . but then the tavern will not spoil a good man any more than the church mend a bad one."

She paid well and thanked the driver as he bowed and backed out the door with a pleasant, "Good night."

Victor's was the face of a man torn by forces – one commanding him to stay, the other to leave.

Ceila ran after the driver and asked him to wait. She then hurried back to the room and proceeded to remove Victor's shoes and socks. She removed his tie and shirt and pulled the sheet over him.

6

Victor blinked his eyes open. The bells of a nearby church tolled the sad intonation of a funeral. He squinted at his watch. It was ten past eleven. He closed his eyes again. His head ached. The room was hot and filled with sunlight. A pair of lovemaking flies buzzed over his head. He swore he'd never do it again. He rose slowly from bed and, wearing only shorts, he filled the coffee pot and placed it on the burner. He headed for the bathroom.

He turned on the light and looked into the mirror. Bloodshot eyes peered back. He tried to smile. The effort was as bad as the taste in his mouth. He brushed his teeth.

Over his second cup of coffee, he saw Ceila's face, could almost hear her voice. He wondered whether he'd ever again love a woman as wonderful as she. His eyes swept the room, searching for some sign of her. He would phone her later. He eased back on the bed and went back to sleep.

He was startled by the ring of the telephone. Fumbling, he jerked the receiver to his ear.

"Victor? This is Ceila."

"Yes, doll."

"Darling, you sound utterly terrible. Anything the matter?"

"No. Not exactly. I got up with the damndest hangover. What time is it?"

"Quarter past two."

"Two! Oh, Christ!" He shot upright. "I'm supposed to check in with the shipping company. If I rush I might still make it."

"No need to rush. This is why I'm calling you. Have you seen today's paper?"

"With this damn aching head, I haven't moved. What gives?"

"Oceanic travel for the remainder of this season is strictly for the birds, my dear."

"And what is that supposed to mean?"

"Hitler's genius has halted all trans-Atlantic shipping."

"Oh – Christ, no!"

"The Germans have closed Danzig and blocked Gdynia. But you still could get a train south."

"And if not?"

"Well, this has always been a home away from home, you know."

Victor lit a cigarette. Then, "Honey, I better get a move on. I'll call you back later. Will you be home?"

"Naturally. Call me later."

He eased the phone down. He drew on the cigarette, his mind flipping cartwheels.

The American Consulate. But the line was busy. He

slammed down the receiver. The line was still busy a half hour later.

Everywhere he went throughout the day, Victor found long lines of people waiting long hours, desperation on their drawn faces. Since the Germans had cut the rail lines at the Polish border, all the railroads and highways heading south were packed.

The hourly radio reports filled the airwaves with border incidents.

Raids by Nazi gangs on various frontiers were charged by the Poles. Trouble flared in the Danzig area, where German sources reported the killing of two Poles. Nazis accused Poles of shooting at German planes in Danzig Bay. Danzig heard artillery fire in the neighborhood of Gdynia. Casualties were announced on both sides.

Victor moved through the crowded streets feeling sterile and divorced from life. He moved like a robot. There was a tremor in his hands and his breath came in gasps with the hot sun burning down across his back. Christ! What a nightmare! He walked faster and faster. There was no escape. He did not see the moving traffic and the actions of people in their business-as-usual attitude. His body ached. A nausea seized him.

Inside his apartment he peeled off his coat and shirt. He lit a cigarette. He sat for a time thinking that what was happening to him had its fantastic side. He was an American. Why should he be sucked into a European mess? He flicked ashes and turned on the radio.

The soft, mellifluent music of Szymanowski was suddenly interrupted by a newscaster speaking in a low, nervous voice, reciting the latest diplomatic setbacks. Something about the Soviets breaking with the Allies. Barring of the Red Army in Poland caused an end of talks with the English and French. He snapped off the radio and reached for the paper.

He read everything, especially the notices regarding shipping. He felt less alone when he read the item: "Americans abroad rush for bookings. Canceled ship sailings leave many stranded. Plan for aid outlined by U.S. Five thousand trying to get out of Europe as consulates in Rome and Berlin give warning."

Victor folded the newspaper before letting it slip slowly to the floor. He rested his eyes on the gray ceiling. It was Thursday, August 31st. He resigned himself to . . . whatever. He reached for the telephone and dialed Ceila's office number. The line was busy. Minutes later he picked up the phone and again dialed her number in a slow, almost reluctant manner. "Hello – Ceila? Are you busy? I'd like to see you after work."

"Love to, honey, but with all this mess, the curator has initiated a speedup in cataloging which could tie us up until late."

"Call me then?" There was urgency in his voice.

"Naturally. And please be careful. I love you."

"Yes – like not getting drunk. I love you, too.'

He set the phone down slowly. He hated the idea of letting her go. He hated this constant parting. He made himself comfortable in the old armchair, picked up the newspaper and concentrated on an item:

GERMAN-RUSSO PACT
AIM IS TO REORGANIZE THE WORLD

A Russo-German pact would permit the Soviets to stand aside while the democracies and dictatorships fight it out; would allow Russia ultimately to act as Europe's arbiter.

As for Germany, a neutral Russia would strengthen Germany in any contest with the Allies and would simultaneously inflict on Britain and

France a diplomatic humiliation and weaken Poland so they would submit without a war.

On the foreground of the present war crisis, this means a fourth and final partition of Poland, and beyond that the reorganization of all Central and Eastern Europe by Germany and Russia for their mutual benefit.

Victor stopped reading long enough to head for the kitchen where he poured himself a stiff shot of whiskey and lit another cigarette. His mind was very much alert when he returned to the newspaper, drawing heavily on the cigarette.

Allies Make War Preparation: France, Britain and Poland, angry, filled with a sense of having been tricked by the Russian-German pact, have quickly regained their composure. The French and the British would be with the Poles should a shooting war start.

Victor finished reading the paper and flung it across the room. He swore aloud. He got to his feet and walked out onto the balcony. He took a deep breath and exhaled heavily.

He studied the street three flights below him. Children were at play in the early twilight. Warsaw and Mokotowska Street were at peace.

How strange to sit back and watch a people go off to war. There were no cheering crowds, no banners waving, no bands, no battle hymns, only obedience, and perhaps muttered curses of protest. There were some rallying calls of "Remember Grünwald!"

These young soldiers going off to the frontier went with a burning hate such as no army had ever known.

The Poles saw through the Germans the moment Hitler asked for Danzig. They had learned from the tragedy of other European countries which had relied on diplomatic bargains and Hitler's promises. The Poles did not believe in bargaining.

49

They told the world they would fight.

For the moment at least, Mokotowska Street was at peace. The phone rang. Victor entered the room and snatched it from the hook. "Hello!"

There was a moment of silence, then Ceila's faint voice: "Darling?"

"Oh – I'm sorry. I guess I just got carried away by those damned reports."

"I've got some sad news, sweetheart." There was another silence. "I don't think I'll be seeing you tonight as we planned. I'll be working right through the night. I'm so sorry."

"I understand. What about tomorrow?"

"I'll call you. Maybe we could have breakfast together, on me."

"With an offer like that, who could resist? See you then. Bye."

"I'll call as soon as I can. Bye."

Victor set the phone down gently. He turned on the small table radio. The airwaves were filled with news reports, many so rapid that he could not grasp them. After some dialing, he finally hit upon a program of Chopin's etudes. He turned the volume up and headed for the bathroom to shower and get ready for bed.

7

He was falling. Through endless space. Falling rocks
screaming like bombs crashing after him. Victor tried to shout
but no sounds came. He tried to right himself and guide his fall.
He felt a jar as he hit bottom.

He opened his eyes. He could not remember where he was.
He had awakened from a nightmare. He was on his knees beside
the bed. He could still feel himself falling as if the world had
opened up. Nightmare! He had been standing with Ceila beside
him at the rocky brink overlooking the Black Canyon of the
Gunnison. The earth exploded underneath him and sent him
crashing down into the deep, gray-blue chasm.

For a moment he thought that he was ill. Delirious.
Everything seemed strange and reversed. He was in a sweat,
and the apartment was gray with the dull morning glow spilling

through the balcony doorway. With effort he got to his feet and into his terry-cloth robe. He headed for the bathroom. The cool water was refreshing. He lit a cigarette and walked to the balcony.

He glanced at his watch. It was six-fifty and the morning sun had started warming the fields. But the street, three stories below, was as fresh as if it had just dawned. Somewhere in the neighborhood a radio could be heard. Here and there, housekeepers with their coats buttoned picked up bits of paper and washed down the pavement in front of houses. Partygoers and prostitutes, fatigue on their gray faces, trudged along the cobbled street.

Victor turned, seeking shelter against the cool, misty air, when the piercing wail of sirens began to rise and fall over the city. Instinctively he stopped and scanned the sky. In the street people on their way to work stopped, their faces lifted. It was only seconds but seemed longer. The drone of distant aircraft could be heard above the screaming sirens. He could see nothing at first. Then there they were, flight after flight . . . silver and black, winging across the sky like a giant flock of wild ducks – ten, twenty, about fifty Polish P-7 fighters. The people in the street continued on their way. Just another air drill.

Victor yawned and stretched. The fighters headed north. He watched. In another minute they would be out of sight. Then suddenly the whole world came apart. The fighter planes, like black darts, began to stall, their noses up, twisted, weaved and dived. Only then did he notice the large formation of planes from the other direction.

Victor watched the air battle from the balcony – something unreal, a deadly game. He stood as if afraid to move. The mass formations split. The attack was on. Every fighter picked his own target, yet all moved in concert.

The fighter planes, outnumbered two to one, dived in with the heedless abandon characteristic of the Slav – all or nothing – as if it were a soccer match. With altitude and sun at their backs the fighters took the German raiders by surprise and forced the Luftwaffe to resort to defensive tactics. The area just north of Warsaw, the vicinity of Jablonna and Rodzymin, exploded into a cadenza of shimmering flashes. The tiny P-7's went into action like a school of sharks, machine guns flashing, darting, striking, rolling over and up and down and up and around and down and up again. Their striking force was so deadly that within minutes the Nazi raiders were forced to scatter and get rid of their bombs in panic. The explosions, irregular and distant, sounded like grumbling thunder.

Not a single German plane reached the heart of Warsaw, and all that saved some of the raiders was the lack of speed and limited firing power of the P-7's. Only a single Nazi plane, a Heinkel bomber, managed to reach the northern outskirts of Warsaw and in haste drop three bombs on a colony of the Workmen's Cooperative before it burst into flames. The air battle lasted only a few minutes before raiders, some with engines smoking, started breaking for home base. Some of the bombers still carrying bomb loads emptied their deadly cargo and machine-gunned any target they could see, skimming home at tree-top level.

Victor became aware of the silence – only the slight tremor in his hands. His face was damp. He felt a faint sickness in the pit of his stomach. It was all over now. The suspense had lifted and his mind was free to reflect on a deadly war swooping down on him. What baffled him most was the sudden knowledge that he was a part of it, even though he merely watched. But it was one hell of a thought that bullets and bombs had no eyes, no heart. They just killed, killed, killed! He hoped the whole goddamned thing would be over soon.

He lit a cigarette and flipped the match to the street, to the bustle of human activity below him.

He leaned over the heavy, wooden, carved banister, thinking how different this country was from any other country in which he had been. In it he sensed a noble, courageous, and proud spirit, akin to ancient Sparta. For the length of time it took him to smoke the cigarette, the whole riddle of Poland was understood. He knew the Polish character – proud and courageous. And though romantic and short of practicality, the Poles were great believers in liberty. Fate had thrown them a curve, their country being between Germany and Russia. Any weak country would have had little hope of perpetuating itself for any length of time between these two giants.

To Victor, this was not the Poland he had imagined it to be. He remembered reading articles and books about the country. So damn little was known of the fundamentals of Polish history. Pick up any American textbook! What reference was made to a country that once was the largest in all of Europe? From an historical perspective it was an anomalous empire, unknown in the annals of other European histories. Surely a history such as this deserved more than just a passing reference to Pulaski and Kosciuszko. Yet what was published was not only completely distorted but woefully incomplete.

Victor thought back to 1935 when Germany proposed an alliance against Russia. The proposal was renewed several times. It would have been to Germany's advantage. She could have thrown all her military power against France and England without fear for her eastern frontier. In the event of a war with Russia, she could have counted on the cooperation of the Polish army in an offensive against Russia from Polish territory.

The Poles rejected these propositions, having no desire to be involved in any German imperialistic plans.

Victor dropped the cigarette butt to the floor and stamped it out with the ball of his foot. He went back into the apartment. He thought of Ceila and reached for the phone. Her line was busy. Slowly he laid down the receiver. He stood, unsure of himself, then turned on the small radio.

Over a cup of coffee, he heard the strains of a Chopin polonaise interrupted by a man's strong voice. Victor listened. It was Mayor Starzynski with words of encouragement. He urged the people to help the soldiers and exhorted the women to fight beside their men, commanding "Go to the slaughterhouse, for the pigs have arrived."

After his coffee the despair lifted. He began to dress. He thought of his plans for the day – but now all of these plans were as the nightmare that had startled him out of his sleep.

He thought of the folks back home. By God, one can blunder *into* this damn thing, but how does one get out?

Twelve o'clock. Several German Dornier bombers managed to get through to the outskirts of Warsaw and thereafter came almost hourly. The Polish force, about one-third the strength of the German raiders, was just as full of impetus as in the morning and managed to scatter most of the raiders. Only a single formation of Stukas managed to get through. The anti-aircraft guns sounded their protest.

That first day there were more than 158 air battles. By nightfall the Polish wing, which originally numbered fifty planes, had only twenty fighters fit to take off again.

Saturday, Victor noticed, was a relatively quiet day, but the third day the Germans grew more inventive. Their raids came from different directions and at different altitudes.

The sharp-edged whining became more and more frequent, followed by the snarl of engines as dive-bombing Stukas streaked like falcons from the sky.

The sunlit Warsaw streets erupted in the metallic pang of anti-aircraft guns, the wail of sirens, the scream of bombs, the drumming explosions. Stark slaughter followed.

In those three days the Poles shot down forty German planes, but by the fourth day the Germans again changed their directions. They came in small formations and at varied altitudes, aiming to sap the remaining strength of the Polish fighters.

It seemed the battle overhead never ceased. The sky rained blazing planes, parts and bits, parachutes; bombs and shrapnel crashed and struck like thunderbolts; machine-gun fire rattled constantly.

The Luftwaffe's tactics were triumphant. The raids were hourly. Polish pilots found no rest. Outnumbered twenty to one, they remained suicidally valiant. Fuel and communication lines began to break down. Nazi formations swept across the sky from north, west and south. What still remained of the Polish air force withdrew to Lublin where the Polish government and most of the foreign diplomatic corps had retreated.

8

Ceila did not know where she was. So many explosions, the wail of air-raid sirens, the groan of aircraft engines. The building shook. The bed and the lamps on the table swayed. Dust drifted in and coated everything gray.

Ceila drew a deep breath. Then a thundering explosion and blinding flash. The building buckled. She was knocked to the floor. Strange, she felt no fear that the end could come so soon. She brushed the hair off her face and struggled to her feet.

The door to her mother's room was closed. She called out, "Mother!" but there was no answer. She forced open the door. "Mother! Mother!"

From under the bed came the voice, "Oh, Jesus Maria. Are they still there? *Ala Boga, Ala Boga!*"

"Oh, God, Mother." A half dozen more shells exploded

nearby.

Just as suddenly as it had all begun it was over. The sirens were silent, and only a crying child somewhere could be heard. To Ceila it was an aching kind of silence, like the stillness before a storm. But there was one comforting thought; for the next few hours there would be quiet on Nelewki Street. She turned and bent over to assist her mother.

"Is it over, are they gone?" asked a whimpering voice from under the bed.

"Yes, Mother, you can come out now."

Her mother pulled herself out, got to her feet and faced her daughter, embarrassed by her disheveled appearance.

"Who said 'War is hell'?" She threw up her arms. "It's far worse!"

Ceila put her arms about her and they comforted each other for a moment. Irritated, her mother started for the bath, brushing the dust from her flower-print housecoat.

Ceila smiled admiration as she watched her mother. Mrs. Rozek was a handsome woman of forty-seven who looked forty. Life flowed deeply in her. A true female romanticist, with that fine, fragile demeanor so naturally repulsed by the course realities of life. She wasn't tall. She carried like a banner her glorious blond hair around a soft, oval face. Her deep blue eyes, when glad emotions swept her, were flashes of rippled brilliance. But this was not such a moment.

Mother and daughter had been close these last few years, almost like sisters. They traveled together about Europe, even shared a coquettish evening on the town. But always discreetly. Her mother never gave Ceila any cause for concern. Still, there were no doubts in the daughter's mind that Mama might have reasons for staying away from home on rare occasions, such as the time she left for a week's visit to Vienna and stayed a month.

And still another time at Budapest. And then there was Rome, when a two-week vacation extended into a full two months. Ceila looked at her watch – ten past six in the morning. An awful way to start off a new day. The nights were still calm, but the days . . . Everyone slept fully dressed, with suitcases packed next to beds.

Slowly she began to shed the dress she was forced to sleep in. The change of clothes made her feel better. She started out for the museum.

Morning was already full. She walked briskly down the street and across Theater Square. A wall of fire billowed from the famous opera house, the cultural heart of Warsaw. Incendiary shells sent twisting columns of smoke skyward.

Stores, shops and offices were still closed, but the streets bustled with traffic as people hurried about their business between alarms. Summer was still in the air, but the cool morning gave hint that autumn was already on the wing this fifth day of September.

She picked her way around a heap of rubble and smashed cement work. There were many dead. They lay where they had dropped like huddled heaps of rags. She could not shut out the sight and sounds of the agony around her. She sensed the implacable calm of her people under duress. There wasn't a trace of panic. Everyone seemed conscious that it was now fashionable to be a front liner.

The streets were full of soldiers, the sound of cavalry hoofbeats and the rumble of many wagons. Here and there wagons were halted to permit the faster tanks, the crowded trucks and heavy cannon to pass. Two-wheeled carts creaked, laden with food supplies and water, all heading in one direction. The carts with the dead moved in the opposite direction.

Ceila proceeded on past Pilsudski Square and the memorial

to the tomb of the Unknown Soldier. A few headless statues and broken columns remained upright. A scene of utter ruin, a vast pile of broken masonry and desolation.

From Pilsudski Square, Ceila entered the Saxon Gardens Park. How beautiful and romantic this park had been only a few days before, overgrown and flowering with a lushness that was almost stifling. She always had a particular affection for the Saxon Gardens, long a favorite of fashionable strollers for its magnificent fountains and proud swans. Now it was only broken statues and an improvised cemetery. Newly-covered graves were marked with wooden crosses and fresh flowers.

Everywhere the stench of fire and smoke made the city a living crematorium. Here and there buildings escaped damage, and Ceila had the impression that the Germans had discriminated between the objects they wished to destroy and those they intended to spare.

Ceila sighed with relief when she found the art museum, scarred with bomb fragments and partly blackened from incendiary bombs, still standing as she had left it the night before.

The museum was being used as an aid station. A long line of people waited at the door, all in need of hospitalization. The line had been growing longer each day. There were sounds of prayer, and the wailing, groaning, cursing of the legless, the armless, the blinded and the dying. Some just stood around, some walked, some crawled and some just lay there waiting for someone, something, anything. The sight was appalling. They were civilians, mostly elderly men; women in the bright colors of summer, and children with frightened sad eyes, wondering what they had done to deserve this.

Above the wailing rose other sounds: "Holy Mary, Mother of God. Holy Mary, Mother of God . . ."

There were only three nurses, an old doctor, and some first-aid equipment. Because of the low stock of medical supplies only the most desperate cases were treated inside. The others had to wait out the day, air raids and all, for their turn. There was no place to go.

The huge bronze doors to the museum were open, but to avoid the crowd Ceila entered the building through the employees' side door. The place was crowded. She headed for the curator's office. The other employees had already been there and left, except for the old custodian trying hopelessly to tidy up.

The curator greeted her with a curt "Thank God you're safe" and moved his chair from the draft. The gray mane on the back of his neck stood out like the feathers on a fighting cock. His face was haggard with red-rimmed, steel-blue eyes and bushy brows. With a trembling hand he removed his eyeglasses and laid them on the table, rubbing the red blotches from the bony bridge of his nose.

He struggled to his feet and walked around the desk. The sound of plaster and broken glass clattered under his feet. He moved slowly, as though convalescing from an illness. His suit hung rumpled over a gaunt frame.

He walked around the room, excused himself, stepped out, and returned. Finally he gave her a side glance and called her name.

"Yes – Sir–" she muttered, walking up to him. "Is there anything I can do? Please do sit down."

"I – I – was wondering . . . wondering and looking . . . how . . . where . . . what can I do?" He shook his head. His arms moved in a wide, encircling gesture. "It's like a mad, mad dream. I simply don't know which way to turn, what to do next, with all this. Where can you bury, where can you hide all this?"

GRÜNWALD

He walked to a shattered window, looked out in anger. "Damn it! If only lightning or pestilence would strike the filthy Nazi souls. They'll destroy it all, and what they don't they will haul away."

Ceila knew how much the curator had devoted himself to the museum and had always credited the will of God for having placed him in this great charge . . . as if the entire museum had been the work of his own hands.

He was liked by everyone. He looked as classical as his categories of thinking.

A month ago he had still been a man in his prime. Always neat and prim, he looked like a university professor, ready with wit and a smile.

But now the violence unleashed by the Nazis had crushed all the convictions of his long life. He cast stupefied stares about the exhibition halls and rooms. Everywhere he looked there were crates of paintings and other art objects. A collection of a thousand years. Many paintings still hung on the walls, including the huge Matejko "Grünwald."

"How is your wife?" Ceila asked. "How is your wife?" she repeated.

"Thank God, thank God," he replied. "I hadn't seen her for two or three days. Yesterday she came here after you left, begging me to come home to eat a little, maybe to sleep." He began to tremble. Ceila helped him to his chair behind the desk. "We had to wait until after the air raid. When we got home – Oh, my god, there was nothing left standing. Gone, all gone like the wind. Just so much smoke and rubble. That fabulous art collection my wife had nurtured since our early days in Paris, gone puff, just like that." He snapped his fingers. "Puff. Thank God he spared her, spared us. She's down in the basement helping the nurses with the wounded." He looked up at Ceila.

"My little woman was a nurse's aid in the last war, you know. But then every woman was, I suppose."

All these six days of bombing he had remained in the museum. He would not sleep, saying, "I'll have time enough to sleep after I'm dead." He kept moving through the huge halls, always alert.

With a few of his closest colleagues – Ceila, Kordian, Lolek and a few of the other museum employees – he had discussed ideas and places where they might hide the collection. They spent hours and hours making records, with detailed drawings, photographs and descriptive reports documenting every item. They boxed, rolled, wrapped and crated as many of the art treasures as possible. There was so much more to be done – and time was running out.

"Why don't you go down and see how Mama is doing? The others have gone in search of boards for crating," he told her. "Nothing much we can do up here right now." He patted her hand and started on his rounds of the museum.

Ceila helped as a nurse's aid. During the first days of the war the fighting was all along the frontiers. After the fifth day, transports of wounded began to arrive. Soon the Warsaw hospitals were filled, and it became necessary to organize more hospitals and first-aid centers. This work was left chiefly to the women, and though the nurses grew in number, there always seemed to be a shortage. Medical supplies and equipment became scarce.

Gas and water began to fail. Baths and sterilizers became impossibilities. Food for the patients grew scarce. More and more, the flesh of dead horses had to be salted and stored during the siege. Electric current was continually failing. Operations often were interrupted. Kerosene lamps and candles often supplied the light to continue surgery.

GRÜNWALD

Ceila made bandages and dressed minor wounds. There was always the cleaning up. Her hands were often spotted with blood. At times she just sat and visited with the wounded.

She marveled at the women who came late in the evenings with pails, brooms and dusters. They were countesses, professors' wives, office workers. They washed and cleaned. It was hard and heavy work.

The long storage corridors and underground facilities at the museum were transformed into emergency units. The depth of the corridors gave protection from the air attacks. Everywhere within the musty halls were mattresses and makeshift cots loaded with dismembered and charred bodies. The smells of antiseptics, the murmur of prayers and shrieks of pain pervaded. There was no deliverance from the frightful whimpering of children.

9

On the sixth day Warsaw suffered its worst bombardment. Many buildings and entire blocks of apartment houses were demolished. Yet the museum remained standing. The bombing continued for three full hours before the all-clear signal.

It wasn't noon yet, but Ceila was numbed. Slowly, using the handrail for support, she pulled her way up the stairway, gasping for fresh air. But when she opened the door, she breathed in only the smoke that blanketed the city like a death cloud. She stood transfixed, strangely fascinated by the flames dancing from the buildings across Malachowski Square.

She turned and walked to her office. She felt tired, so tired. Perhaps she could snatch a few winks of sleep. With fumbling fingers she undid the top two buttons of her blouse and flopped into the large stuffed chair. She tried to relax, wishing she could bathe. She wanted to wash off the stench of war. She closed her eyes. Her head eased to one side.

But almost immediately the clatter of running feet burst into the room.

It was Dana, the young girl who lived in the apartments across the street from her own. The slim twelve-year-old spoke between gasps.

"Your mother – it's your mother."

"My mother?"

"I think, I think – she's dead."

Ceila held on, burying her face in the child's blond hair that fell long and straight over slim shoulders. Each supported the other. Their bodies shuddered.

Ceila withdrew. "It's all right now. I think we better go." She reached for the pink sweater draped over the back of her chair. They looked out into the street. It appeared safe enough.

Ceila tightened her grip on the young girl's hand. "Stay close to me, honey." They picked their way around broken slabs of pavement and bomb craters.

Ceila tried to shield Dana's face. What she hadn't considered was that the girl had already passed this way. What bombing hadn't leveled, the incendiary bombs blanketed with fire. Bodies lay everywhere like oversized rag dolls.

Apartment after apartment was a smoking, flaming death-trap. Men and women jumped from windows; parents threw their children out into the street rather than have them roasted to ashes or be buried under the debris.

Ceila hastened her stride, pulling the girl after her as they passed the bloated carcass of a dead horse. They hurried across Saxon Gardens. The lovers and laughing voices were gone. People in the park were digging graves.

When they got to Nalewki Street, Ceila couldn't believe her

eyes. What that morning had been her home was now crumbled brick and mortar. Men were searching the debris for their families, unmindful of bleeding hands and blinding tears. A row of broken bodies lined the still-standing buildings.

Dana ran off to join the group of children huddled around two weeping old women.

Ceila leaned against the wall; the tears flowed freely.

"It's not right. It's not right. No – no."

Her knees gave in. She slumped to the ground. She reached for a piece of brick and held it in her trembling hand. She stared at the ruins and felt the loss that lay inside.

More than just her mother. Everything she knew and understood. It was all there. All that a mother could be and do, pride and love. How many times had her mother said she would never leave Poland. Not as long as she was alive. Now it was all gone. How strange.

Ceila managed to get to her feet. Her hand felt the weight of the brick. She tossed it back into the rubble. She started to walk away with a single backward glance. She walked away, away from what had been home.

She got word to Victor. He hurried over. The last few days he had worked with the fire-fighting and rescue team in his area. He was surprised at her coolness. She had managed the final arrangements with assistance from the curator.

The burial took place the same day that rescue crews found what was left of her mother. The funeral party threaded its way to the cemetery. The wooden coffin was laid to rest in a continuous trenchgrave partly filled and still being extended, about two meters wide and three feet deep.

Victor stood just behind the small group of intimate friends who surrounded Ceila. Her face reminded him of his mother's when they buried his father.

GRÜNWALD

Ceila's mother did not have to suffer. The war was over for her. A priest said a few words of prayer and made the sign of the cross with holy water over the coffin. They lowered the casket. Everyone in turn dropped a handful of earth. Ceila asked to be left alone for the remainder of the day. They arranged a place in her office at the museum next to the room occupied by the curator and his wife. She and her mother had always been close, but Ceila had been a free and practical woman. She had felt that religion was understandably useful for some, but she never filled her life with religious rites. She sought out experience. Any truth was better than make-believe. There was more worth in the comprehension of love in all its phases than in all the mysticism of religion.

10

Ceila was in her office when she heard men's voices above the sound of her typewriter. Lolek appeared, his voice urgent. "The curator would like to see you."

Kordian, Lolek and two strangers in business suits stood around the curator's desk. The curator was studying a communique from the Foreign Office. Ceila thought this strange. Most correspondence came through the Cultural Department. The curator handed her the report. She studied the newspaper clipping.

REWARD — RM 2,000,000

GRÜNWALD PAINTING — JAN MATEJKO

The item was in four languages: German, Polish, French and English. Offered besides the reward money was German citizenship and a passport and safe conduct to any desired destination for one's self and family. All information was to receive full and prompt attention and be kept secret to protect the informers. The address and telephone listed were those of the warped genius, Dr. Joseph Goebbels, German Ministry of Propaganda.

The curator looked at Ceila, then at the two visitors.

"I'll be goddamned!" Kordian paused. "Wouldn't you expect something like that from the filthy Bache?"

"Do you think they would destroy the painting?" asked the curator.

"It's as clear and simple as the nose on your face," said the younger of the two strangers. "Since when have the Nazis become so interested in boasting about the Grünwald to the Germans?"

The curator looked at Ceila. "What do you think about all this?"

"I don't like it. It doesn't sound good."

The gray-bearded, balding gentleman with the professorial manner took the paper from Ceila's hand and, pointing at the press release said, "You can judge for yourself." He pushed the press release at the curator. "They'd like to destroy the Grünwald at any price."

Curator Bozinski read the item for the third time. "I suppose you are right, but what do they hope to gain by such a dastardly act? Who are they trying to fool?"

"Only themselves," Kordian shouted. He was shaking. "They think if the lie is big enough, even they could swallow it."

"It's important that we keep this quiet." The bearded man stood up straight. "It's a rather unpleasant task for anyone."

"How are you going to keep anybody from shooting off his mouth?" For the first time Kordian smiled.

"We hope to be able to appeal to the people for their public-spiritedness," the man replied.

"How?" Kordian asked.

The stranger shrugged.

The curator walked out from behind his desk. "What can we expect further? What are we to do?"

"At the moment I have no idea," replied the stranger, adjusting his glasses. "It should be within the next day or two, at the most."

"We are now in the process of evacuating, and there might be some delays and confusion," said the other with flat Slavic features. A little shorter than average height, thin lines across his flat, broad forehead, the brown eyes sunken under the heavy, bony brows, he kept pulling his lip tight, as though locking in his thoughts.

The curator reached for a cigarette and nervously for a match. The stranger lit it for him. He sputtered, "What in damnation are we supposed to be doing while you wait to make up your minds? Bureaucracy! – Bah!" He saw the two gentlemen to the side door. Then he scurried back to his office, summoned the others and started down the hallway toward the main gallery.

He halted in front of the Grünwald canvas. Lolek had to spring aside in order to avoid a collision. The curator exclaimed, "How in the world is anyone to hide a thing as large as that?"

"I suppose the first thing I'd suggest is to get it out of the city." Lolek's remark came as a surprise to all.

"There it is, like a full-blown page out of the history books," said the curator. "To the Germans, Grünwald is a symbol of defeat. To the Poles in their victory, Grünwald remains a constant source of hope and pride.

"Grünwald! How hearts did quicken to the sound of Grünwald! How could anyone afford to forget, even though it happened in another existence? For more than five hundred years the battle cry of Grünwald to the Polish people was like yesterday – nothing about it remote or alien to them. Grünwald! – an echoing cry of another time, but certainly not of another world. In his Grünwald Matejko portrayed on canvas what the Nobel Prize Winner Henryk Sienkiewicz did in his multi-historical novels. By his work, Matejko was able to uplift hearts and reinforce resolve in their struggle and constant invocation to preserve and to fight. His canvas gave great justice to the words of Sienkiewicz's novel *The Knights of the Cross*.

Anger and hate, so alien to the curator, now swelled. "Who directed the course of a bolt of lightning? Is it the law of nature?"

Ceila noticed how tired and old he looked, pushing himself to the brink of collapse. Slowly, head bowed, he trudged back to his office.

Early the next morning the phone rang. The curator answered. He said little – mostly listened. His face turned first crimson then gray. Slowly, very slowly, as though it were heavy, he placed the receiver on the hook.

"It's what still remains of our foreign office." He swallowed, fitted the glasses on the bridge of his nose. "Our government, along with the foreign diplomatic corps, has withdrawn to Lublin. It's all up to us now: the destiny of the Grünwald painting is entirely in our hands."

The curator was no longer a part of anyone's scheme. He appeared calm. He stood again before the Grünwald canvas. Overhead, the aircraft. Around them, exploding bombs. The curator's thoughts were on saving the canvas from the Nazis. How long before German agents would be at the door?

72

He assigned some to remove the canvas from the wall. He directed others to make a crate of solid oak large enough to encase the rolled canvas.

Kordian urged Lolek to move faster. Lolek retorted, "It won't matter how much we rush if a bomb hits this place." He stopped by the side door. He was knocked to the floor. The blast was so close that the building shook. Glass splintered. Mortar dust fogged the air. Spitting dust, Lolek rose to his feet. "Just as I said. What's the big rush?"

They hurried off in search of horses and wagon.

Ceila looked in at the basement first-aid station. For the next hour she comforted patients and managed to quiet the children.

That evening the curator, Ceila, Kordian, Lolek and three others met.

"There's no need having the whole world know about this," the curator advised. "We've been together from the beginning. The fewer we involve the better."

They discussed the route to be taken. They set departure for tomorrow night after the nine o'clock air raid. The dark would provide cover, and there would be less activity in the streets. They would proceed over the Poniatowski Bridge which remained intact. They would cross over to Praga and proceed along the road parallel to the Vistula River. Other bridges might be blown up farther down the river. They would head for Lublin then on to Lwow and the Rumanian border. With the combination of the museum's funds and their own, they hoped to buy themselves out of any unexpected encounters. From Rumania they would proceed by boat to England. They would carry as little as possible and a food supply of smoked sausage, smoked ham and rye bread.

Ceila waited until Kordian and Lolek left before she asked the curator, "Do you suppose it would be possible that our

American friend go with us?"

"I would think so. He's got to find a way out of the country somehow. It's mostly my fault that he's even here."

Then the curator asked casually, "Does he love you?"

"Very much."

"Why doesn't he marry you then? He's been treated like a brother, always welcomed."

"He asked and I said no – at least for now – does it matter?"

"No, I suppose not. Marriage is not always the answer to everything." He pondered before he continued. "This – war could but be the beginning of another world war. Battles are no longer fought at the front lines, and what the aircraft and the scientists are brewing for us could be worse than the work of a dozen witches. What sort of man is your American?"

"Consientious and imaginative. Strong and proud. I'm sure he could help, if need be."

"Yes – I suppose we could always use an extra hand."

Ceila nodded. "Always." She marveled at the curator's composure. The nervous gestures of these last few days had vanished, as had his diffident manner and querulous voice. He was the soldier of old, in full command of himself – there was nothing like action to perk up a real man. And so it was decided that Victor would join them.

11

Ceila lay down on the couch in her office. The museum felt
cool. The many shattered windows caused drafts that stirred the
warm air. The only light in the place was the dancing red and
yellow reflection on the walls from the burning building across
the way. Who needed hell? She closed her eyes.

She was annoyed when footsteps approached her room.
Then Victor poked his dark head in. He walked in and sat down
beside her.

"I had to lie down for a spell," she said.

"You've done wonders as it is." He regarded her. The blue
silk blouse outlined the fullness of her breasts. Her pleated skirt
folded casually high above her knees. She was barefooted.

"You be careful you don't cut your feet," he said, "with all
this broken glass about."

"That's why you are here – to protect me."

"Till hell freezes over." He bent over and kissed her.

"Well," she said, "Hitler certainly made a personal call here today."

"Came knocking on the door?"

"That he did. He's even touched our lives at the museum."

"Now suppose you tell me all about it."

She told him about the Grünwald communique. Victor asked, "How much is that in American money?"

"Seven hundred and fifty thousand dollars."

"Christ! For three quarters of a million dollars and a deal like that, who wouldn't be tempted to sell his own grandmother to the bastards?"

"That's just what we are afraid of. Everybody knows that the painting is here – not only the Poles, but students and tourists, most of them Germans."

"Three quarters of a million dollars could sure go a long way."

Ceila repeated her conversation with the curator.

"Great, sounds wonderful," he said. "I sure can't just sit around doing nothing." He got to his feet and began to pace the room.

"It won't be easy, out in the open with the Nazis machine-gunning everything that moves."

"But anything, anything, as long as we are doing something." He sat down beside her.

September the 7th. No hint of autumn. The sun shone bright in a cloudless sky. People scurried along in the hot air with faces toward the sky. Everyone at the museum was listening to the radio. The concert was interrupted and the impersonal voice announced another air raid.

The Polish Suicide Battallion at Westerplatte was holding out after days of shelling and bombardment, the announcer told them. But across the rest of Poland, Germany's heavy forces had advanced across an 800 mile front. Nazi planes had tried from the beginning to destroy the bridges over the Vistula River, but so far no bombs had struck. The last Sunday, all Warsaw turned out on the streets, ignoring the air raids. The happy news that Britain and France had declared war had dispelled the fear that they might have to fight alone. Crowds danced and sang in wild jubilation.

The curator, his wife and museum employees returned that evening to remove paintings from the walls. They crated and wrapped many art objects. Shortly after eight o'clock they gathered in the main office to listen to Mayor Starzynski's speech on the radio. In pre-war days he had been an architect-engineer in the city planning department. After the sixth day of war when the government left the capital the mayor was put in charge of the citizens, prepared to fight, to set an example for the free world. Through the years of Poland's dismemberment and all the wars, Warsaw remained a symbol of Polish unity.

He began his speech:

"Citizens, another day of warfare is now over, in the course of which there have been so many massive bombardments."

The curator's wife began to cry. Ceila bit her lip to refrain from breaking down. The Mayor continued:

"The bombing of Warsaw must have profound repercussions. The ruins will disappear. We will reconstruct them. Warsaw has been destroyed more than once. Revenge will be bitter. Hitler's lies have no foundation to Germany's policy of violence and extermination, with all that follows: theft, looting and massacres.

"In closing may I reiterate the words of Neville Chamberlain in his appeal that we defend the right. It is evil things that we shall be fighting against – brute force, bad faith, injustice, oppression and persecution – and against them I am certain that the right will prevail. And with the help of God, right must prevail."

The curator moved to his trembling wife and put his arms around her.

Victor cast a sidelong glance at Ceila. Her eyes were closed.

"Come." Victor helped Ceila to her feet. "Let's see what we can find that Hitler hasn't bombed."

It was the end of the seventh day of the war. They walked toward the exit. Victor turned and asked, "I wonder what the folks back home are up to now?"

Her eyes were fixed on the street. How could anything possibly remain standing. She muttered, "How is this all to end? How? How?"

Victor replied, "How? When is what I'd like to know."

The hand that Ceila gave Victor felt cold and frail. They walked in search of a restaurant, deep in an ancient stone wine cellar. Her face was a small pale triangle between mussed hair. The loss of her mother had taken its toll. But her footsteps did not falter – chin high, eyes sad but undimmed, she picked her way.

They moved down the street. Every foot of the way they encountered people with the same determination, fighting fires, caring for the wounded. Everywhere people were cleaning up after the air raids – fighting back, each in his own particular way.

About a dozen people were in the restaurant. It had never been heavily patronized before the war, but now it was quite popular – thick stone walls, soft candlelight; between sips of beet soup, weak coffee and cheap wine, one could forget the war.

The menu listed a number of meat selections. They all tasted the same – the sweet stringiness of horseflesh.

Victor reached for Ceila's hand. "In war people seem to have more time for each other."

"We always had time for each other." She leaned over and pressed her lips to his hand.

She smiled, then let her eyes wander. A woman was holding a child firmly around the waist. An elderly man comforted his woman; her head rested on his chest. Two men played chess on a wooden crate near the candle. Only a direct hit could have interrupted their game.

Strange how the people had installed themselves for good in their cellars. They brought down furniture, spirit-lamps and candles. They cooked, ate, slept and prayed here.

They ate and took time for a cigarette over a glass of red wine. Victor suggested, "Come, let's head for home, if it's still standing."

She said nothing, and they went out into the night and another burning hell!

People scurried like rats out of hiding, in all directions. Victor watched the faces. There was no sign of hesitancy or faltering. There was no cowardice or treachery. To look at the dead was to see the corpse of the Polish romantic. From the dead, from the sufferings, an awesome thing was being formulated which no weapon or system could stop; the resistance movement. Instead of dividing and destroying the nation, the Nazis had united it!

The streets still had their own special melody. The hubbub of crowds, mostly women and children selling everything from buttons to old clothes. A ragged child snatched a parcel of food from a passerby and devoured it as he ran. The newsboys, despite constant shelling, managed to get the latest editions to their regular stations. Here and there a body lay covered with newspapers. Legs protruded, swollen or very thin. Some had died where they had fallen. Others were left by relatives or neighbors to avoid burial costs. Everywhere were hurriedly dug graves covered with flowers.

The apartment building was still standing. It was a wonder. Each time more war torn. The gas and the water had long since been turned off, but there was still electricity.

He tried the switch and a dim light from a table lamp lit the apartment. He made sure the blackout curtains were drawn and started for the kitchen. "I have wine, but would you care for something stronger?"

"Yes."

"Yes – what? Which would you prefer, the wine or the whiskey?"

"Whiskey." She collapsed on the bed and kicked her shoes off. "I take mine straight these days."

She rolled over to watch him disappear behind the kitchen door, then turned on the radio, hoping to shut out the sounds outside. The music was warm and welcome – a flowing Strauss waltz. It reminded her of happy moments in Vienna. She rolled over on her back and stared at the ceiling. "I wonder what the people of Vienna are doing?" Victor entered with two glasses in hand and seated himself on the edge of the bed.

"To the poor people of Vienna," he said, handing her a glass.

"To all the poor people in all this sad, crazy world." There was no remorse in Ceila's voice. He pressed his mouth to hers.

She looked childlike, small, helpless. Her hair came around in bright folds to cradle her face. Her eyes closed, her lips partly open, her bosom rising and falling. Before he knew it she had fallen asleep. He took the glass from her hand. He lay down beside her and cradled her in his arms. Sleep came. With sleep came strange dreams in which she was standing protectively over him.

12

At the museum the next day, Ceila and Victor could hear the argument long before they approached.

Kordian and Lolek were at it again. They had finished crating the Grünwald painting.

"Maybe we could trade that canvas to Hitler in exchange for peace," Kordian said.

Lolek didn't think that was funny. He called Kordian a Gypsy lover. "Any Gypsy whore is twice the person that you'd ever be." Kordian gave his retort emphasis on Lolek's foot. Lolek grabbed a hammer and went after Kordian.

"Fascist," Lolek screamed.

Kordian turned white. He took a step back. He trembled a little.

"You stupid ass. Talking like that could get your neck

broken!'' Slowly he began to move forward. "Put that hammer down before I . . ."

"Stop! Stop!" The curator came running. "What the hell? What are you trying to do, turn this into an insane asylum? You fools! You'll have time enough to fight Germans, but for God's sake not here. No, not here. No! No!" He grabbed the hammer from Lolek and glared. "I'll see you two in my office."

In his office the curator looked like an angry school teacher. He walked across the room with hands deep in his pockets and turned swiftly. "One day soon you fools might have to fight. I only hope you will know how. I don't want to see any more of this stupidity. Do you understand?"

It was time to start moving.

"Since yesterday, I've given the Grünwald considerable thought. Our only hope is to get the canvas out of the country. We could join up with the government in Lublin, move on to Rumania and then to London. If it stays here I'm afraid the Germans won't leave a stone unturned until they find it. We'll have to move fast before too many people learn about this. We leave tonight. We'll meet here at eight. And Kordian–" he eyed the sulking artist – "Sometimes I worry about you."

Kordian apologized. "Sorry, I didn't think the sorehead would take things so seriously. I'll keep an eye on my friend that it doesn't happen again."

"You'll what!" Lolek exploded.

"Nothing." Kordian smiled and ambled out of the room.

"Kordian!" the curator called after him. "See that the others meet here in ten minutes."

The working staff filed into the office. None smiled as they grouped around the curator. "We've been associated for a long time, and I've been most happy to have enjoyed so many loyal friends. I hate to admit it, but I'm forced to leave for a few

weeks. Most of you will remain on your jobs as usual."
The curator spoke slowly and before he was through they
were all in tears. When he had finished, he shook hands with
each before dismissing them.

All that day the curator was busy. He analyzed every
chamber, room and corner, making mental notes. He was on the
move again.

The problem of transport remained. A truck or van would
attract too much attention. A four-wheel wagon would be more
suitable. It was the customary vehicle in Poland – a long, low
cart used to haul hay and wares to market.

He'd tell his wife when she brought his bowl of soup as she
did each afternoon.

Promptly at noon, the curator's wife took her seat across the
desk from him. He told her. She asked, "You sure you want me
along? What if I should fail to prove useful? What if I might be a
nuisance? It's such a long trip, and by wagon, yet."

"Nonsense!"

"Only if it's the wish of all of you, then I'll go."

The curator smiled. She had not changed despite the tragedy.
She remained solemn and mildly aloof. Almost childlike. She
retained much of her former beauty – her slender figure, the
whiteness of her skin.

"I think this war is horrible," she said. "Sometimes I'm so
frightened. What is to become of us? I believe in God, but how
can there be so much hate in the world?"

The curator did not answer. He'd die for her if only to relieve
her of this agony.

Their marriage, though childless, was filled with so many
memories that they never seemed at a loss for something to talk
about. They had always shared the same room, the same bed.
She made him comfortable at home, clean as a new duckling.

GRÜNWALD

He was kind, appreciative, faithful. They were far from being wealthy, but she never found herself in want. It was a terrible loss, the bombing of their apartment with all its treasures of some of Europe's great artists – most of them personal friends. She thanked the good Lord for having spared their lives, then moved into the museum basement to help the victims.

The nine o'clock raid came and went. The moving hour arrived. None seemed eager to leave. They were turning their backs on a most wonderful way of life. With their bags and a few belongings and a small food supply they took their places aboard the wagon.

Kordian was up front at the reins, with Pani Curator seated at his side. Behind, were the curator and Ceila. Lolek took guard post at the rear. They would pick up Victor on the way.

The air raid had been extensive. They were more than an hour late when Kordian finally eased the wagon out of the museum building.

Within a few blocks they encountered a fallen building blocking the street and were forced to backtrack. On all sides, desolation. The night was aglow from burning buildings.

Rats and half-wild cats roamed the ruins. Wild dogs, singly and in packs, fought each other over human and animal flesh. Broken water mains spouted fountains into the air and the stench of broken sewage pipes pervaded. Buildings collapsed without warning. Burning gas mains lit up the debris. The wagon creaked through the ruined city on its quest for sanctuary for its cargo.

13

Victor made ready. In five minutes he had packed his old black leather suitcase. He shaved in a cup of cold water and changed into travel khakis. He put on a brown woolen sweater for cool nights.

In the kitchen he found a vodka bottle half full, took a long swallow, then another. He glanced at his watch – at least an hour before the pickup. He walked out on the balcony, first assuring himself of its rigidity.

The air-raid sirens started screaming again. He scurried down the stairway and hid under the concrete arch supporting the stairs. He hadn't time to make the cellar before the bombs began to explode.

When the sirens finally wailed their reprieve, Victor hurried back to his apartment and again reached for the vodka bottle.

He fixed himself a stiff drink, made himself comfortable on the bed and turned on the radio. Only a single station responded. He turned the dial and got another faint response. He stood the radio on its side and the speaker came in reasonably clear.

"Germany's armies from East Prussia have been delayed in their march toward Warsaw." The commentator's voice grew self-assured with the report that there was still hope, with the brave detachment holding on in the Baltic stronghold at Hel. With reinforcements from the east, Warsaw's defenders were digging in. And there were still the rains to hope for and Allied pressure at Germany's back.

Meanwhile, German columns smashed on eastward toward Lublin and Lwow, Poland's remaining lifeline: the roads and railroads to Rumania.

Reports of Russian armies on the eastern border did not worry the Poles. They felt Stalin was merely making sure Hitler did not forget to stop when he reached Russia.

The commentator decried the Nazist breach of International Protocol. German planes attacked Lublin where the Polish Government had withdrawn from Warsaw. A cabinet meeting was called when the city was bombed and strafed with machine-gun fire.

The commentator switched to the activities of the Allies, but noisy interference forced Victor to turn the radio off.

He wondered how his friends were doing. He began to feel sleepy. He fought off the agonizing desire to doze. He couldn't miss the rendezvous. Surely they would not leave him behind.

No farm cart could be comfortable for any distance. Then he thought of Ceila. He hated the air raids. He hated the Germans. One could forgive the plundering of a conqueror and even violence, but how did one justify the piecemeal destruction of an entire city?

He fell into a deep, exhausted slumber.

A hurried clump, clump beat its way up the steps. Victor bolted upright. Someone was coming after him!

Kordian's hulk cast a shadow in the doorway. He stood wavering, a wheezing sound in his throat.

"Victor!" he yelled, groping in the darkness.

"Sorry, old boy; guess I dozed off." He reached for his sweater and suticase. "Sorry I put you through this." He nodded toward the bottle. "Help yourself to a drink, it's the best I can offer." He pushed the hair off his face, then gave the Pole a conciliatory pat on his back.

Kordian reached for the bottle. "We were delayed some by roadblocks. We've got to hurry. It'll be daybreak before long. They're waiting for us at the Square of the Three Crosses." He took three stiff swigs at the vodka. He turned to speak, but Victor was already bolting down the stairway. He seized the bottle and started after him. "I'd sure hate to get caught on that bridge when those goddamned Germans start the day off."

They walked rapidly up Mokotowska Street. It was deserted except for a few shadowy figures.

Then everything came to a halt. Necks craned toward the black sky. Sure enough, there was that low drone. Victor and Kordian began to run.

They started across the square. Lolek was waving to them from the main door of St. Alexander Church. The others had already taken cover inside. The flame of a little lamp flickered near the altar. The smell of incense mingled with dust and sour, sweaty bodies.

Victor pushed through the crowd, looking for Ceila. Everywhere people stood and sat and sprawled. He tripped over legs and heard curses. There were wounded on stretchers on the floor, groaning and begging for water, but all murmuring ended with the first screams of Stukas, then bombs. The church had been hit before and the noise of collapsing masonry splintered under the vaults. Any near hit could be the last for those inside.

It was not a long raid, a sporting run for the Nazis to start hell-burning to light the way for bigger raids soon to follow. The ambulance men arrived and asked the people to leave. The crowd filled the streets. Most of them hurried to the Vistula River to fill their pails. The sky was no longer inky black. A faint steel blue on the eastern horizon blurred with smoke.

Lolek led the two to the farm cart where Ceila and the curator and his wife waited. The team and wagon had weathered the raid in the debris of what was once the Ministry of Transport. The building had suffered a direct hit a few days before.

They embraced. Kordian passed around what remained of the vodka. Kordian again took the reins with Ceila at his side, while the curator and his wife slumped behind them. Victor joined Lolek toward the back. They headed straight up 3rd of May Avenue and onto the Poniatowski Bridge.

14

Kordian steered the wagon onto the bridge where refugees pressed along the walls. Long before daybreak they started to gather in numbers. The sun winking on the horizon brought the traffic out. Hundreds of wagons and carts, cars and trucks; people on horseback and on foot, all moving toward the bridge. Soldiers in trucks shouted at the moving mass to give way, even made gestures with guns.

Kordian eased the wagon forward. They hadn't far to go, maybe thirty paces at the most.

The air-raid sirens started to scream.

"O, Jesus," Pani Curator breathed out.

All forward movement came to a halt. Hundreds of angry voices, the frantic drivers with heavy hands on bellowing horns. Stomping feet of the crowd swayed the bridge.

"Why don't they move?" Kordian yelled. "We'll be caught here like sitting ducks. It's murder."

"The fools." The curator stood up. "In their panic they've created a jam. We can't go forward or back. God help us!"

Ceila turned quickly to catch Victor's eyes. "Quick, under the wagon!" He helped her.

"The filthy sons-of-bitches," Kordian mumbled, quickly fastening the reins to the seat. "Those filthy sons-of-bitches!"

Lolek helped Pani Curator to the ground while the curator managed on his own.

"Damn it!" he mumbled. "A few minutes and we'd have been off this damn bridge."

The crowd waited, the sea of heads facing the steel-blue sky and the first sounds of low humming aircraft.

Every action created an immediate reaction, multiplying the confusion of angry voices and frightened faces.

High in the expanse of sky glittering formations moved like wintering geese. The planes grew larger.

Kordian and Victor tried to calm the horses while the others hid under the wagon. Victor noticed a commotion not twenty feet away. "What's all the shouting about?"

"I don't know."

An army captain bellowed to a burly civilian standing next to a small pickup truck with the hood up. Victor understood a few words: "dog's blood" and "stupid." Then Victor saw the carcass of a dead horse, a splintered wagon and load of spilled logs. He turned to Kordian. "The truck must have run into that horse and wagon."

"And here we are. The stupid bastards," Kordian swore.

Above, the planes' wings waggled the signal for attack.

Someone yelled *"Niemiec!"* The shouting diminished as the officer pulled the man's jacket down over his arms, binding his elbows.

"A German at the wheel caused the pileup," Kordian said. They watched the captain pull out his revolver from the holster and shoot the man's brains out. He shouted a command and soldiers hurriedly disposed of the dead man and pushed the vehicle to one side. Other soldiers and civilians pulled at the dead horse and attacked the lumber. But it was too late.

Closer, closer the planes dived until Victor could see the swastika markings on their wings. He pressed his body to the floor of the bridge. He could almost see the pilot's face and felt the gunsight trained at him.

The sky was alive with the snarl of motors, the whistling of bombs. The bridge shuddered. Ack-ack thundered and the machine guns clattered. Clods of earth and water bounded hundreds of feet high.

Some of the bombs missed. Others did better. The bridge was full of smoke. A truck filled with soldiers was hit and bodies flew like broken puppets.

Other soldiers under shouted orders of their officers set up machine guns behind their trucks. In their cross fire two sharp-nosed planes crashed into the river. Three others nosed drunkenly skyward, black smoke trailing from under their bellies before they rolled over and crashed out of view.

A third and fourth flight of planes streaked in. Again the sweet smell of burning flesh and molten metal; the screams of men and horses. The planes came back again and again.

The bridge held. The sky over Praga blurred in the smoke. The raid lasted only a few minutes, but it seemed hours before the planes nosed upward and disappeared.

People ran, they crawled, they fell and lay still; they prayed and they cursed. The flies spread quickly. Once again the crowd began to move, inches at a time.

Both the horses had been hit. One lay still, whining with a throaty sound. The other, half mad with pain, kicked aimlessly, shrieking and fighting to get to its feet. A bullet from a lieutenant's pistol ended the agony. Strong backs helped push the wagon off the bridge and onto the parkway.

It was a harrowing two-hour wait before Kordian could find two sound animals. More people than horses had been killed. Kordian had several animals to choose from.

The bridge was filled with bodies. Relatives and friends carried them to the edge of the bridge. Horses with empty carts in tow milled about until taken in hand.

Finally, with two sound horses again in harness, Kordian led them out slowly through the crowding refugees. Momentary relief came as they moved forward. Kordian drove a wild course among the shell holes and buildings that collapsed about them.

The streets were a river of ghostly shapes lapping against each other. The heat was horrible. There was no panic, only a steady tide. Overhead the sky was blue and the sun bright. It held no promise for tomorrow.

An old man with outspread arms tried to board the wagon, but one such exception could mean that others would attempt the same and soon the mass would force the wagon to collapse.

Lolek harshly fought the stumbling man off. He uttered a cry and fell face down into the dust. The mass moving like robots stumbled and stepped and drove over the body, rushing on like an animated sea.

At times they came to a complete halt only to start again at an agonizingly slow pace. Kordian urged the team on through the refugees. Six children were in a cart pulled by a mule, all piled atop the bedding. Their father was away fighting somewhere. Their mother had been left dead at the bridge. Friends advised the youngsters to go ahead; they would see that she was buried.

A blond girl of fourteen, the eldest, sat reins in hand, crying. The young huddled close together, all shabby, their faces pale. Ceila turned her head to avoid their glances.

Some looked very funny, hauling chickens and bedsprings and ridiculous assortments of household goods. Others were not so funny, such as mothers nursing their babies on breasts long since sucked dry.

Kordian had but one thing in mind: to get far out of Warsaw before nightfall. The old farm wagon rocked and ground its way. The ride was wearisome. But on they drove, east, then south toward Otwock, where the road became less clogged with refugees. Sometimes they rested, hidden in the trees along the road. Time and again Kordian stretched and moved on with a reassuring glance at the sky.

"Jesus, Jesus," Pani Curator murmured.

"What now?" Her husband gave her a quick glance.

"Jesus, Jesus." She looked straight ahead, her eyes wide.

"Are you all right?"

"I don't know."

"What's the matter, then? Should we stop?"

"No. No need to stop."

Kordian turned to the curator. "Any vodka?"

"For the lady."

"There's nothing wrong," she replied. "I don't need anything."

"Never you mind." Kordian's words were direct.

"A little vodka," Kordian advised. "Pani Curator, there is nothing better for an upset stomach. I know, it's been an old family remedy."

The curator handed her the bottle. She refused at first, but when her husband was about to raise his voice she took a short sip.

"I'll be all right after a while," she said.

She was fragile and evidently growing weaker. She hardly uttered a word of complaint or bitterness.

She had not believed that the war would come. When it did, she was confident that Poland would win. Now she could not close her eyes in the face of defeat. Oh, God, was the privilege of living asking too much?

The curator placed his palm tenderly against her cheek. She tried to smile, glanced at her watch and said, "It has been such a long day."

"Very, very long, my dear," he replied. "You sure you're not too tired?"

"It's too soon to stop. We still have so far to go."

Time and again the wagon had to pull off to the side as they let columns of brown-uniformed soldiers march past, all heading toward Warsaw. A regiment of lancers went by at a smart trot with their harnesses jingling. Small groups sang as they marched behind battle flags and colored banners.

When the planes came down, the bursting shells ripped the road with orange flames. Shrapnel plowed into man, animal and machine. The civilians pressed amidst the troops, burrowing into the ranks as if soldiers never died. Neighing horses struggled to their feet. Women screamed and children wailed.

In one rush for cover, something struck Victor, knocking him to his knees. When he saw that he could move, he stumbled into a ditch. He lay still, dazed with the taste of blood in his mouth. Ceila shook his head.

"Are you all right?"

"I'll be all right." He spit blood. A fragment of flying debris had cut the side of his lip.

The crowd diminished. The curator at the reins guided the team around a sharp right-hand turn. Off to the left a village was burning, mostly hidden in smoke. Midway between the village and the wagon was a large potato field where two women supervised nine children digging potatoes.

Out of nowhere three fighter planes on silent wings at treetop level exploded with machine-gun fire.

The wagon lurched across the ditch and into the forest. The curator tugged at the reins. The frightened team fought the bits. Kordian leaped to the ground and managed to bring them under control.

The roar of the planes returned. Those in the potato field stood as if undecided what to do next. Machine-gun bullets ripped the dirt closer and closer. Not until the bullets were upon them did one of the women scream and fall to the ground. The children doubled over like black balls against the green potato stocks. Not one of them tried to run. They did not move as the planes came back again and again. Only after the planes nosed up from their kill did a black ball shake convulsively, before it lay still again.

The two women finally got to their feet. Only one of the children, a boy of about eight, started running toward the village. He took a few strides and spilled headlong. A large group emerged from the village in haste.

Victor turned to Kordian. "Why didn't they run for cover when they first saw the planes? They could have made it."

"Did you ever try to outrun a machine-gun bullet? There wasn't a tree or rock they could hide behind." Kordian cursed. "I've never felt so miserably helpless in my entire life. I'd have given anything – anything, to have stopped those bastards. Those filthy bastards!" He spat at the ground. He led the team out of the forest and back onto the road.

They made themselves as comfortable as possible, with the

curator and his wife up front. They rode on in silence.

The curator said, "Not too far now, maybe five or six kilometers on the other side of Otwock."

"Wonderful. I'll be glad when this day is over," said his wife, glancing at her watch. "We'll be in the village before dark, thank goodness. Are we going to stay there?"

"Not if I have anything to do about it." The curator hesitated, "We're staying at an old friend's home, a small country estate where we so often went hunting. Wonderful hare and fox country." He smiled a little.

They bypassed as much of the town as possible. Bombs had torn up the roads. Trees stood with tops snapped off, leaves wilted and brown. Everywhere abandoned wagons and carts piled high with belongings. The dead lay in heavy dust where they had been struck down in flight. Small groups of homeless huddled around fires, shouting out, asking for news.

A smoke cloud hung over the town. The old silhouette of buildings and church spires had toppled into piles of rubble. Landmarks had changed.

They passed Otwock. Half an hour later they rolled through a small village where the continuous stream of wagons had ripped the road's surface. Weary horses strained. Old men and women fought at the reins, cracked whips, cursed, entreated and sometimes led the horses. The curator reined the team carefully around a spot in the road near where German planes had bombed a children's sanitorium. About thirty of the young ones lay dead, half buried under the ruins.

They dragged on, past burning cottages, craters and litter, avoiding the farm animals that wandered across the lane. Cows bellowed to be relieved of the milk in untouched udders. They passed dead and rotting horses, cows, pigs, goats and dogs, gas-ballooned stomachs transforming them into monsters.

15

The night was cool and clear. The moon and stars shone brightly. The road was a dull gray ribbon with ruts and rocks black under the sky. Silhouetted shrubs and fencing resembled strange monsters. They could expect a wild beast to spring out of the darkness at any moment. Only the rumble of the iron-bound wheels and bridle jingle. Even the horses acted nervously, tossing their heads – a gurgling snort from one, then the other, then only hooves muffled in the dust.

Through the fringe of forest they could make out the long, low lines of the villa, with a steep roof to shed heavy snows. The plastered white wall glowed grayish-blue through the vines and shrubs. All the rooms were on the ground floor. It was typical of most country homes where, with a few quick changes, any room could be transformed from a bedroom into a salon and vice versa. In the old days, the nobles rode about continually, for hunting, for war, business and pleasure. They took with them rugs and skins and bedding and made themselves at home anywhere.

The curator brought the wagon to a halt, his searching eyes piercing through the dull shadows under the moonlight. He inhaled deeply. The cool September air spread thin. The odor of apples and pears came from the orchard with the sharp smell of manure from the barn.

"This should do for the day." He turned to the others. "Safer out here in the country than in any town." He guided the horses as close as possible to the door, still under the protective cover of pines.

Kordian asked the others to wait. He went in alone. It was pitch black inside. The damp indoor air felt cold after the intense heat of the day. He smelled burnt wood, acrid earth and dust, and the animal fat used to grease hunting boots. He lit a match. Other than four solid walls and a roof, there was nothing else. The place was void of furnishings. Straw was piled in two of the corners where some previous travelers had made a night of it. He wasn't exactly pleased, but it would have to do.

One by one the others uncoiled themselves and climbed out of the wagon. They stretched their arms and walked around to work the kinks out of their legs and backs.

Kordian and Lolek hurriedly unhitched the team and watered them at the low stream wandering through knee-high grass. Kordian reached into his pocket for some sugar cubes and awarded each horse its share before hobbling them to graze under the orchard.

The curator lit some candles and started a flame in the huge stone fireplace. Victor brought in piles of additional straw and turned to help Ceila, but she reminded him it was a lady's chore to stack the straw. She piled it to make a bed fit for a king and shaped a pillow for the two of them.

They hadn't said much to each other all day. There always remained that problem of trying to stay alive. To stop was to give up; to lie down was to die. Victor just had to do something, say something.

"I could get more straw," he said. "Do you think this will be sufficient for this hard, cold floor?"

"If you like. We could use more I'm sure."

She turned and smiled in the dim yellow candlelight; there was a sweet calmness about her face. He went outside, knowing that she was glad the day was over. At this moment the war was far, far away.

She laid a blanket on the floor, then a plain tablecloth, then knives and forks. The curator handed her a bottle of red wine. She put out some glasses and bread and salt and pepper.

There was no need to cook anything. All had been prepared. It was a matter of portioning the food out. They ate noisily and appreciatively – fresh ham, hard boiled eggs, plenty of black bread, glasses of wine. It was dramatic, by candlelight.

Supper was hardly over when they heard the drone of bombers. Lolek got up and opened the door and stood. The others joined him. The sky filled with the glow of softly falling flares in the direction of Warsaw. It was a gorgeous sight. The flares burst into daylight brightness. Then the bombs fell where the flares glowed. Like distant thunder they heard the explosions. Cities, towns and villages were on fire all over Poland this night.

The curator turned to his wife. "Well – mama, you have seen living hell. Now maybe it's time to sleep."

Tomorrow was another long trek. There wasn't much to do now except sleep, but Kordian wasn't ready to crawl under the blanket. He approached Victor standing in the doorway smoking and said, "Cool, but still too nice a night to go up in smoke." The Pole jerked up his head toward the sky. "Let's you and I walk down to the village. Who knows, the night could yet prove interesting. Need to stretch the legs a little, anyhow."

"You've convinced me." The American smiled.

Kordian went back into the villa to tell the others. Ceila cried out,"He can't go." Then she started to laugh. "One of those village beauties might steal him away from me."

"No, no, no. I wouldn't permit it," Kordian roared back. "I'd steal them for myself first." It was the first time anyone had laughed for days.

They departed, with Kordian in the lead, figuring on a twenty-minute walk to the village. They walked through an orchard smelling apples, manure and dry straw. From time to time Victor could feel a fallen apple crush under his feet. The smell like apple cider filled the night. He almost ran into Kordian, who suddenly stopped and appeared bewildered.

"Walking around like this in the night," he said, "a man could get himself shot."

"Thanks for telling me, bub. Where do we go?"

"There is an old cellar bar," Kordian smiled, nodding. "I used to know the Gypsy barmaid there. What a lay, what a lay. She'd rather screw than eat."

"Nothing the matter with that."

They walked out of the protective cover of the orchard. A deep blue sky wide with bright stars provided a faint source of light. The black silhouette of the village stood out against the skyline red from burning buildings. They were about a block from the village when the dogs started barking. Lights went on and a few doors opened. They could see the outline of armed men looking out into the night.

They entered the village as though it were home. To have hesitated could have proved dangerous. They headed for the cellar bar. A dull light shone through the partly opened door. A number of men stood about, others sat on their haunches against the wall on both sides of the door. Peasants and villagers, broad shouldered and long armed in their white homespun shirts, watched them with small eyes out of wrinkled, broad faces. Their pistols, old rifles, scythes and knives were ready.

Kordian recognized one and then another, and they were welcomed as old friends. After a short visit the two learned that the villagers were holding court over a number of captured Germans and Polish-born Germans who had caused trouble and spread untruths and panic amongst the people. There wouldn't be any drinking, but sure as hell there would be some hangings before this night was over. The villagers couldn't understand why, but the war had come and their homes had been bombed and their fields burned to the ground.

"Come," Kordian pulled at Victor's sleeve. "You might learn something from real life that you can't learn from any textbook."

They inched their way through the crowd down the narrow stone stairway. Two more men recognized Kordian. Their brown teeth showed smiles as they shook hands. The only sources of light were oil lamps suspended on chains from the heavy rafters. The stench of stale ale, tobacco smoke, sweaty bodies and just plain earth permeated the place. Some men sat on the bar next to those leaning against it. Others sat on upturned barrels, but most just stood along the ancient stone walls.

Except for a slight murmur from time to time, all were quiet. Only the speaker's voice sounded. Kordian nodded toward the bearded village headman seated behind a small table as the presiding judge. Seven German prisoners, two of them in tattered Polish officer uniforms, stood on trial. With the exception of the elderly man wearing the clerical collar, they were all young, in their late teens and early twenties. Victor gazed at the Germans, their arms bound behind their backs and the hangman's noose dangling over their heads. Two of them didn't seem old enough to have done much of anything. The feelings of the Poles against the Fifth Columnists were bitter. The speaker, with his great gift of delivery, intensified the hatred. He spoke slowly and very determinedly.

"These are people without any set of principles, the dregs of humanity who leached on the blood and Christian decency of their neighbors. The insidious, evil influence of Nazism found suitable breeding ground amongst the thousands of Germans born in Poland. Professing themselves to be Poles, they were accepted as brothers, but in their hearts and minds and deeds, they dealt only in treasonous activities."

The man who read off the accusations was constantly on his feet. From Warsaw, he was a former attorney presently with Polish Intelligence. Even out of uniform he had a kind of arrogance. With his hat on, in a dark leather jacket, he could be any one of a million refugees. He was grotesquely broad and tall, with a flat face and contemptuous dark brown eyes flashing.

"This treachery was all the easier since these German colonists scattered across the country were not only organized in various groups but were active in every sphere of social life. They are to be found everywhere, in our factories, on the farms and in our offices. In all professions and enterprises, in business and on teaching staffs. They number into several hundred thousands, all active in conspiratorial espionage and diversionist activities. It is their evil contributions which have made matters so much more advantageous to the German armies, moving like well-trained troops amidst the refugees, spreading panic and defeatism."

The village headman, as judge, listened to the accusations against four of the captives standing in the center. Two of them were in Polish officer uniforms, the other two in civilian dress, heads bowed. The judge's face was red, and the large gray handlebar mustache quivered. From time to time his lips twitched at the folds of the gray beard where the mouth should have been. He resembled an ancient Norseman, distinguished by the mass of white hair on his head, with a wide, flat nose and soft gray eyes. With large veined hands, fingers gently tapping against each other, he listened. He probably remembered facing a similar predicament when, in his younger years, he had fought the Russians and Cossacks, the Austrians and the Germans, sometimes in the uniform of one country, then another. The passing years made his memory vague, but the comrades that he had seen face the firing squad or hanged probably numbered in the count of the gray hairs still on his head.

"With such agents," the prosecutor went on, "our country has been infested with nationalists of German descent. Speaking our language and acquainted with our country they have been caught in the act of diversionist activities.

"I will not burden you with all the minute details of their operations. Their code word is 'Echo,' since the word is everywhere written and pronounced in the same way. On the two in civilian clothes was found a list of names and addresses of Germans who live in Poland and to whom they could turn. On the bodies of dead German airmen is to be found similar information. On these four, as on all captured or dead subversives, was found a piece of red or blue material about the size of a handkerchief with a large yellow spot in the center."

Slowly he moved toward the table at which the village headman listened and from it took another exhibit and held it over his head. "Sometimes a light-blue brassard with a yellow spot in the center, or a swastika. They carried them under their coats and shirts or as arm bands.

"They mixed with refugees, making it very difficult to be discovered. They have been found in Polish officer and noncom uniforms, or as Polish railroad officials and city police. But mostly attired in civilian clothes, as workmen, beggars, priests and even disguised as women!"

He paused and held his breath. For a moment there was an angry howl of voices. Slowly he walked behind the two prisoners in civilian clothes and deliberately shoved them forward as if to separate them from the two in Polish officer uniforms.

"These two," he said, when his trained ear told him that sentiment had begun to move his way, "had been captured while shooting refugees along the road from ambush, making light sport of human lives. They had also killed wounded soldiers and especially officers. Working in groups from two to ten—" he raised his voice above the excited sounds – "they fired at Polish troops, they burned supplies, they cut telephone wires. They have been known to mix mustard gas in water used for drinking and washing. They spread false reports and give signals for flight. They caused accidents along the roads and bridges, blocking them in time for air raids with lorries, wagons, cars and trucks."

An angry murmur of swearing voices drowned out the speaker's words. Some in that crowd had been on the Warsaw bridge that morning.

Victor and Kordian exchanged glances. He felt peculiarly stirred with a distinct kind of fear, standing in the midst of a near hysterical angry crowd. He felt a gnawing hate for everything European, its treasons and betrayals, its hates and passionate persecutions.

"Please! Please!" The village headman was on his feet, arms waving. "Please!" All was silent again. The elder turned to the prosecutor. "Go on, sir. Please continue."

Briefly, unemotionally, the prosecutor told them that ever since the invasion of Czechoslovakia the Germans had prepared their agents. At first they came by auto and took up positions, contributing vastly in hastening the German invasion.

He told how, after the war started, they passed themselves off as wounded Polish soldiers and had themselves evacuated to the interior. They had secret documents hidden under the false bandages and in the linings of their uniforms. Sometimes no documents were found, but German money was almost always on them. They worked with German deserters from the Polish army.

"This leaflet," he said, waving the paper in his hand, "leaflets like this they distributed. It reads as follows: 'The Polish Army is broken up. All Poland is under German occupation.'" His voice threatened to break, but eyes bright and with a slight quivering of his lips, he went on, "'To obtain an honorable peace, arms must be laid down immediatley. The Polish soldiers fighting in the rear of German armies will be treated as ordinary bandits and shot. The Germans are bringing order and peace with them.'" A faint smile of irony crossed his lips. "My brothers, I ask you, what peace and what order, for whom? The Germans!"

The speaker told how the parachutists played a leading part in subversive activities. They generally descended in the evening while bombs were still falling, armed with revolvers, electric lamps and explosives. Most of them descended on the banks of the main rivers near the objects they were to blow up. Provided with small transmitting radio sets and bicycles, they sought out the minority groups who put them up and facilitated their tasks.

When the speaker seemed finished, he walked to the table and stood. "We must"– his voice deepened – "You must seek out these traitors, these murderers of our women and children and our men in uniform. These filthy swine who speak of peace and order while they bomb and burn our towns and the helpless villages such as yours. These agents must be destroyed! We are no longer our brother's keeper! They must be destroyed as you would exterminate the vermin that would invade your homes!"

Victor was leaning against the stone wall, his eyes closed, his mind probing the implications of the horrors he had just heard. Kordian was looking at him, his eyes half-closed. Victor looked up with a swift searching gaze and nodded as if he understood it all. His eyes swung back to the village headman and watched as the man's lips twitched under the fold of his gray beard.

The old man cleared his throat, shook his head angrily and extended a brown gnarled finger at one of the men in the crowd. "Stopa. Take ten men and hang them."

The men wasted no time. The crowd was on its feet. A shout of approval went up.

16

The four prisoners were hurtled out of the building. The village leader and the prosecutor held a short conference in muffled voices. Sometimes their voices surged, only to sink to a murmur again. Finally the old man cleared his throat. He looked about the room before directing his gaze at the German teacher, a lean man of about twenty-four, and the youth of about seventeen beside him.

"We'll proceed," he said, "with these two next." He turned to the prosecutor and said in a weary voice, "You could proceed without any necessary preliminaries."

"Who would ever give a second thought," the prosecutor began, his tone beginning to bristle as he walked to where the youth sat. He was a boy of about seventeen. He took him by the arm and gently led him toward the center of the room. "To a young boy such as this playing in the fields? His being there is as natural as the swallow nesting in the shrub next to your cottage. And yet," he snapped, "he is as deadly as the swiftest bullet."

There was a murmur about the room. The speaker signaled for the teacher to be brought to the center. He shifted his gaze from the youth to the other. The youth was the youngest of the Germans, small, almost boyishly delicate. His shock of blond hair intensified his sunburnt face. His small hands, tied in front of him, burned a deep tan by the sun, seemed more competent for a musical instrument than a gun.

"I hope that no one here," said the speaker, calm, as though he were in his own living room, "in this tragic moment in our country's history, is so naive as to think that a boy as young as this hadn't been trained to murder and for terrorism." Flinging out an accusing finger within inches of the boy's nose, making the youth flinch, he said, "Most agents have been recruited from the youth groups of German origin but born in Poland. After a number of weeks of training in Germany, these individuals with a thorough knowledge of the Polish language were charged with special missions to be carried out in their own particular areas. Sometimes very simple tasks, like painting white crosses on the roofs of German colonists' houses and buildings, to distinguish them from the others. Or painting chimneys white so that at night these chimneys could be lighted with various colored electrical light signals in accordance with the agreed code.

"These two were caught while signaling to raiding aircraft by stacking rocks in the fields in the form of an arrow pointing directions.

"Living in danger," he went on crisply, "could be exciting to a young man. It also makes one exceptionally alert to many things, but it also tends to cause a little relaxation and even some carelessness that could prove fatal, as in this case. On this one"– he pointed at the teacher, then pulled from his pocket a piece of paper – "was found this telegram which read: 'Mother dead; order wreaths'. It was the signal for them to begin their subversive activities.

"Frightening, isn't it, all these little things so easily over-looked by the innocent and the foolish." His voice rose. "But just the beginning," again calmly, "just the beginning in the conspiracy to destroy our country, to destroy us! This same man whom your children called teacher is but German Wan-derledhrer or Itinerant Teacher. Trained in Germany, he returned to Poland. Like his kind, we went to the Starosta, your village administrator and to others and talked of the cruelties of the Nazis and expressed joy at returning to their 'beloved country.' But he and those agents like him remained in constant touch with those in Germany. Most of these enjoyed great esteem among their Polish neighbors, all the time working hand in hand with the local German tradesmen who secreted wireless transmitters in their homes and places of business. This one, with perfect knowledge of Polish, frankly admitted that he was a German born in Poland and educated at Warsaw. He lived in this district for generations and had always been regarded as one of their own. This is gratitude. This is the honor and the order they speak of, and," he paused, "And our ticket to hell!"

There was a short pause before they were aware that the prosecutor had stopped talking. The silence held as though they had been instructed not to make a sound. The seconds seemed to lengthen.

"Take them out and hang them," rose the elder's voice, indignant and with heat.

The approach of the hostile, armed crowd was swift. As they passed, Victor noticed the boy was weeping. His shoulders shook and his fists were in his eyes. One of the peasants came behind him and gave him a push so he could drag one step after the other until they were out of the building. From outside came the distant howling of an angry wind of bitter voices. Victor watched as the earnest faces looked up at the stairway, simple and twisted as if by fear but determined that death would be swift. Six had gone. Only the pastor remained.

There was so much tension in the room that it felt as though some might leap at the throat of the German in the clerical collar. He sat near the table, a passive arrogance on his face, a firm contempt for the modulated murmurs about him. Once again the village leader stood up and held out his long, bony arm.

"There is still work to be done here," he said, and the prosecutor turned grimly.

"Whom can we trust?" The prosecutor paused before walking slowly toward the prisoner. "When there are murderers amongst us in priestly robes, the churches and those who preach in them are no longer holy, nor are they free of the blood of our countrymen. There are those like this priest who, under the cloak of their priestly robes, have spread treason and a most contemptible betrayal of our land. There are those like him who have plans for the conquest of our country and the final goal of the destruction of our society while still carrying the cross before them as did the blood-thirsty Teutonic Knights at Grünwald."

The prosecutor gently took the pastor by the arm and led him toward the center of the room. The pastor's face was still rebellious. A slender man of about fifty, his hands tied in the back with a leather strap, he bore the traces of his ordeal. His cheekbones were prominent, his temples hollow, and the long, gray hair hung loosely over his ears. The stubble of beard made his face haggard, his mouth thin with only his eyes showing life. There was something even romantic in his appearance. His thin, long nose flared with every breath, giving him a kind of Wagnerian air. The eyes, large and lustrous, slate-blue but the eyes of a captured bear, glowed with fire. His dark suit was ragged and covered with mud and grime. He had served as an observer for the German artillery from the steeple of his church.

"This is a strange friend we have here." The words were deliberately blunt. "A strange bedfellow indeed. God, how he must pray all night to save all those poor souls he has sent to hell."

For the next few minutes, in clear, measured tones, the prosecutor went on to explain the pro-German activities the pastor headed.

He told how the pastor was associated with numerous German consulates over the country. From these centers an entire German staff of advisers and pseudo-officials, really intelligence officers, supervised subversive activities. They went about instructing the German farmers to stop selling their grain. They were preparing provisions bases for the time German troops would march into Poland. Every day, more and more large stores of petrol that had been secreted were discovered.

The prosecutor went on, "To the pastor and the Germans, the refusal of other people to submit to their jurisdiction was a sin. In their minds their way of life was the only way. The task was not so much to change them as to bring them into some kind of harmony and understanding."

"Change!" cried the pastor. "What do you know of change or harmony? What do I care what you do with me?" His voice shifted, fearful at one moment, vindictive the next. "You will all soon follow me to the same grave you prepare for me. The

Germans will bear down on you until you lose all desire to live! Personally, I sympathize with you, but if Germany is to expand, we have no other choice but to exterminate you. The wolf is not to be blamed because God created him as he is. That is why he is killed at every opportunity."

An angry voice in the crowd yelled back, "Keep a civil tongue!"

The village headman hesitated a moment before he said, abruptly solemn, "No German or Pole will, as brother, be bound so long as the earth turns around. Take him out and hang him."

The pastor began to jabber in German and in Polish and, as if that weren't enough, shouted in Ukranian. His voice went on in some chaotic murmuring until he realized that it was all for nothing. The final judgment for treason was hanging.

He glared back, his eyes bulging. He started to shake his head as though trying to say something. He made strange sounds and the veins stood out on his face. His skin turned white. Then he stood quiet, his chin resting on his chest.

The crowd moved in. A peasant turned the pastor around to start up the stairway, but he wouldn't move. The peasant's jaws clamped hard. He cursed, then gave the prisoner a hard push. When the priest still refused to move, another grabbed him by the neck and called for a rope.

The pastor leaped back, snatching another second of life. Tears blanketed his blue eyes when two men put the noose around his white neck. Then they jerked it forward. He half-stumbled behind them, up the stairs and out of the building into the night.

Victor and Kordian watched the pastor fall free through space from the dry limb of an oak tree. The rope snapped taut, breaking his neck. Death was quick.

Victor then saw the other six hanging from surrounding trees. In the stillness of the night the body of the pastor joined them, swinging slowly back and forth. Some men snorted. Others cleared their throats and spat as if to rid themselves of a disgusting taste. The murmur of the crowd soon diminished and the sound of retreating feet died away in the dark – to home, to bed, to sleep perhaps. They looked over their shoulders in a passing glance at the swaying bodies.

As they walked away, Kordian noticed Victor's grave expression, then glancing at the stars he said, "I wonder if the stars still shine for those seven back there hanging from the trees. Nothing in this world is more still than death."

When they got back everyone was fast asleep. Victor found Ceila curled up under her blanket. He lay down beside her and pulled the blanket over the two of them.

The floor was hard and damp and the straw didn't make for a very good mattress. But Victor couldn't feel sorry for himself after all the bombings, machine-gunning and now the hangings. And tomorrow much of the same, but now – sleep. He began to feel heavy with it. He finally closed his eyes.

17

Ceila was cold – that penetrating cold of morning in the rolling country. She buttoned her sweater and wrapped herself with the long shawl. She felt hunger. She looked up. It was comforting to see the sun rise bright over the forest.

Only two weeks ago there had been champagne and caviar and all kinds of tasty dishes and dainty pastries, sausages and breads by the dozen. All that before the bombs started falling.

They had just passed through a large pine forest near Karczew and had been on the road since dawn. Planes droned high in the sky. Formation after formation, innocently small like silver stars, flew southeast in the direction of Lublin and Lwow.

They rounded a curve and slowed down at the roadside chapel where only yesterday someone had placed fresh flowers.

Then the farmstead came into view.

"A most prosperous looking estate," Ceila said quietly, "for this part of the country."

She did not take an eye off the place as they approached the farm with its neat large living quarters, the well-kept barn and sheds, much of it connected with stone Gothic arches. The black forest lay just off to the right and the orchard immediately behind the stables.

Two farm dogs barked and rushed at the heels of a young man pushing a bicycle through the wooden gate. The dogs halted, stiff-legged, and barked as if they wanted to leave with the boy as he started to pedal down the road. Their heads turned, tails no longer wagging. They noticed the wagon approach. They raced alongside the fence, barking, slobbering belligerently, until the wagon passed.

They caught up with the figure on the bicycle when the road started a gentle climb. As they passed the young man, he waved and smiled. He speeded up until he came alongside and grasped the side of the wagon to let himself be pulled upgrade.

"Good morning," the young man greeted Lolek: "Cool morning, but it looks like another hot day."

"Not a cloud in the sky." Lolek glanced upward. "How far are you going?"

"Just down the road a piece to see a friend." They made their way in silence. The youth noticeably eyed the long wooden crate, his blue eyes very much alive under the neatly combed shock of light brown hair. His lean figure was neatly attired in tan trousers and a heavy woolen sweater. He had a definite air of competence and usefulness.

Lolek surveyed him coolly. Strange to be of military age and yet bicycling down the road. He must be younger than he looks.

"That's a strange looking box," said the youth. Lolek made

no reply. The young man asked, "Where are you headed for?"

"Next town,"Kordian replied. "You live here?"

"Very prosperous," Lolek said, looking back. "Must be nice to live like that."

"Oh, I've seen better." The youth glanced around at the others until his gaze rested on Ceila. "Where are you from? Are you city folk? Warsaw maybe? Refugees?"

"You don't look like country yourself," Ceila smiled.

"Still at the university," he replied, "but with the war and all, you understand."

Ceila stared at the youth. He looked familiar in a vague way. That short, upturned nose. She stared so intently that he turned his head. She was almost positive that she had met him somewhere before.

They rode on with the youth holding on, pedaling leisurely. Toward the top of the incline the dust wasn't so bad, and a slight breeze drifted in to the left. They plodded on as quickly as the horses could pull. When they reached the summit at the next crossroad, the young man thanked them, and waving goodbye, skirted to his left down the narrow dirt road and disappeared.

Hours went by. The white dusty road ahead was pitiless. The sun, like a burning ball of fire, hung close. From time to time, squinting into the sun, they moved about, seeking comfort, trying to stretch arms and legs and work the kinks out of their backs. Most of the time there was silence, with only an occasional murmur of tired disgust.

They heard a sound that made them forget the heat and aches and pains. It was the sound of a plane starting down for the kill. There was only time to pull off the road and dive for the ditch. Victor grabbed Ceila and pulled her down, shielding her with his body. The silhouette against the pale sky was growing larger and larger. It was a single Messerschmitt. The snarl of its motor grew louder and closer. Victor had only one wish, to burrow deeper into the ground.

It came down, growing in the dive. But it held its fire. When it began to pull out, its swastika-marked wings were hardly ten feet above the wagon. Still its guns remained silent. The plane pulled up into a gradual roll before it started to circle back – down, down, down. It roared overhead, even lower this time. Still its guns remained silent. It pulled up steadily. The angry hum grew fainter. It was gone.

"The filthy sonofabitch," Kordian spat, running out to restrain the frightened horses. "What kinda fuckin' game is he up to?"

There was a soft sound. It was Pani Curator, sobbing. She sat on a clump of earth on the edge of the ditch, rocking back and forth. The curator was standing beside her, patting her head gently. "Mamus – Mamus – don't cry. He's gone now, Mamus, Mamus, don't cry."

She sat sobbing. Day by day her energy was being sapped.

"Oh, Christ!" Kordian shouted. "I thought that was it! That bastard – he was out of ammunition, or just another observation plane. I'd have given my life just to have spit in his eye, he was so close."

"You know" – Victor looked at Ceila, then at the others – "I feel like I've seen that young man on the bicycle before, and just now Kordian mentioned an observation. . . ."

"Could be!" Kordian shouted. "The country is overrun with Fifth Columnists. It could just be, could be, we can expect most anything on this road from here on."

But there was still terror on Ceila's face, shaking the dirt and grass out of her hair. Finally she shook her head from side to

120

side before an amused twinkle set in her eyes. "Hell should prove a pushover after this." Her voice seemed calm, but it had the tinge of foreboding doom.

They rode on again. But now the hot sun began to sink and the heat of day was broken and all the sounds seemed to follow them in the memorable September afternoon.

They passed a small cluster of birch trees and off to one side a small religious roadside shrine. It seemed neglected. It had been some time since anyone had lit a candle or replaced the flowers. Perched on one of the tree branches, a golden oriole made a strange, melodious song. It was the first bird they had heard in days. It was Lolek who first noticed the clear, sorrowful, symphonious grace of the bird's call. After some effort he managed to simulate the sound, and was rewarded and amused by the oriole's reply. This cheered everybody.

They passed into the cooling shade of some tall poplars. They rode on with the slow but steady clap, clap, clap of the horse's hooves almost in rhythm with the call of the bird and Lolek's whistle. Kordian, at the reins, started singing. It was picked up by the others, first the curator, then his wife, finally Ceila.

> *A little bird flew past the guelder rose,*
> *Gray were his flickering wings*
> *Don't cry, dear girl, don't cry, my only one.*
> *Is the world so small to you?*

The voices rose, tinged with sorrow:

> *Fly, little bird, high;*
> *Fly, little bird, far,*
> *To my only one, my only one.*

Victor felt alone because he did not know the song and could not join them. He understood it was a sad song about love. Victor looked at Ceila's face and sensed the nostalgia and deep emotion. She was singing with the others. Something in her proud, graceful manner made him wonder. What happened to the previous signs of hopelessness, wretchedness and adversity? Yes, her eyes were tired, but they held their healthy fire of aloofness and insolence. What a patrician standard. Perhaps it was in this almost boundless fortitude that she found her defiance against the horrors of war.

He was baffled by the smile she gave him. She looked so very young and so preoccupied with her singing. Her voice had a delicate ethereal beauty. It was not entirely a voice of depth; after all she was no professional, and yet quite remarkable that such clear and steady notes should come from one so tired and tortured within. Philosophers profess that music opens before man an unknown realm, one which has nothing to do with the world about us. Entering it, Ceila left behind all her emotions, surrounding herself only with inexpressible nostalgia. And though the song was sad, in its beauty she found happiness.

The melody encompassed Victor. The deep chords fell like tears. A solitary voice lamented and the others joined in.

> The grove restless, the grove restless
>   the boughs hum;
> The yellow leaves fall from the trees.
> They've taken my sweetheart
>   and I'm alone in the world;
> My family urges another on me.
>
> Fly, voice over the dew,
> Over the green meadows,

Over the Vistula, over the Dunajec;
Tell my beloved that I wander here
And that I am heartbroken.

Fly, little bird, high;
Fly, little bird, far
To my only one, my only one;
Have him return, have him return
For they urge on me one whom I don't love.
My darling, my darling, so far from me,
Let my tears flow to you.
Though the sun be wide and far in the sky,
You are even farther.
You won't return to me, nor I to you,
My voice will not reach you.
Sad is my life for we are apart.
Sad am I without you and sad is my fate.

The sun stayed motionless for a while as they moved out of
the cool arches of the poplars. Singing and talk ceased. There
was only the thudding of the wagon wheels. As the sun once
more began to retreat westward and the shadows of the
approaching forest grew longer, Kordian reined in the team.
One by one they got down. They took up their blankets and
prepared for the night.

18

The sun came up bright and bold. Ceila found the cold air scented with dew and morning fragrance. She sat there with the blankets about her and watched the red sun explode on the horizon, as though the day were anxious to match blood-letting. She had slept well and was in high spirits. It would be good to get started as soon as possible. Every hour on the road brought them closer to Lublin.

She put her shoes on and eased onto her feet. She adjusted her skirt and sweater, took the pail and walked quietly toward the river.

When she returned, they were all still in their blankets. She set the pail down before seating herself next to Victor. He looked like a small boy curled up, still fast asleep. She watched him for a long time. When the others began to stir about she bent over to kiss him on the cheek. She nudged him gently on the shoulder. She shook him and he opened one eye, then the other.

"How long have you been up?" he asked.

"Not long – but you sure did miss a wonderful sunrise." She brushed her nose against his.

"Thanks a million." He yawned. "I slept like a log."

"That you did – a big, big log, with all that snoring and jolting."

She tickled his nose with a blade of grass. The morning air was clean and cool. He turned over on his side, playfully pulling the blanket over his head.

She jerked the blankets off him. He snapped to his feet. He took a deep breath of fresh air. He stretched. The others were all up and moving about. He slipped into his shoes, adjusted pants and shirt, and joined them in putting bedrolls together. The country seemed at peace. "Would the planes come today?"

"They'll come," Ceila replied in a quiet voice; "sooner or later they will come. They always do."

She was startled by the flutter of wings. A flock of sparrows flew in unafraid. There were forty or fifty of them. They appeared as if from the ground. Pani Curator immediately threw a handful of bread crumbs. The curator showed displeasure. This was his department. He proceeded to distribute the crumbs himself. The sparrows responded to him. They pecked at the crumbs, crushing each to bits and then picked again, three quick flicks of the tail to each peck.

Happily they flitted about the place, hopping and skipping like butterflies.

How much Pani Curator resembled the sparrows. She was dressed as if in mourning, attired in black from head to toe. Her hair was black except for the silver slip on the right side of her head, and the big black eyes shone under the heavy black eyelashes. Only her face and hands showed white.

The curator suggested they get ready to move on. Beyond the forest the country was as dead as the village and towns they had passed: scorched fields of barley, corn and wheat, black traces reaching like tiny fingers toward the pale cloudless sky. He looked up and down the vast, dusty fields that stretched out of sight. Here and there a small stone bridge spanned a dry stream. The only green was the forests, and here and there an unscorched orchard. It was all a yellow-brown sea of burned fields. The sun was coming up fast, another hot and dusty day.

The endless white road stretched away through cuts in the rolling country, circling around and through the forest and dipping into flat valleys. It no longer simmered with the promise of life but wound along like a giant snake slithering into despair.

A cloud of dust in the distance headed rapidly toward them. Whatever it was seemed so utterly small, hardly a fly with all that dust swirling skyward. Victor pointed it out to Ceila who was brushing the grass out of her long hair.

Ceila alerted the others. It was some time before they could make out two motorcycles sputtering through the dust. Ceila sighed in relief, walked over to Pani Curator and chatted before she turned to Kordian. "Nothing to worry about. I'd recognize those Polish uniforms anywhere."

They all moved out of the fringe of the forest. The motorcycles stood out more clearly. They all looked at the curator and back again to the road. Not until the curator smiled did they feel it was all right. But why all the haste in that rapidly advancing dust cloud?

"It could likely be some couriers or staff officers. They might pass in a big hurry or even stop to ask questions. In any case, there isn't much to worry about way out here."

The roaring from the road grew louder. The curator turned to his wife. "Don't let it worry you," he comforted.

Lolek nervously smoked a cigarette and kept looking down the gray road. "Don't suppose," he inquired in a quiet voice, "that maybe the war is over, do you?"

Kordian bent over as if to pick up a large rock but instead threw a pea-sized stone at him. Lolek hardly responded as it bounced off his shoulder.

The roar was close. Sometimes the cycles disappeared from view. They shot into view again. One had a sidecar with two officers. Another officer rode the single cycle. Leaping out of the dust, they were there, roaring to a halt as if they knew exactly where to come.

They looked friendly as they dismounted. The captain had a smile on his face. Like most Polish officers, they appeared confident. They were tall and slender. The captain walked with his head bent low as if careful where he placed his next step. He turned from side to side to his lieutenants, who plodded close beside him. They had machine guns strapped across their fronts and pistols at their sides. Their brown uniforms and hats were tinted with dust.

They walked proudly. The youngest of the three, when he looked up for a quick moment, startled Victor. The face was familiar – something about the width of the shoulders, the clean-shaven face of a lad hardly twenty. Probably commissioned only last summer, looking very smart in the new lancer uniform, the four-cornered hat cocked smartly over his right eye. Victor would have sworn he had seen him before, but then these officers in uniform all looked alike at a distance.

The captain, very straight and tall as he moved into the circle, removed his hat and with gloved hand wiped the dust from his eyes and brushed his blond hair casually before putting the hat back on. His eyes, when he looked up smiling, were dark blue and confident.

"Good morning, sir," the captain said, holding out his hand to the curator.

"Good morning," the curator replied. His politeness seemed strained. "What can we do for you?"

The curator extended his hand. That instant the old observing eyes caught something in the captain's look, something furtive – the guilty innocence of a boy caught in a lie.

The captain with his aides moved toward the wagon and superficially examined the contents before he approached the curator again. "May I ask where you are going and what do you carry?"

The curator advanced a few short steps. "No trouble at all, at all. We've been bombed out. We're heading down the road. As for the wagon, just a few of our personal belongings, that's all. Why do you ask?"

"We've been authorized to be on the lookout for a particular item." His voice was brisk. "I gather you are the spokesman for this group. May I see your papers?" Smiling, he held out his left hand, the right resting easily on the butt of the machine gun.

The curator pulled out some museum papers and correspondence and gave them to him. The two lieutenants looked over the captain's shoulder and raised their eyebrows. They eased their weapons down to their sides as the captain murmured, "Curator Bozinski, hmmm, Warsaw Museum." He folded the papers and returned them. He hardly seemed impressed: "And your group?"

"My wife and associates."

The captain scrutinized each member. He was squinting into the harsh sun, a dark stubble of beard on his chin. There was that contemplating stance about him, arms folded across his chest. Victor could have sworn that he had also met the captain.

The captain proceeded to inform them that he and his comrades had been ordered by their government to locate a certain painting and asked, addressing the group in general, whether any of them knew anything about a certain Matejko painting, "The Battle of Grünwald."

When no one spoke, the captain looked at each individually, then at the curator with a grim, suspicious stare.

"If you are in possession," he said abruptly, "I think it would be wise for all concerned that this painting be surrendered to the military who are authorized to safeguard the canvas."

"Impossible!" the curator cried. "I know nothing about the painting and if I did I'd never release it to anyone without the proper documented authorization."

None spoke.

"In that case," the captain said quietly, "I compliment you on your wisdom." He eased the machine gun across his stomach, grinning broadly at the old man's fortitude. "After all, one can hardly trust anyone these days, now can one?"

The two exchanged stares. The captain appraised the situation, noting where each stood, glanced toward the pasture where the horses grazed. He ordered the young lieutenant to fetch the animals then turned to the curator. "I don't suppose then that you would have any objections if we look for ourselves? No need to act hastily. We have all day." He advised the other lieutenant to pry open the wooden crate.

As they watched the young lieutenant mount his cycle and start for the pasture, Kordian approached the captain.

"Would you care for a cigarette?" he asked, reaching into his shirt pocket. Kordian looked toward Victor. As he pulled out the pack there was a blue handkerchief with a yellow circle. As he lit the captain's cigarette he quietly said, "Echo."

The captain withdrew momentarily, then smiled and said

"Echo." He stood his ground. "These are strange times we live in; one never knows what one's own brother might do these days." The officers started to move toward the wagon. Kordian moved toward them. The Pole inhaled deeply, then swiftly he turned to Victor, his face grave. "Why don't you help the lieutenant? There isn't anything about an Echo that he hasn't heard before."

Victor got the message. He was nearest the wagon.

None from his group was armed, and he understood that it was up to him to act. Only Victor and Kordian fully realized their predicament. It was up to him.

Ceila stepped forward and looked calmly at the captain. "Don't I know you? You seem so very, very familiar. I'm almost positive we have met before."

It was evident that she caught the officer's fancy. He eased his gun down and moved toward her. "Very probable," he said. "Warsaw has long been . . ."

"I hardly realized you came from that part of the country," she said.

"Oh, yes," he began briskly with a smile. "I am a graduate of the University of Warsaw."

"Yes – even your voice seems familiar. My name is Ceila Rozek; and yours, captain?"

"Alexander–" his voice was hesitant – "Alexander Nowak." He clicked his heels.

"I know we've met before. I remember that night as if it were only last week."

He withdrew cautiously. There was a faint smile on her lips, her face luminous and beautiful.

Kordian, noticing the captain's interest in the girl, turned again to Victor. "Help the man with the crate. Don't just stand there, help the man." He gave a shifting glance at the submachine

131

gun where it had been placed by the lieutenant as he went about inspecting the cargo.

Victor walked slowly. His hands trembled slightly and the muscles of his legs felt tight. Then, as if from a great distance, he heard Ceila ask the captain, "Have you ever been in the Club Dragon in the Old Town?"

Instantly Victor remembered the three officers at the Warsaw nightclub and the insult that infuriated Ceila. The lieutenant was still trying to pry open the crate with his dagger. He was as familiar as the young one who had gone after the horses. He was the youth on the bicycle only yesterday morning.

He felt cold and uneasy as he started to move toward the wagon.

The rattling of the submachine gun was most assuring. All the hate seemed to leap out of him with the bullets that ripped the captain in two, then the lieutenant at point blank range. The captain's eyes went white and glassy before the blood spurted at the sides of his mouth. He fell back, legs and arms thrashing. The white face of the lieutenant twisted in surprise. Five, ten, twenty shells. A heavy trigger finger held fast at the easy mark. The lieutenant slipped to the ground, his hands digging into the pit of his stomach, murmuring between lips gurgling blood, *"O Gott, mein Gott!"*

"That other bastard!" Kordian bellowed, snatching the gun from Victor's limp hand. Lolek undid the gun from the waist of the captain, and the two ran and leaped after the third Nazi. He was approaching with the horses in tow and was hardly eighty meters away when the shooting started. His eyes popped in disbelief. With a single trained motion he slipped the submachine gun from his shoulder and in a single burst felled both horses. He ran for his cycle, firing at his pursuers. With a rapid stroke of his starter foot he had the motor sputtering and in a yellow cloud of dust made a zigzagging escape with bullets kicking up dust flakes.

Kordian saw it was too far to hit a moving target. Lolek was still shooting. "Don't waste your bullets," Kordian said.

Victor propped himself up against the wagon. He wiped the sweat from his face. He inhaled deeply – the fresh air with the faint sweetness of the pines. He had a feeling of essential rightness about it all. Still, he felt sick within. He had none of the trained emotions of a soldier with a gun. All his anger had gone. He felt no exultation at the sight of the upturned face and the blank eyes of the Nazi in the captain's uniform. A large horsefly alighted on the lips where blood oozed out of the mouth.

Victor hadn't seen Ceila walk toward him. Now she took his hand in hers. He felt life pouring back into him.

"I was scared," he said. "I was so scared I might botch up the whole works."

"We'll make a soldier out of you yet." She smiled.

"Or a corpse."

"You held yourself like a real man."

"Maybe from where you stood. But you should have been inside my boots to really know how I shook."

19

Kordian and Lolek ran to where the horses lay, still alive but of no use. Kordian turned away cursing. The enemy was everywhere, even where there were no battlefields. "Blood of dogs!" he swore heavily. With quick flash of purpose he aimed the gun at the horses; their eyes blinked at him just before he pulled the trigger. It was quick, but his eyes watered and his hands trembled. He took his time walking back to the others, his head hanging heavily.

"Thank God, thank God," came from Pani Curator.

"Thank God for nothing!" Kordian cried. "Thank Victor!" Then his voice grew quiet. "For a while there I didn't know if he was going to do anything but maybe fill his pants." He grinned at Victor. He walked to the curator, patting the weapon in his hand as if it were a toy. "For the remainder of the trip, these are part of our rigging. The forests and roads are crawling with German rats."

He said, "Lolek, we can't stand here forever. With the horses dead everything is as normal as hell will ever be. Come . . ." He looked speculatively in the direction of the nearest village. "Come, we'll see how good you are at running down a pair of thoroughbreds."

"You sound quite sure of yourself on rounding up some horses," Lolek said, taking a piece of smoked sausage and a hunk of black bread which Ceila handed to him.

"You know," Kordian laughed, "it would be like finding a woman without a hole the day we couldn't find a couple of horses in Poland any time of the year." He grabbed his rations. "Come, we'll have a look."

They were off down the road and crossing the stubbled fields, jabbering away like a couple of schoolgirls. It was evident that, despite the differences between them in ideals and opinions, they would always remain comrades.

"Do you suppose this was all stupid from the start?" Lolek asked. "This war and all its friggin' miseries?"

"Stupid!" Kordian turned on him passionately. "Your little brain must be stricken from the sun for you to think like that. There is still England and France, and maybe even Russia. We'll drive the swine out yet."

"Yes, but when winter comes—" Lolek's voice was soft and thoughtful. "Winter is coming, and what then? My belly aches already from hunger. My bones hurt and my eyes always feel like there's sand in them."

"Shit!" Kordian turned in anger. "You talk like a traitor. A fish out of water makes more sense than you do with your stupid talk. We are not fish. We are Poles fighting for our land. You talk like we should submit like all the others to those friggin'

Nazis, to give up our way of life, right or wrong. Never, never, never!"

"Yes, it's good to speak about freedom and all such madness, but it's been days since we've had any news. What's the good of all this misery? God only knows what the future holds."

"God?" Kordian cried. "What in the hell has He got to do with it?"

"It's been days since we've had any news." Lolek's voice sounded weary.

Kordian didn't answer. The village came into full view, deadly silent, proof enough that war had come and gone. Nothing moved, no dogs, not a living soul in the narrow streets. The whitewashed, thatched-roofed houses all seemed abandoned.

They hurried on, past upturned carts and wagons littering the way, their cargo picked clean as if by vultures. Everywhere blackened trees, trampled fields and bomb craters.

The first sign of life was an old peasant and a four-year-old boy, their mouths open in silent curiosity. The old man's loose gray blouse hung over trousers tucked into his boots. They sat near some old willows beside a dry stream. The noise of winging cranes rose in the direction of the sun, and the two gazed as the flock flew southward to another life. Only a single bird remained, standing on one foot, the wings too old for flight, watching as his friends disappeared from sight. There was an old cart wheel atop a high pole for storks to nest on, but it stood empty. The storks which brought good luck and prosperity had long since taken flight to a safer land.

Kordian and Lolek waved greetings. The pair seemed as simple and as true as the earth. Then Kordian and Lolek decided to part company so that each could search a section of the village. As Kordian turned he gave the old man and the boy a passing glance. With them, the Masters of the World had been entirely successful.

Nothing moved. Kordian stopped to decide which direction to take. He heard the bellowing of a cow behind the ruins to his left. He hastened toward the noise and found the animal partially buried and burned under some smoldering timbers. The cow was beyond help but, as he turned to leave, he noticed the gray horse in the next stall. The fallen timbers had blocked it in. Except for nervous and frightened prancing, the animal looked sound. It was a large, well-shaped horse. It stretched out its neck with bloodshot eyes on Kordian. Suddenly the gray pulled back its neck, its nostrils wide, ears back. The jittery animal gave him a second look and neighed a little.

Slowly Kordian approached the animal. "Easy boy – easy. Come, old one." The horse looked sound enough. "Come here." He held out a sugar cube through the fallen timbers. The animal sniffed at Kordian's palm. At last the gray took the cube and let himself be patted on the soft part of his nose. "Easy, easy," Kordian mumbled. "You'll do for now. We have a way to go, you and I, old gray."

The animal stopped shaking. The low voice and gentle touch had a calming effect. Now came the problem of freeing the animal from the stall. The fallen timbers were too heavy to lift. Kordian walked around to the far side and found some loose boards. Before long the two walked out as friends, Kordian leading, still talking to the horse.

He rode the animal bareback for almost an hour about the village and the surrounding countryside before he chanced upon another horse unattended, half crazed with fright, nostrils flaring. The large black carried a nasty wound on its right flank. It reared back on its hind legs, gave a shrill neigh and, kicking, darted away for a short distance. But seeing them approach, it stood nervously. It was some time before the black stopped shaking and took the sugar cube from Kordian's palm.

They rejoined Lolek. They were heartily welcomed when they returned with the horses. They soon learned that the black stud had a terrible fault. It bit and kicked at anyone who approached it. It took all of them to put it in harness. It was almost noon when the stones rattled, the chains jingled, and they started to roll.

20

Kordian swung the wagon wide to guide the team carefully around the curve of the dense pine trees. The white dusty road shimmered heat waves and snaked out of view. Ahead was a woman on foot. She seemed some kind of apparition, small, alone. She carried a bundle in her arms. She walked very slowly and, surprisingly, was soaking wet. As they approached she waved and called, "Please wait, please wait."

She looked like a madonna, from the long white gown to the light blue shawl covering her head, partially concealing dark hair that fell loosely about her shoulders. The lines of her face were perfectly carved. She moved with the grace and carriage of a noblewoman. The bundle she carried was wrapped in a white blanket. It was dry, yet her clothing was wet.

They hesitated. After these last few days, whom could they

trust? As they passed she just stood, seeming to care little whether they stopped or not. Then Pani Curator pulled at Kordian's sleeve. "Please, a minute can't hurt any."

He reigned to a stop. The woman shifted the weight of the bundle in her arms. Her voice sounded sincere. "You could never cross the river. You should retrace your route back to the next crossing and take the road to the right where there is an old wooden bridge, where you might cross. I'm almost positive it's still standing and, if not, at least the water is not so deep there."

There was no emotion in her weak voice. The words rang true. She seemed in every respect a real lady. But who could tell? This could be another means to waylay them somewhere along a strange country road.

"Where did you come from?" the curator asked. "And where are you going?" He had traveled these roads to Lublin before and thought that he knew the country quite well. Should she so much as hesitate or slip, it could be the difference between the truth and a lie.

"From Deblin and on my way to Sobieszn," she replied, trying to conceal her fatigue. "It is along the way. I'd be happy to show you, that is, if there is room for myself and my baby."

Slowly she unfolded the blanket and showed a red-faced sleeping infant, hardly more than a week old.

"We'd be only too glad to help you." Pani Curator tried to be polite. "But how do we know that you speak the truth? We have been taken for fools before."

"I'm so sorry." The woman withdrew the baby, embarrassed for her efforts. Her voice still soft and understandable enough, she said, "If this is what must be, it then must be." She proceeded to cover the sleeping infant's face from the harsh sun before she looked up at them. "I regret that I have no way to prove what I say is the truth. There is only your trust in me."

She stood her ground proudly. Yet she semed very much in need of help.

"I think we should aid this poor woman," Ceila said abruptly. As if all were of the same mind they started to move about to make room. Lolek jumped off to help the woman.

Kordian reversed their heading and started in the direction she had advised. After a time, at Ceila's innocent inquest, the stranger introduced herself and went on to explain her present predicament. Her voice was intense and compelling without any effort toward drama. She told them she was of a noble family from Krakow and was the wife of a captain whose whereabouts at this moment she did not know. A few days ago she had had the baby boy at the hospital which only this morning had been bombed. Many were killed and wounded, but the wing of the building in which she was hadn't been as badly damaged. She took her baby and walked away from the horrors at the hospital.

"But why are you so wet?" Ceila asked.

"At the river," she replied, "the bridge had been bombed out, impossible to even walk on, let alone take a wagon across. In crossing the deep river I had to hold the child above my head to keep him dry. You can imagine–" she cuddled the bundle to her bosom – "how long my darling baby would last swaddled in a wet, cold blanket. I would die first before I would see him suffer." She held the sleeping infant to her face.

In half an hour they were back at the crossroads and took the turn to the right. An hour later they were at the site of the old wooden bridge. The stranger's route was straight ahead, she told them. "Maybe another half hour's walk, but I'll be all right now. Home is just down the road a way." She smiled. "And it will be good to be home again. They'll be rather surprised to see me, but glad, I'm sure. I'll get off here now. Thank you, thank you very much."

The wagon stopped rolling and Lolek helped the lady off. "Are you sure you'll be all right now?" he asked.

"Thank you," her voice was warm. "And the best of luck. Just keep on this road after you cross the bridge. It will follow the river for a way and soon angle toward your destination." She returned their waving goodbyes and slowly started the climb up the rolling country road.

The wagon bumped and jarred along the dirt road through yellowing meadows with knee-high grass. A fitful September wind came over the fields and blew the women's hair and whirled pieces of grass and straw into their faces.

The tree-lined road ran beside the Woierpoz River, then climbed in a graceful sweep. In the distance at its narrowest and highest it blended with the pale blue sky. The ghost of a golden sunset filtered through the trees outlined against the sky. There was a melancholic peace.

They rounded the hill. An immense forest lay ahead. The warm glow of early evening was on the fields – splashing colors, tints of orange and gold and red, long shadows of purple and blue.

They rolled to a stop and Ceila turned to Victor. "Let's go for a swim. If we hurry we'll still have some light left."

"Sounds great. You lead the way."

She took him by the arm and led him through the pine forest toward the river. They came to some rushes and clusters of blackberries. She reached for them among the tangled branches. They were large, soft and ripe, and full with the season.

When she had her fill they moved on with thoughts of escaping the heat of day. The sun splashed golden rays through the crowns of the pines. Suddenly she slipped from his grasp with a short shriek of delight and darted off on her own.

"I'll see you at the river, " she called back. "That way you shan't blush as I undress."

She gave her skirt an upward flip and ran, scurrying under the low branches and around the brush. A gentle wind brushed out her hair as though she were propelled by the wind. She flashed back a smile and called for him to hurry.

The river was fairly high at the rocky narrows and invitingly clear. It gave off a gentle whisper. Fallen leaves moved leisurely toward the locust trees. Shrubs bowed low, hanging over the water. The blossoms hummed with bees, the air perfumed with the fragrance.

The world seemed at peace. She gazed into the water then slipped out of her shoes. She put one foot in, then the other. She laughed with glee as she pulled back and almost tore herself out of her garments. With that happy feeling she stretched her arms wide and high up toward the sun. With a skip she leaped into the cool water.

She surfaced like a fish and immediately plunged back into the depths. The water was a silvery silt on her naked body. It felt so clean. Her body was no longer tense. She swam faster and faster, almost as if it were possible to swim away from war and trouble.

But to swim away from familiar faces and familiar places? She must first cut herself from life. She was not yet ready to die. The world was still far from being so utterly hopeless. One dies only to have served. She swam quietly and smoothly, feeling nothing of the world bent on suicide. She gave herself to the moment.

Victor found a conveniently low stump to sit on, aware of the sun on Ceila's darting form. He waited for her and helped her out by the hand. She shut her eyes, happy that he did not leave her alone, feeling his kisses and hands about her body. She finally pulled away, shook her head rapidly from side to side to rid her hair of the water. When she opened her eyes again she saw a luminous, quivering blue sky through the tall green-leafed ceiling.

She cocked her head and listened to the chorus of grass-hoppers, crickets and frogs. "Why didn't you come in the water? It was simply divine. I feel like a new person."

He didn't answer. She dressed quickly. He helped with the snaps and hooks. They walked hand in hand, watching the squirrels dart across their path. Ceila laughed when one of them stopped a few feet away and sat up on his tail, with little hands meeting across his breast, his nose quivering. At last they lay down in the short grass, warmed by the rays of light streaming through the canopy overhead. She lay on her back, still panting from the swim.

She leaned toward him, her breast soft against his chest. He kissed her moist, parted lips. She closed her eyes and in the stillness felt him hold her close.

He held her like that for some time. He was her world, warm and alive. When she opened her eyes she saw the pine forest soar up into the sky like the arches of a cathedral. The sunlight splashed its translucent rays like a sheet of gold reaching into the depths of the forest. A horsefly buzzed above; like a small toy plane it alighted on the toe of her shoe.

The war seemed far away. What did yesterday or tomorrow matter?

He leaned toward her and eased his mouth to her lips. Living on the edge of danger made him want her even more.

"What are you thinking about?" Her voice startled him.

"How calm and peaceful it all seems."

"Like a different world – so quiet, like dying."

He eased back, taking her with him until her head rested on

his shoulder. Her hair touched his face. He listened to her breath. There was a comfortable longing warmth in her body. He listened to her voice. "Why can't we glide on like a fallen leaf upon the river, washed and clean and eternally comforted by the sun, lured on by the rapids?"

She closed her eyes but not on memory. So many happy winters with friends and familiar faces among the Carpathians, in the Tatras. Gliding through forests on a sledge and where Zakopane and the best ski runs were. Where the golden sunlight and the long blue shadows played upon the eternal snows and glaciers.

She sat upright. There was no snow on the ground. She closed her eyes again and leaned back into his arms.

He put his lips against her throat, her ear, her parted lips. All the intimacy of the yesterdays. They made love – an unconditional devotion to one another.

They lay side by side. The strain of the day ebbed. The darkness of the forest gradually closed in about them. Finally he put his hand on one of her breasts and gave it a gentle squeeze. She did not move. He could feel her heart beat.

She broke away after a while. "We better be getting back to the others. I forgot to tell you, these forests are not exactly safe after dark. There are bears and wolves in these woods."

"Thanks!" Victor jumped to his feet. "Now you tell me." He looked very serious.

He helped her to her feet. Arm in arm they walked back to camp. Just before they entered the circle, he drew her close.

"I love you more and more each day," he whispered, then kissed her on the mouth. Then he said, "This could not end, never. I'll never leave you."

21

In the morning the cold was more penetrating than ever. Kordian helped Pani Curator up to the front seat next to her husband. The curator, reins in hand, thanked him. Kordian unbuttoned his jacket and scratched at his ribs. "This cold is bad enough, but an empty stomach is worse than lice."

They had eaten sparingly and hurriedly. They should be in Lublin sometime late in the afternoon. Kordian looked at the sagging underbelly of gray clouds and watched the golden light of the rising sun. A gust of autumn wind sprang up, saturated with the damp scent of the soil. When the wheels of the wagon rang over the stones, Kordian heaved himself aboard.

For comfort and warmth they all snuggled a little closer. Ceila had pulled her hair back and covered it under a flowered scarf as the peasant women did. But she looked nothing like a

peasant. Victor had placed a blanket over them. Kordian and
Lolek renewed their discussion on the merits of war. Soon they
were at it hot and heavy. Any moment they might strike out at
each other. Lolek finally jumped off the wagon. He said he
would rather walk than listen to Kordian's stupidity and insults.
But Kordian continued to shout at Lolek.

"Jesus Christ! What man is there who wouldn't fight for his
country? Look at you! Where would you find such woods, such
fields and such wonderful women? To die for them is to die
happy. The enemy has swept over our land before, and our
fathers showed them the better end of the sword. You yellow-
bellied dog! You should be proud to fight for your home, your
land!"

"What land? Where is your home now?" Lolek shouted
back. "You talk like some patriotic ass!"

"My friend," Kordian began soothingly, "you and I have
known each other for many years. Yes, we've quarreled, and
bitterly, yet as friends no one has more happily shared a bottle
or a loaf of bread. I just don't understand you. I don't think
you're stupid, but I'm beginning to think this war has turned a
screw loose in that hard head of yours."

"You're not as clever as you think," Lolek said. "Sometimes
I wonder whose side you're on."

"Would it make you any happier if I told you?"

"Don't jest with me!"

The curator turned, shouting, "Damn it, the hell!" He pulled
in the team. "Lolek! Here, you have that much energy to waste,
you drive!" He handed the reins over. The morning sun began to
dissipate the gray clouds; but the warmer it got, the more
Kordian's temperament began to show as he started professing
his passionate love for his country.

"It was in these lands that my first teacher was nature and not the printed word." He stopped long enough to seek out Victor's attention. The artist's old enthusiasm had returned. "It was in these borderlands that I first watched the life of the birds in the swamps, the crooked willows and the colors in the wild fields and the golden fields of grain."

"It was Kordian," Ceila said, smiling at Victor, "who perhaps was the first to paint the buzz of the bee in flight towards the daisy. And made the wind in the painting rustle in the stalks of sunflowers and the rain beat on the windowpane."

"Yes–" Kordian said slowly. "I've always wanted to paint all the sounds and all the bustling clatter of real life. Of lovers and buxom wenches laughing, little children at play and old men dreaming in the twilight."

Victor listened. He was aware that as the hours passed, so did the miles, until they were deeper and deeper in Lublin country, the heart of Poland. Here was the birthplace of many of its great intellectuals, writers and statesmen. As Kordian had seen it, in the spring it was beautiful, primarily an agricultural area with highland forests that stretched all the way into the breadbasket of the Ukraine. As far as the eye could see, fields of grain lay like a sea of golden waves under summer breezes. Yes, the winter nights were long and cold and it took great fires to heat the cottages, but the larder was always crowded with the best pork and beef to keep a fighting man going for months.

Lublin was on the international trade route early in the eleventh century – reaching from the Baltic to the Black Sea; the bloody thoroughfare from China to central Europe. The city thrived on a brisk international traffic and endured countless invasions, including those of the Khans and Tamerlane. The city walls still bore the scars of the Tartar Batu who introduced gunpowder to Europe.

"After the Mongols and Tartars," said the curator to Victor

specifically, "came the Turks, the Cossacks and Russians. All had at one time or another ravished this land by fire and sword like heated lava – and left it fertile with their blood and bones.

"After centuries of frontier wars, a highly spirited breed of men of great bravery sprang from these borderlands. A race of knights-errant who, with their great love of adventure, were ready to join anyone's struggle in the name of freedom. Naturally, it was here the adventurous and nomadic streak in the Polish temperament blossomed and made Grünwald possible."

Victor was familiar with Poland's history, always described as terrible and magnificent. Terrible because of Poland's unfortunate geographic position and the insatiable covetousness of her neighbors. Magnificent because of the indomitable spirit of its people in their undying love for freedom and their constant readiness for sacrifice.

Throughout the centuries, Poland repeatedly reaffirmed her claim to the title of the defender of Christendom and Western civilization. In the strict sense, Poland was a shield interposed to ward off any menace. Sometimes the shield was pushed aside or beaten down; but as long as it was there something could always be saved.

For some time Victor sat quietly and listened as the conversation drifted over to the Grünwald incident and its similarity to the present crisis. Then Victor asked the curator how the battle of Grünwald came about.

"During the Crusades, Poland had its hands full beating off the Tartar hordes along its southern borders. At the same time, along our northern Baltic frontier, we were harassed by the pagan Prussians. 'Prussia' is from the Polish 'Po Rus,' which means 'by Russia.' Numerous attempts by Polish princes to bring these fire-worshippers under the Christian helm met with failure.

"The real fundamental issue between Poland and Germany actually dates back to the Crusades," said the curator. "You see, after the Crusades, the German knights were not permitted to return to their homeland like the knights of the other countries. In a deal with the Pope in exchange for their services as mercenaries, they were granted land and a castle on the island of Malta, taking the name of Teutonic Knights. The Hungarians were the first to call on them for aid but soon asked them to leave when, having disposed of the Tartars, these German knights turned on the host. The Poles learned too late of the knights' treachery when requesting their assistance in bringing Christianity to the pagan Prussians. This order was called the Knights of the Cross because of the black crosses on their white habits. In a matter of time they accumulated great power, extending their domain along the shores of the Baltic. Sustained by a wide network of monasteries they rapidly gained a vast influence and popularity over most of European knighthood. Their rallying call to battle against the pagan Prussians, then against Lithuania, gained great support, especially in France, England and Spain."

Here the curator became loud and vehement. With gestures and arm waving, he continued. "Having murdered most of the Prussians and taken the rest into captivity, the Order took on the name of Prussians and eventually turned on the Poles. When opposed, they charged Poland with conspiracy with Lithuania to exterminate not only the Order but the whole of Christendom. This propaganda increased after the Polish-Lithuanian union, when pagan Lithuania voluntarily became completely Christian in 1386. This union in effect repudiated the existence of the Teutonic Order on the Baltic – the only one of its kind in Europe, forming a state wholly provided by imperial and papal privilege – presently Prussia. War became the Order's only trade and sport. But those lies and their treachery availed them nothing. No emperor or pope could turn plunder into a deed of reverence or make a noble act out of murder and rapacity. They were no longer a truly Christian order but a kind of sect of heresy of the worst kind because they were cloaked in a religious habit.

"So you see, after nearly two hundred years of wars and political intrigue, it finally led to the battle of Grünwald. It was one of the greatest battles of the Middle Ages, yet so little is known about it. Most history books devote hardly more than a passing reference, while most German histories ignore it completely, in spite of the fact that it had far-reaching effects. They charged that their defeat was because of Poland's collusion with pagans, and this constituted a threat to the whole of Christendom. Like Hitler's propaganda, they spread lies that the Poles were the enemies of Europe."

At this point Kordian drove the point: "These same aspirations have been voiced by Heinrich Himmler when he wrote: 'We shall extricate ourselves from any war, and the Poles destroyed, and their nation, which for 700 years has been an obstacle to our expansion to the east, which has been in our way since the Battle of Grünwald.' "

"Thus," the curator continued, "the concept of murder that has been so deeply rooted in the German mind is not new, but many, many centuries old. According to the German concept, the Poles are the main culprits in preventing them from accomplishing their dream of a great German empire."

22

They rounded the summit of the country road. Far off above the dark line of trees they sighted smoke that marked the city of Lublin.

"Another hour at the most." The curator sounded enthusiastic. "So far so good. We've finally managed to make the first leg of our trip. Now all that remains is Lwow then the Rumanian border."

"Yes – but don't forget," Lolek said, "that's three times farther than we've already come."

"We'll have to move much faster than we have," the curator said, "if we hope to catch up with the government officials."

"There is no telling where they might be by now," Kordian added. "I'll be glad when we turn the Grünwald over to them."

"We've been very fortunate so far, thank God," said the

curator. "I'd give my right arm just to know what happened to that young Nazi who managed to elude us."

Kordian said, "By now, I'm sure those goddamned Germans have a full report on us. There is no telling what in the hell they could be planning for us next."

A disturbed silence followed. Pani Curator broke it. "Oh, God. How will it all end?" The cool air stirred the strands of her black hair, so strikingly black against the white skin.

"It shan't be long now," Ceila said. "We should be crossing the border in a matter of a few days; then freedom, and, who knows, maybe even America."

"Hardly," said the curator. "Mamush and I must stay, even return to Warsaw in utmost haste. We still have a responsibility, you know."

Ceila looked at Victor. He tried to smile but it was forced. She snuggled closer to him. She still wore the flowered scarf around her head and face to keep the harsh sun from drying her skin. She gazed into the boughs of the trees overhead.

They rounded the country lane. Lublin became more distinct. It was more like a giant wall of smoke than a city. The billowing gray coiled and rolled like a snake above the shimmering silhouette. The old cathedral, one of its steeples damaged, stood clearly visible above the rooftops, as did the towering Krakow Gate from which they could soon tell the time of day by its eighteenth-century clock. The red-white flag waving in the breeze from the summit of the tower could be seen for miles.

In times of war, roads did not expedite traffic. They edged through a piteous spectacle of refugees – pale, drawn faces and squinting eyes against the glaring sun. They trod like actors across a stage. It was the sight outside Warsaw all over again, only in reverse. They streamed in a solid wave toward the city.

Many were soldiers who had been in battle, some still in

complete uniforms, but most in tatters of what they could salvage, borrow and steal, most of them bandaged, the blinded aided by the lame. Everywhere, crying children separated from their parents, mothers calling for their children.

It was a grotesque task for Kordian. He urged the team around abandoned vehicles and bomb craters, cut across fields, bouncing ever closer to the city gate. Its arched entry was jammed with bodies. The thick stone walls had long since outlived their usefulness, but there was still hope at the sight of the armed garrison manning the gallery that circled the seven-story tower.

The walls dated back to 1341, when Tartars sacked the city. King Casimir, honored with the title of "The Great," relieved the siege. To prevent such recurrence, the walls were built with a few well-guarded gates.

Lublin, surprisingly, was not so heavily damaged – so many streets and so many parks, churches, schools and museums, and so many centuries of labor and love in that enormous effort of building the city. But Lublin's thousand-year age was showing. During the partitions the Russians confiscated everything. One of the conditions of the peace treaty with the Bolshevists was that everything had to be returned. But, as after any war, most was lost and what was returned was in such poor condition that it could never again be used. They'd even taken the marble from the walls and decorations over doors and windows.

A cluster of buildings on the highlands near the center of the city was the administration center. Here were numerous large banquet halls and offices, a radio station and newspaper office.

Krakow Street was bright with sunshine. Everywhere they looked they saw rubble in the streets, glaring empty windows. The squares and parks were no longer leafy and green, but gray and pitted with brown earth where the dead had been hurriedly buried.

The selection of objectives for destruction left no doubt that the Germans intentionally bombed structures of historic interest and artistic value which had no strategic purpose.

Kordian drove to the art museum through streets where dark crowds hurried like thieves from building to building.

The gaunt facade of the museum was unchanged. The window blinds were down. The heavy ornamented doors hadn't been opened for days – only the fresh white scars of shrapnel, dust and rubble.

Lolek made the rounds of the doors and found them all closed.

The curator suggested, "We'd better proceed to City Hall. Someone there should direct us to Professor Woda."

Once again Kordian started the team down the street and they soon became a part of the crowd, growing thicker. Minutes later he pulled up on the far side of the square from City Hall. He tied the reins, jumped off and with Lolek close at his heels walked quickly toward the wide stairway leading up to the gray stone building.

Inside was chaos. Men in business suits and officers stood in groups, some talking in hushed tones while others shouted. Messengers moved briskly about, waving papers and asking questions from desk to desk. Office clerks and secretaries emptied files of important documents and papers into wooden boxes.

After a half dozen inquiries, a woman at one of the desks informed them that the professor was in conference. "And, I'm afraid," she told them, "that he'll be in there for some time yet."

"But it's important that we see him," Lolek said.

"Sorry, but he's busy. It'll be at least another hour or two." She pointed at some chairs. "You could sit down or come back later."

"Listen, lady, this is most important," Kordian said, looking down as she shuffled some papers. "We've come a long way and can't just sit waiting around."

"No – no – no–" I'm sorry," she snapped back. "You can't disturb them."

A man came out of the chamber and hurried across the room. Kordian stepped into his path.

"What is it?" The man looked startled.

"We've just gotten in from Warsaw on a matter of grave importance for Professor Woda. We found the museum closed. We must see him."

The man hesitated, studied the two, and replied, "We stopped for a minute to stretch our legs. Come, we'll see what the professor has to say."

They followed him. Kordian winked at the woman behind the desk as they passed. She did not smile. The man closed the door behind them.

It was a large, sunny room, the walls decorated with flags and paintings of heroes and battles; bookshelves crowded with volumes. A large crystal chandelier hovered above the mahogany table, surrounded by at least twenty red velvet-covered chairs.

The professor stood next to three other gentlemen. Woda stroked the gray slip of mustache and shifted his gaze from one to another. He was as straight as the last time they had seen him but had a lot more gray hair. He wasn't as fastidious about his attire and appeared worried. Upon seeing them he smiled and waved.

He excused himself and with arms extended approached them: "Kordian, Lolek, so good to see you." His voice was warm but the expression in his green eyes was full of anxiety. "What brings you here?" They shook hands and wrapped their arms about each other.

"We're here with Curator Bozinski," Kordian said before slipping into a whisper. "With a prize package the pigs would sell their mothers for. The curator is waiting and anxious to see you."

"We've brought the Grünwald painting," Lolek said.

"Good, good, but–" He glanced back at the table where the men were returning to their seats. "This is an emergency meeting with the City Council – hmm – let me see–" He hurried to the table. After a short exchange he returned.

"You two go on," he said. "I'll be only a few minutes at the most and will join you."

He opened the door and let them out. "I'll join you in just a minute."

Five minutes later, when the professor still didn't appear, the two walked slowly out of the building. There was a look of grim determination on Kordian's face. Lolek was overjoyed. Their luck, their wonderful luck, had held up and, thank the good Lord, at last they would be rid of the Grünwald canvas.

They stood there joking under the massive columns, when the wailing klaxonhorns first sounded the alarm. Almost as suddenly came the roar of low-flying aircraft and the screams of falling bombs. They stood there as the explosions sent the air splitting apart in a red flame. They clung to each other, each with arms and body shielding the other. When the next bomb struck, the building shuddered like a dying animal. They seemed so alone when they went down with the facade of the building disintegrating around them. Masses of granite, brick and mortar covered them.

Still another flight of bombers discharged bombs. Then the Stukas took over, cutting down everything that moved.

The curator and the others sought cover. They saw their two

comrades disappear under the collapsed building. The curator grasped his wife and pressed against the stone wall near the entrance.

Soldiers stood their ground and fired back. One of the Stukas was hit. It nosed sharply upward, trailing black smoke. Like a wounded bird it winged over, then slowly began to spin earthward to explode.

Ceila and Victor hugged the ground as close to the wall as they could. The earth trembled with exploding bombs. Shrapnel whirled freely, killing and ripping.

Finally it ceased. There remained the sounds and agony of the dying. For some time Ceila did not move.

Victor, seeing that she was unhurt, bounded off in the direction of City Hall.

Ceila felt pain in her head and weight across her legs. She tried to withdraw her right foot. Slowly she opened her eyes.

Sprawled across her legs was an old woman's torso, head and one arm still attached to shoulders. The mass of rags and tattered flesh was a mottled bloody red. Ceila swiftly kicked out from under it. She wanted to scream. Instead she gave a sickly cry then started to crawl on her knes.

She stood up. She walked to the wagon and braced herself against it. The curator and his wife appeared. All the crying woman could say was "Jezus Maria, Jezus Maria." Her hands were clamped tight in prayer.

The curator scurried off toward the bombed building. A crowd pressed in. The ambulance corpsmen and police restrained them.

The curator elbowed his way to the nearest officer. "Is there anything, anything we could do for them?"

"Hardly," the man replied, looking up fearfully at the gaping building. "More of the building could come down. It'll be some time before we get to them."

He walked back to the wagon. He found the others grieving over the end of their two close friends.

"It was the will of God," Pani Curator said. "My dearest, don't torture yourself so much. It was the will of God." She pressed her frail body up against him.

What could he say when he was so full of hate and anger? How could he fight back? His face distorted, he pulled his shoulders straight and in a trembling voice said, "Jesus Christ! Give me a gun, give me a gun! I'll kill every sonofabitch of a German that walks the face of the earth."

"No – no–" Pani Curator put out her hand over his mouth: "Please Tatusu, do not speak in such terrible anger and not in the name of Jesus Christ! Please don't, please!"

"Christ!" he cried back almost as if it were a dirty word. "If this is life – if this is living, where in the hell are Mary and Joseph and all the saints! This is war, woman–." He pulled himself free and walked toward the horses. He buried his face against the warm, wet neck of the animal. It stood still, as if it understood.

"I too have seen war," the wife said. "And I would like to see more of God." She moved toward him. "But seeing you like this, listening to you, I have a dreadful fear for all of us. This is not like you, not like you. I have always loved you and I know you and understand you. This is not like you."

She stopped long enough to watch as Victor rejoined them.

"You know best." Her voice broke. "Do as you like, my dear."

The curator looked at her. He was about to say something when Professor Woda walked up. They greeted each other warmly. The curator told about the tragic loss of their comrades and the purpose of their mission.

It was agreed that they would meet after dark behind the museum.

With the curator at the reins, the wagon rolled down the street. Even the horses seemed to have sensed a loss. They plodded, heads bobbing low with each stride. None of them wanted to believe that it happened, yet it had happened.

At the art museum the professor met them as agreed. He was nervous but determined, and Ceila had a warm feeling in her heart for him. Lublin was crawling with Fifth Columnists, *Volksdeutsche*, Ukranians and Nazi sympathizers.

It was difficult going for a while with just the three men, but they finally managed to move the heavy crate inside the building.

Professor Woda led them to his office. He did everything possible to make his friends comfortable. He apologized that he had no spirituous refreshments on the premises, but when he bowed himself out he reminded them, "I'll soon do something about that. In the meantime, ease your weary bones for a short while and I'll go and see about finding you a place to stay." Still bowing and smiling he backed out the door and was off.

In a matter of a few minutes, much to their surprise, Professor Woda, gasping for breath, burst into the room. "We're very much in luck. A student friend has agreed to move in with a friend of his and let you folks have his place. Fortunately, it is but a few blocks from here and we can move right along."

The professor quickly locked the door behind them when they left. They all boarded the wagon, rounded the corner and were out of sight of the building.

When they got to the apartment Professor Woda found for them, the curator beat his fists against his head and cried: "Why – why did they have to die?" He pushed himself past the others and flung himself into an old wooden chair. "Why – why – why?"

There had to be answers. Their lives, Poland, Grünwald, the days of war, and now they must die. Everything was marked by events, not seconds and minutes.

Pani Curator knelt down before him. "Please – please – don't torture yourself so – so–"

Ceila found some tea and put water on the stove to boil. The professor excused himself and hurried off to find some food.

23

The apartment was on the corner of a street of carriage houses. On the top floor it commanded a splendid view of the streets below and the gray-black rooftops and chimneys. There was a large living room and dining area and kitchen. A large sofa made into a bed, which the curator and his wife shared the first night. The back room served as a bedroom and study furnished with an old wooden bed, a writing desk and some bookcases. A bathroom down the hall was shared by three families.

Their morning meal was the first hot food they had had in days. It consisted of tea so strong it was almost black, soft-boiled eggs and large slabs of black bread.

Late that morning Professor Woda came and inquired about their immediate needs. Pani Curator put the teapot on the stove.

GRÜNWALD

The curator wanted news. What about Warsaw?

"It's sad, but there is still hope. The German drive has slowed down. The city is surrounded on three sides, but our armies are moving as fast as the clogged roads permit." The professor tried to sound optimistic. "The President, the government and some of the military commanders are all in the regions adjoining the Rumanian frontier, where the mountainous area is full of Polish troops." He explained that an even larger force had retreated to the marshy lands in the vast Polesie District near the Russian border, where they could hole up in good positions for the winter and harass the Germans.

The curator paced the floor. From time to time he stopped to reset the eyeglasses over the bridge of his nose. "How? How could it happen twice in our lifetime? We already fought a war to end wars."

As the professor talked, Victor walked to the window and watched the commotion in the street. The flood of travel-weary refugees continued. The air raids and the bombings were one thing, but the German slaughter of civilians was another matter.

"What are your plans?" the professor asked the curator.

"Mamush and I will be starting back to Warsaw in two or three days."

"But why? What good can you do there?"

"We had hoped to join up with the government, but that is out of the question now. All we can do is leave the Grünwald painting in your hands. You'll know what to do. There is still time. There is still the chance that we could get through to Warsaw and the museum."

The women left to see what they could find for the next meal. Victor sat near the window. Professor Woda nodded. "I'm sure you are glad that your wagon trip has finally ended."

"Yes–" Victor smiled. "We all are, I'm sure."

"How true," the curator agreed. "Hell every foot of the way." Victor drew on his cigarette. "How much longer before we move on?"

"It is difficult to say," Professor Woda said. "As you've just experienced, it's difficult to travel these days." The professor started to pace. "I doubt that we could receive any assistance from the fleeing government, as they have their hands full as it is." Staring at Victor he spoke slowly. "It's not only too late to join them, but the Germans have been bombing the highways, railroads and bridges hourly to hinder the exodus across the Rumanian frontier. The only other alternative," he said, "is to bring the matter up before the city council here. They have been meeting almost daily. They would be the only ones in authority now."

Victor leaned back in his chair, his eyes closed, his mind probing. There was a long silence when he thought he heard his name.

"Did someone call me?" He opened his eyes and saw the two men watching him with a searching look.

"We're concerned here with more than just getting you safely out of the country," said the professor, his eyes intense. "We not only feel responsible for your safety, but wonder whether we can trust you. For that matter, you should have left with the American Embassy a week ago."

Professor Woda smiled, transforming himself from a harsh and challenging individual into a friend.

"Let me be quite frank with you, Mr. Zabel. We have no way of knowing that you might, perhaps, for reasons of your own personal safety or for money, talk to the Germans. You are an American, after all, and have no ties of any kind here. You have nothing to lose and everything to gain by talking, should they ever pick you up."

"No ties," injected the curator, "except for Ceila. I'm positive that for her convictions he'll think twice before he talks. I feel sure his intentions are to have her leave with him when he goes."

"I'll be perfectly frank with you," said the professor. "I hope you will, for the sake of everyone concerned."

"I've known this gentleman for some time now." The curator lifted his head proudly, stood up and crossed the room to stand before Victor. "He's encountered hell and was pressed into a war not of his choosing."

Victor weighed every word. His gaze moved swiftly from one to the other. From their expressions, they were unhappy he was here.

"You have been quite candid with me," he said in a weary voice, "so I'll be equally frank with you. I'll do anything you wish and you needn't fear as to what I might do. One thing for sure, I have no intention of leaving here without Ceila."

"And if she refuses?" Professor Woda snapped.

"That – only she can account for."

The professor gave a short laugh. It was genuine. "You are a brave man, a good man and, as the curator said, this is not your choosing. But you needn't fear. We'll find a way."

"I'll never be a threat to you."

"That, I'm sure." The curator smiled. "We'll work it out somehow. You Americans are hard to keep down, you know."

The morning of the third day after their arrival the rescue squad uncovered Kordian and Lolek, their bodies battered to a pulp but their arms still protectively around each other.

Late that afternoon Ceila leaned against Victor. Together, standing next to the curator and his wife, they watched as the two black pine boxes were lowered into a common grave. The priest crossed himself and chanted, "Merciful Father—"

Professor Woda was beside the grave. Around him clustered a few friends of the two artists. Bells tolled in the distance in the hot September air. Tears ran down perspiring faces.

When it was over and they had turned to leave, a sudden wind tossed and tangled Ceila's long hair which was hanging loose over her shoulders. Strands blew across her face. She put her arm around the weeping Pani. They walked away without a word.

The sun was already low, and the heat of day had subsided by the time they returned to the apartment. They ate in silence. After dinner when the dishes had been put away and the shades lowered Curator Bozinski turned to Victor. "Now, don't you think you could use a drink?"

"I think we all could," Victor replied, reaching for Ceila's hand as she was putting the table in order. "I'm sure you'll join us. And Pani Curator." He got up to get the bottle, bowing before the woman sitting very much alone: "You'll have just a little one, just this once, yes?"

Victor did not wait for an answer but hastened back with four glasses and a half-filled vodka bottle. They had one drink, then another. They talked about the two friends far into the night.

That night, their eyes closed and the desire to sleep almost beyond endurance, no one slept. Their minds as a unit dwelt on Kordian and Lolek.

At six in the morning, Ceila gave up trying to sleep. In the dim steel-gray glow of daybreak, she rolled out of bed. Slowly, not to disturb the others, she dressed warmly and put on the teakettle to boil. She got into one shoe. Victor lifted his head. "What time is it?"

Ceila turned her eyes toward the clock on the shelf above the stove. "Almost six-thirty. I think I'll go out early and see what I might find at the old market. We're in need of provisions and maybe a small bottle of wine for dinner."

"But isn't this a bit early?"

"I had to get up. I didn't sleep a wink all night." Ceila bent over and mussed his hair: "Who knows, I might be lucky enough to find some fresh meat other than smoked ham. Don't you think that sounds good?" She kissed him full on the lips.

"With a kiss like that, I better let you go. You be careful, now." He pulled the bed covers over his head when he heard the door close softly behind her.

24

Professor Woda did bring the matter of the Grünwald painting before the Lublin council, but other matters were more pressing. The city was struck by two more air raids. The right wing of the museum was bombed, destroying five halls of archeological and natural history collections. In the last raid, Woda's home had been demolished by incendiary bombs. With his wife and sons he moved into a corner of the conference room at the museum.

A committee finally visited the gallery. The canvas was unrolled to its full splendor. But so many had ideas as to the course to be taken that they disbanded without reaching any decision. Late that same afternoon the city suffered another strafing, but it proved to be more of an harassing action and less damaging than the others.

Late Sunday morning they all met at the museum to discuss the matter, all but Professor Woda. They could only wait. Ceila proceeded to pull the blinds up on a few windows and admired the bright sunny day. The streets were filled with churchgoers. Small groups stopped to visit. Less than a month ago, these same people clung to the belief that the decency of mankind would protect the humble, the weak and unprepared.

Ceila turned to the others when she saw the professor. "Here he comes now."

He came rushing with his gray hair flowing. From the manner in which he pushed the crowd out of his way, she knew something was up. Maybe it was good news, Ceila prayed. Just this one time . . .

When they opened the door for him he was breathless, his face white: "Oh God! The Russians, the Russians!" He gasped, falling onto the nearest chair. "The Russians – the German radio reports that the Russians have invaded the country along the entire length of the eastern border."

The report left them paralyzed and silent. Not a wink of an eye, not a whisper, hardly any sound of breathing.

"It's a lie!" The curator's voice pierced the silence. "It can't be true! Just more Nazi propaganda!"

"Hardly," Woda answered, his words barely audible. "It's true enough. As we listened the Germans announced it as another victory for them."

"But how is it possible? Does it mean the Russians have declared war? Are they coming to help us? How reliable is the report? Where have they crossed? How many?"

Everyone began to talk at once. Pani Curator retreated and sat down in the corner, sobbing. Victor hurried to her side, but she turned him away. Wringing her small hands, she rocked convulsively. Ceila put her arms about the woman's shoulders.

She too was crying.

Curator Bozinski held his ground in front of Woda. "How – reliable is the report?"

"No one could believe what they heard at first," the professor said. "Finally we heard a report made in Russian, Polish and Ukranian. It said the Soviet soldiers were coming as friends and liberators and for the Poles not to resist them as they were coming to protect the White Ruthenians and Ukranian people from the enemy. The report urged for the union of all Slavic people as brothers."

"What enemy? Protection, who from whom?" roared back the curator.

Early the next day, Curator Bozinski and his wife completed their preparations for their return to Warsaw. Victor stood slightly apart and watched the group bid them farewell and good wishes. So many outstretched hands to hold for a moment, so many kind words. The tears welled up in Ceila's eyes as she embraced the frail woman.

"I hate to see you go," Ceila said. "You have all been a family to me."

The two kissed each other again and again. Pani Curator held Ceila tightly in her arms.

The curator shook hands with Professor Woda then turned to Victor with his hand extended. "Well, young man–" his voice was firm. "Goodbye. Go with God and the best of luck to you. Maybe you'll come back again some day. You are always welcome, you know. It can't always be like this."

Victor was surprised by the casual manner of the curator's words, as if this was just another farewell and they would be seeing each other again soon. As they shook hands all Victor could say was, "Of course, of course, goodbye."

The curator turned to the women and touched his wife on the

shoulder. "Come Mamush. We've a long way to go."

Pani Curator quickly dried the tears and blew her nose. She shook Victor's hand and wished him Godspeed before she turned to the professor.

The curator gave Ceila a bear hug and planted a kiss on each cheek, mumbling, "You take good care of yourself now, and be careful; I want to see you again soon."

Victor helped Pani Curator up onto the seat while the curator, with last-minute instructions from the professor, took his place behind the reins.

Then only their backs could be seen above the bobbing heads in the crowded street. The gray sky brought a breeze to the dry coolness of autumn.

Professor Woda pledged himself "to guard the painting and to protect it from the German invader and to keep its whereabouts a secret." The secret sign, which was also to serve as a password when the canvas was handed over, was a visiting card with the curator's signature. Three such visiting cards were made out. One remained with the curator, one was to be passed on to a representative of the government, and the third was left to Professor Woda. He could only relinquish the painting to the individual who could identify himself by one of the cards.

Since the arrival of the canvas at the museum could have been known by others, countermeasures had to be taken. Woda decided to use the recent evacuation of the government as a decoy and make believe that the Grünwald painting had been taken along into exile. At the repair shop he ordered a huge roll and a covering of boards. He requested a young lieutenant in charge of a government transport column to make the fictitious transfer of the fake canvas. As soon as the lieutenant got out of town, he was free to dump it into the nearest ditch. The important thing was to stage a noisy exit and farewell, which was completed with Ceila and Victor assisting.

It was nearly seven o'clock that same day. Victor sat near the window leafing through a magazine, and wishing Ceila would wake from her late nap. He was anxious to move on, especially now with the Russians in the war. He felt very much alone.

There was a knock on the door.

"Who is it?"

"Woda."

Victor opened the door. Ceila heard and sat up, rubbing the sleep from her eyes.

"I'm sorry," Woda said, regarding her. The fullness had returned to her face. Her soft hair fell loosely. The tan sweater outlined her breasts and her skirt rested just above her knees. She was barefooted.

"Oh my gosh," she said, "I must look a fright." She pushed her hair back, slipped into her shoes and hurried off to the bathroom.

"It's frights like you that I need more of," said the professor. He placed two bottles of red wine on the table and walked to the kitchen for glasses. "I could have some wine. How about you, Victor?"

"Have I reached the age of consent?" Victor smiled.

"We'll make an exception in your case, but only for today." Woda shook his finger at him. He popped the cork off and filled three glasses just as Ceila returned.

She sat down on the couch while Victor and Woda pulled up chairs to the table. They toasted the safe return of Curator Bozinski and his wife to Warsaw. Woda got to his feet and shaking his head said, "Our situation is growing worse by the hour." He stopped to take a deep swallow of wine. "I called

175

again on the city officials, and after two hours of deliberation, we finally agreed to construct an appropriate shelter in the museum garden to conceal the canvas."

"But couldn't that prove dangerous?" Ceila asked.

"Could be, could be," Woda replied. "It can't be just any hole in the ground. It'll have to be deep enough to be bombproof as well as waterproof. If it's to repose there for the duration, however long that could be, it'll need to be well protected. Dampness and mold would soon rot the canvas. It'll take some planning and work."

"A fresh hole would be easily detected by searching parties," Victor said. "And I'd imagine that the museum grounds would be the first place they would look."

"How true. You have a point there." Woda twirled the glass between the palms of his hands. "We certainly can't rush into this thing. It'll take more planning."

"Does it have to be in the museum garden?" Ceila inquired. "Elsewhere at least it would be away from prying eyes, and certainly any forest would be as good a place as any to get lost in."

"Get lost is right." Woda looked at Ceila. "You've at least helped salvage part of the idea. But should something happen to any of us, who would ever find it again? Whatever the plan, the canvas will have to remain within the city. It's not exactly a needle in a haystack, you know. With the waterproof box, the contents will be more than fifteen feet long. Such a hole would be large enough to bury ten men. Yes, a project of such magnitude would attract attention in the museum garden. The city is filled with *Volksdeutsch*, Ukranians and Nazi sympathizers, not to mention the traitors who would sell their own flesh and blood for such a price. Sooner or later, someone would find out. We must, we must seek elsewhere."

Victor studied the professor, a natural in his capacity as head of the art museum, a respected teacher, historian and writer. Calm, honest and patient, he was often introduced as the "great," being one of the most learned men in the country.

The professor sipped his wine, smoothed his gray mustache and walked toward the door. "I must be leaving you two now," he said. "More work tomorrow. The doors are always open, stop by any time. Good night." He bowed and closed the door behind him.

Two days later there was no time left for talk and planning. "The Germans! The Germans are coming!" The shouts echoed through Lublin's streets.

A yellow-gray dust cloud mounted like a solid wave across the western fields, moving ever closer. It moved out of the forest where a bloody struggle had raged for forty-seven hours, with the Nazi Panzers moving ahead like prowling monsters.

Victor and Ceila heard the rumble like a train crossing a bridge. They stopped and looked at each other then turned to peer down the street. First the mounted cavalry, then the roar of motorcycles with the dark figures in German helmets crouched low. Their carbines and submachine guns lay across their laps. Their helmets and uniforms were coated with dust. They rode freely, looking about from side to side as if on parade. They came four by four, in line.

Then came trucks, their angular frames ripping leaves from the shade trees along the street. Finally, tanks, their motors pumping, the ground quaking. Victor could feel Ceila tremble.

"Let's start for home," he said.

Ceila wouldn't budge. Still they came, the antitank company, the signal corps, the staff cars and service troops. A death-like silence fell over the city.

There weren't many people in the streets, and those that were there pressed against the walls of the buildings and stood in dark doorways. The children ran away. Most of them peered out from behind closed doors and drawn curtains as the cavalry galloped into the city square and lined up in formation in front of city hall. Immediately behind them, motorcycles and tanks ground up into position. At a signal from an officer, the soldiers leaped from their cycles and carriers and pointed their guns across the square as they raised the German flag.

The children were the first to return, staring with dirty, tear-stained faces at the black and gray monsters.

Victor stood in silence. A twilight breeze swept the leaves and dust in the streets and threw it into their faces. He buttoned up his coat and with Ceila clinging to his arm they walked to their flat.

Once inside, Ceila said, "They've come at last. Maybe it's for the best. Here in Lublin at least, the war is over." She undid her coat, threw it over a chair and walked to the kitchen. She poured water into a teakettle and placed it over the burner. There was no time to lie down now. She walked to Victor. "You're so quiet." She put her hands on the back of his shoulders and leaned on him. "This is all so maddening. Damn Hitler and his politics."

Victor turned, taking her in his arms. "Darling, what about us? Don't you think we should have been on the road long before this?"

"We should have been a lot of places before this," she said. Again she started moving about and putting things in order. "We'll formulate our plans just as soon as things settle down a bit."

Victor was about to say something when there was a loud and urgent knocking on the door.

They exchanged glances. The knocking grew more urgent.

Ceila eased toward the door. "Who's there?"

"Madam, please—" answered a male voice. "Professor Woda sent me."

She opened the door and recognized a face she had seen in the museum shop. "The professor needs you. He said to come quickly!"

He was breathless. He had evidently run all the way. He had none of the flat Slavic features. He was black haired, white at the temples, with a rather long face and thin pinched nose. She had seen his face among the Armenians on her rounds about town.

She turned to Victor, as if beseeching him to say something, do something. But he just stood there.

"Where is the professor?" she asked. "What does he want of us?"

"At the museum, madam," the stranger replied. "You must come now." He looked unhappy, folding and unfolding his cap.

She felt frightened, but she asked herself, how else could this man have found them if the professor hadn't directed him? A cold wind struck one of the window shutters. It helped her decide, with the coldness that swept across her body.

"Come, something's happened," she said to Victor.

25

They ran up the wide marble stairs, and halted in horror. The main hall of the museum was a shambles. The paintings, sculptures and showcases remained in their places, but the floor was a mess. The professor was at work making it even worse. They stood there, not knowing what to make of it. He was rushing like a madman. He worked his way toward them, ripping and flinging the contents of an old pillow.

"You seem very disturbed." He smiled. He continued tearing away at the feather beds, straw mattresses, anything he could lay his hands on. He shouted at them. "Don't just stand there, help me!" Still they stood, stricken.

"I'll explain," he said, shoving a feather bed at them. "Go at it girl, have fun." He blew a handful of down into Ceila's face and laughed. "This is the only idea I could come up with. We have no time. Under this whole damn mess is the Grünwald canvas. It's the last place anyone would think to look for it."

In less than an hour, with additional touches, the main hall was transformed into a messed up dormitory for refugees in transit. For the balance of the night and far into the early hours of the morning they rounded up refugees from the streets and brought them to the museum.

The refugees packed in with all they had been able to salvage when the bombs fell. They were mostly older people and small children. At first they stared in awe at the exquisite decor of the huge hall, at the chandelier and the paintings. Then they proceeded to make themselves at home amidst the marble sculpture of ancient Rome. It was strange to see a woman bathing a child in a fourteenth century marble bowl, an old man trimming his beard in front of a Roman Caesar, holding a piece of broken mirror.

Though the night was chilly, the windows were open to let out the stench: the perspiration, dirt and breath of hundreds. The floor became even more littered with rags and paper. From every section of the building came the sounds of children and of people trying to make themselves comfortable. They sprawled everywhere, in every conceivable postition, groaning, snorting, and muttering.

Professor Woda, Ceila and Victor were more gratified than fatigued when the sun came up that morning. There was a faint smile of contentment on Woda's face at the madness that had transformed the palace. They stood looking with compassion at the tired faces and bodies – still in their heavy coats, hats and boots because they feared that to remove them was to lose them. Little did any of these people realize that, sandwiched between some old canvases and under all this mess, was the Grünwald painting.

Professor Woda thanked Ceila and Victor for their assistance. Ceila's calm deserted her. She felt sick. Tears squeezed out of the corners of her eyes. She bid Professor Woda goodnight, turned and walked toward the door.

Victor led her by the hand. Her hair had fallen over her face. She was weeping softly. She asked, "What's the matter with me?"

"It's been a hard night, darling," he whispered. "A breath of fresh air and you'll be all right again. We'll have some tea and a bite to eat. That should perk you up some."

The two had hardly been gone an hour when the Germans surrounded the building. The SS Officer was polite as he greeted the professor with a curt "Good morning." They had come to search for Polish government officials. They had reports that members of the fleeing cabinet had stayed at the museum.

It was difficult to appear calm, but the professor managed. He said, "Yes, they did stay here for three days but have long since gone."

The firm, quiet tone of the SS Captain carried a lot of conviction when he demanded that he and his men see for themselves. Woda conducted a score of SS men and soldiers with drawn guns through all the rooms and basement of the museum.

"Pigs!"remarked a junior SS officer, his eyes scanning the mass of refugees.

"I can't understand how people can live like this," remarked another.

"Pigs – pigs."

The grating sounds of boots on the marble and stone echoed through the halls. Doors were flung open by heavy rifle butts, but the rooms were silently dank and empty. For his cooperation,

GRÜNWALD

Professor Woda received a certificate that he was in the clear. He watched them drive off. How human these Germans were after all. This was his first direct contact with them. These Nazis were no devils. Except for over self-importance and the urgency to bark like mad dogs, they seemed quite human. There still might be hope. He turned, rubbing his tired legs to restore the circulation, and walked back into the museum. He dropped down onto his pallet and fell into an exhausted sleep.

Five days passed. Victor had little choice but to make the most of it at the flat. The escape from Poland wasn't going to be simple. There were others just as desperate to leave, and there was Ceila, now that it was decided to leave together.

The weather was growing colder by the day, and the reports grew more alarming, with many arrests and beatings. Everybody could feel the German pressure. Still there was no panic.

Victor looked at his watch. Six o'clock. Ceila had been gone almost three hours, rounding up what food there was still to be bought on the open market. He hated to see her go every time. He always wanted to go along, but she didn't think it was safe. There was always the fear that he would be recognized as an American by the Nazis. There was always that certain something about Americans that stood out in any crowd.

He tried to read but found it difficult. He had already napped. It wouldn't be completely dark for another hour. He rose from the couch and went to the window. It had been a week since the Germans had taken the city, but there was still fighting in outlying areas. Every day he heard the grating sound of boots and the muffled sound of slurred feet as another column of prisoners was being led back, weary, unshaven, with little resemblance to the Polish soldiers he had seen before the war. Now and then a fresh German infantry company, marching off, would burst out in lusty singing in contrast to the silent column stumbling along in the opposite direction.

Victor turned from the window. It would be another one of those slow nights. They would sit up for hours talking over a cup of tea. He walked out onto the small balcony in the cool air. He wished Ceila would hurry back.

The outdoor air sharpened his wits. His eyes scanned familiar roof tops, streets and alleys, looking for the unusual. But it was all the same, with dark figures scurrying along into dark doorways.

He was alert to every sound, from the muffled drum beat of booted feet, to the slurred dragging of the wounded, even to the wind in the tree tops. But what he knew best was the sound of Ceila's heels and the slow shuffle of the Professor's heavy step.

It was Ceila's quick, light click, click, click, the tapping of heels that always made him sigh with relief. They spent more time together now, and when she had to leave, he spent most of the time worrying about her.

It was from Ceila that he learned of the real tragedy of Poland.

Warsaw had finally surrendered. The war was officially over, except for the last Polish stand at Kock, not far from Lublin. Two days later, September 29th, came an official German-Russian partition of Poland. The Soviets sent the Red Army to occupy Eastern Poland, thereby creating a buffer between Russia proper and the Germans. Poland had again ceased to exist, except for the government in exile in Paris.

The first few days of occupation were fairly good ones for both the Germans and the people, but before long the Germans started to demonstrate an iron-handed policy. There was no attempt at winning the people over. The Nazis believed that any sign of decency would be mistaken for weakness.

At first the German soldiers got along better with the Jews

than with the Poles. All the Jews could speak some sort of German. The soldiers chatted with them and patronized their shops. But in a matter of two weeks, as the political occupation took over from the military, this changed.

A large three-story office building facing the square was the administration center for the Germans. A smaller building across the street, with a number of sentries, housed the German General Staff. All civil rule was taken over by the Gestapo.

The people started back to their abandoned homes and farms. Once again crowds moved on the roads, returning to ruined villages, towns and farms.

The area around Lublin had always been self-sustaining; the wheat fields, the pig farms and orchards were a main part of the bread-basket of Poland. Now it was rapidly being stripped by the Germans. Whole villages and fields were burned whenever defiance flared up. Slowly, resistance groups were organized, and a growing underground started to unite. Almost everything that was to be bought was on the black market.

The generals settled down in the castle in old Lublin. The forests around the city abounded in deer, fox and boars. Here the generals had hunting grounds. Bloody traces of the hunted appeared. The shots heard were less and less from hunting parties and more and more from the Gestapo execution platoons.

Victor was waiting for Ceila at the door, a glass of wine in his hand.

"I was beginning to think you'd never get home."

Her arms were loaded down with foodstuffs. "Did you miss me – just a little?"

"You worried me. You were gone longer than usual. It seemed like days since you left."

He filled another glass of wine. He helped her with her coat and put the food away.

I don't know if I should even mention this," she said. "I just can't understand what's happening in this world."

"We've seen just about everything, why should you be so shocked now?"

"It was terrible," she said. "Three German soldiers had a rabbi cornered at a building. The brutes made him shit in his pants before they let him go. . . . I suppose you had another boring day. I'll make it up to you by cooking a wonderful dinner."

In the tiny kitchen she told him more of her visit across town. "It's becoming worse by the hour. I have nothing but utter contempt for those damn Volksdeutsche."

"I don't understand."

"Like beasts, they change with the wind. Now that the Germans are here, they claim to be Germans, and if the Russians were to come tomorrow, they would become Russians. I would prefer real Germans to those traitors." She paused. "There is a terrible fright in the city. Every day more and more people disappear behind the walls of the old castle. Now, along with all the goosestepping, these damn Volksdeutsche, after helping destroy the country, are lining up for their rewards. Working with the filthy Nazis, they're reporting the people who did their duty. Oh my God, is there no end to this treachery and murder?"

"How did you learn about this?"

"It's all people are talking about – in whispers, of course. Every day people hear shots from behind the walls of the old castle. Reports are that special Gestapo squads are murdering our leading citizens. They have started a program of liquidating all the intelligentsia and are making the country into a gigantic slave-labor camp."

26

It was Professor Woda's first visit since the night he set up the dormitory.

"Nothing could be more tranquil for a man's nerves," Woda said, "than uncomplicated companionship."

Victor took Woda's coat. "Care for a drink?"

"If for medicinal purposes, yes," he laughed. "But to get drunk might be an even better idea."

"What will it be?" Ceila asked, assisting him to the only stuffed chair in the place. "We have a wide selection tonight. Wine or vodka?"

"Vodka," he replied. Victor walked up with three glasses and a bottle.

"Hundred proof." He smiled. "Guaranteed to burn any rust

right off the pipes."

"Sounds fine,"Woda said.

"Anything new?" Ceila sat down. "Have they bothered you much?"

"Yes and no," Woda replied. "I used to wonder what I'd do when they finally arrived. One must move like a cat, adapting oneself to every opportunity." He took a deep swallow. "After a short functionary inspection they ordered the museum closed. You can imagine my displeasure at such harsh demands, so what could I do but start pleading? What about all these poor refugees, including my family? They finally agreed I should have a few days to find a place. You could imagine how that night I slept more peacefully than I have all those preceding nights. Honestly, if anyone ever told me that one day I'd be sleeping on top of the Grünwald painting, I'd curse him as a complete idiot. And here I was, with my whole family. But yesterday the Stadthauptmann's personal aide came for the keys to all the other halls, and we're still quartered in the main conference hall. Little by little the refugees are starting to go back to their homes. But things aren't what they seem on the surface. I fear for the future."

"But the war is over," Victor said.

"That is what they are saying and want us to believe, but what they are doing is hardly the same." Professor Woda went on to explain about the great surge of humanity pouring into the Jewish area, with further transports expected daily. "The question of an enclosed ghetto has been voiced. The Poles naturally objected to the authorities since the enclosed settlement would cost them their Jewish contacts. Daily there are Nazi acts of provocation designed to create bad feelings between the Poles and Jews.

"Community activity has ceased completely. Everyone

looks only after his own needs. With supplies rapidly disappearing from the shelves and all sources shut off, the black market has doubled the prices. It's terrible, absolute chaos.

"I heard our people were putting together a list of persons collaborating with the Nazis as each day more of the intelligentsia are arrested, never to be heard from again." Woda took a deep swallow before continuing.

"Life is rapidly becoming a vacuum. Today they closed down the newspaper offices and arrested the publishers and editors. The publication of books and booklets has been forbidden, as have all other forms of literary and artistic activities. No more theater or concerts. All music of Frederic Chopin and Moniuszko has been forbidden."

"Impossible!" cried Ceila, rising abruptly to her feet. "These are not people, they are beasts! I hate them! I hate them! – if I were only a man I could kill!"

Both Victor and Woda looked on helplessly.

"I'm sorry," she said finally, slipping her coat loosely over her shoulders and walking toward the door before she turned. "We'll be needing a few things for tomorrow." Both knew this was only an excuse. Both knew she needed to walk and think.

Victor followed her to the door. "Don't be too late," he said gently. "I worry."

"I won't," she replied. She kissed him on his mouth lingeringly. She turned and was gone.

Victor walked to the window and watched as she disappeared down the street. He turned and said, "I'll be glad when we finally leave this place."

"Yes – I can understand how you feel. Just as soon as matters settle down, I'm sure you two can make your move. It shouldn't be too long now."

Ceila came out of the street and started across toward the old market square. A blinding sun forced her to move in the shadows along the buildings. When she reached the far side of the square she saw a group of men being herded together by armed soldiers for forced labor at the aircraft factory which was being dismantled for shipment to Germany.

She stopped at the sixteenth century cathedral. One of its domes had been damaged by an air-raid. She had visited it once before, its Renaissance chapels and tombs, some of the most beautiful relics in Eastern Europe.

Again the sunlight blinded her. She squinted against the glare and sought out the shade. She proceeded around bomb craters then slowly picked her way around a labor crew of bearded Jews patching a stretch of sidewalk with gravestones torn from the old Jewish cemetery.

A few pedestrians, their heads pulled low, seemed in a hurry. Everywhere German soldiers leisurely viewed the windows and displays of wares difficult to sell elsewhere.

Lublin, with its finest historical tradition, had been transformed into a German city. German banners were everywhere, with huge portraits of Hitler. The parks and squares and street names were being changed to German.

She passed shops with empty shelves as gray and dusty as the windows. She passed a small open-door flower and novelty store. It was empty except for some potted plants, and to her surprise, some fresh red roses. It was too much to resist, too much to be without such a small gift, if only a single red rose. She felt a wonderful ripple inside herself. She took her time and found the one rose that was proper. She could only afford one. Only a woman could understand such a simple thing, so deep, so red, full and rounded, just beginning to unfurl its soft, velvet petals.

She paid, clutched the rose in her hand and walked out,

somehow feeling safer than she had in weeks. She sniffed at the deep fragrance. She would present the rose to Victor. They would nurse it along. She was suddenly completely happy.

She heard a commotion – shouts, whistles, screaming female voices. She stopped. Soldiers had picked up a large number of young girls. They were being led to the center of the square. The Germans tried to drag someone out of the crowd. More shouts and screams rose above the soldiers' demands for watches and rings. A number of German officers stopped to watch, delighted.

An elderly woman clutched frantically at one of the soldiers, trying to get one of the girls away from him. She was clubbed to the ground and lay there twitching and groaning.

The girls were being herded like cattle to the high school building which had been closed the week before. After a medical examination they would be put at the disposal of young German pilots who had just arrived. Some of the girls were sent to hospitals as blood donors. For the last few days now, the high-school dormitories to which the girls were taken had been used for an elementary course in debauchery. Only German officers had access to the place.

A group of people gathered near where Ceila stood, watching, unable to act. From the midst of confusion someone screamed, "There she is! That's her! That's her!"

The crowd grew, tightening as they began to close in. The screaming male voice grew louder and closer. "Arrest her! That's her!" People looked this way and that. Ceila was curious. Then she realized that all the faces were looking at her.

The crowd began to run. She panicked and joined them. She could feel her heart pounding faster amidst the rushing mob of white faces. The crowd pressed on, darting into doorways of buildings and shops. Older folk were knocked down and trampled by those that followed close behind. More shouting and yells and whistles sounded as the number of German uniforms grew. Huge police dogs barked.

Ceila darted into a doorway, pushed and crowded by the mob. She ran up three flights of stairs, following others, until the mob pressed so tight that she could go no further. Along the corridor one of the doors was forced open and she, too, was pushed into it.

She began to feel faint. Above the noises rose the clatter of hobnailed boots on the stairway. There were shouts of German cursing: "Raus!" More shouting, whistles, the ugly growling of dogs, and the smashing down of the door. "Raus! you swine, Raus!"

Ceila had been pushed to the far corner of the room and could not move. She did not know how long she had been trapped there before the Germans apppeared. Shouting, and by force of fist and toe and truncheon, they drove the people from the room and found her. She stood alone in the corner.

Ceila's lips were dry and fevered. She looked down. She had not realized she had been clutching tightly to only a stem. She had a blurred glimpse of a living thing that had been ground to bits under the hobnail boots.

A young officer in an SS uniform burst into the room and began screaming, "It's her! It's her!" He stamped across the room, seized her by the hair, and jerking her head back, shouted, "She's the one. One of them. It's her! She was one of the group with the Grünwald painting! They killed two of our officers!"

She recognized the young man with the upturned nose on the bicycle – the one in the Polish officer's uniform at that Warsaw nightclub. The one who escaped on the motorcycle.

"You come with us!" He gave her a push toward the door, into the corridor, down the steps to the street, and into a waiting car.

She had a glimpse of their faces, hard and impassive, eyes hidden under the peaks of their caps where a death's head glittered. Seated up front, sneering at her, was the young officer with the ugly, short, upturned nose. She knew that to be a member of the Elite Guard was an honor, not only to the man, but to his family.

Her apprehension mounted as they sped through the city. From the facade of buildings she saw the white eagle being removed and a huge black flag with the swastika replacing it.

The big car sped on. The city fell away. The car slowed and stopped before the large gate to the old royal castle. The castle had its day of glory in the time of knighthood and raiding Tartars under the Khans. It was built by King Boleslaw and reinforced by Casimir the Great in the year 1341. The four sides were rimmed with parapets from which soldiers could shoot down on the enemy. In the center of the courtyard stood the ancient church where the Lublin Union was signed between Poland and Lithuania in 1569. For many years the castle had served as a prison.

The Gestapo had appropriated it. An enormous scarlet flag with the swastika centered in a white circle hung over the gate. Uniformed sentries in black polished steel helmets held bayoneted rifles at attention. At the proper signal, the car proceeded slowly through the gate. The car stopped at a large door marked "Gestapo Headquarters."

"Raus! Inside!" said the pig-nosed officer.

One of the SS men remained with her when the young officer disappeared behind the door. Ceila fidgeted. The eyes of those passing watched. They resembled robots in their spotless uniforms and highly polished boots.

The door was flung open and a man in uniform motioned for her to enter.

27

Ceila felt tired when she sat down. There was a slight tremor in her hands. Her eyes darted nervously about the large, damp room. She had visited the castle once before.

She recalled the purpose of that visit. The castle had been converted by the Russians into a prison and the Poles continued to use it as such after the enemy had been driven out of the country. The Gothic church was the purpose of her visit. It was old – old even for Poland – rebuilt by King Jagello in 1410, who commanded the forces that defeated the Teutonic Knights at Grünwald that same year. After the partitioning, the occupying Russian soldiers whitewashed the walls and history gradually forgot the chapel existed. Years later, the whitewash chipped off, revealing part of a fresco-Jagello and the Virgin Mary. Immediately the Russians began a systematic destruction, chipping away at the stone and peppering the fresco with tool marks.

A commission arrived from St. Petersburg and, after investigation, announced that this historic relic was a Russian chapel with Byzantine frescoes and had to be saved. The destruction ceased. The Poles, happy over the event, never bothered to argue the true ownership. Byzantine? Russian? Not until experts set to work, patiently peeling off the whitewash, did the fresco show clearly that it was the work of Master Andrew of Wilno, court painter of Jagello.

An officer appeared in the doorway and motioned Ceila to follow. She held her breath, expecting some torture. The deep-stained paneling of the ancient walls gave off a comfortable golden glow. The room suggested nothing but permanence and cold efficiency. There was the usual huge desk and leather upholstered chair. Another chair, a simple wooden one, faced the desk. There were colored portraits of Hitler, his hand extended in the Nazi salute, and a photo of Himmler. There was a huge stone fireplace off to one corner, but it had been some time since anyone had built a fire there. On the mantel were a few mementos, among them a sword, some family photos and a book. There was still another door, a heavy door, very much like the first through which she had entered.

So this is it, she thought, confronted by the Gestapo agent seated behind the desk going through some reports. Things like this always happened to others.

The officer looked up. "Would you please have a seat," he said, his thin lips curled in a faint smile.

Ceila's mind whirled without direction.

"Would you please remove the babuska," he said without looking at her.

She complied, nervously toying with the scarf. She felt as

though she had a part in a play.

"Well, what do we have here?" He got up and asserted his authority by dismissing the guard. He walked from behind the desk and leaned against the edge, smiling.

"I'm Gestapo Commissioner Gossberg." He introduced himself unpretentiously. "I'm here to work out the means by which Poles and Germans can live in unity. When two countries are no longer at war they should live as one, don't you agree?"

He was tall, slim and impeccable in his uniform with a single row of ribbons. There was an ease about him and a clipped, precise speech. This was an authentic product of Nazi education, a graduate of Ordensburg. In every respect the genuine specimen of a Prussian Junker.

When she did not answer, he continued, "Fate has a strange way of selecting individuals to perform a role in history. I, for one, have no patience with feminine heroics; do you understand?" His blond head tilted to one side, gray-green eyes seeking her out.

"Yes, sir." She looked up at him.

"Good, I'm sure we could be friends." He rose from the edge of the desk and lighted a cigarette. He walked with a firm, regimental stride.

"No harm will come to you as long as we understand each other." He turned and his voice became hard: "When I ask you a question, you answer as simply and as precisely as you remember, without any hesitation. There is no need for heroics or for tears, just a simple answer, do you understand?"

"Yes," she replied in an unwavering voice.

"You're an American. You're not like these Poles."

"You are speaking of my people."

"Ha–!" He had not received the reaction he had hoped for.

"Do you know I could have you shot!"

"Yes."

"Take it as you wish, but whatever you do, do not make it difficult for yourself, do you understand?"

What a strange procedure. Nothing like what she'd expect from an interrogating German officer.

"You are a beautiful woman, an American, as you might say. This war hasn't been easy for any of us and not for you. Let me help you the way you deserve to be helped. Passage to America, money, fine clothes."

When she did not answer he sighed. He walked quickly behind his desk and stood contemplating her coldly. Her flesh crawled as he ran his eyes over her body.

He seated himself and asked her to empty the contents of her bag on the desk – the usual collection of odds and ends a woman carries.

He feigned sympathy, sighed again as he pushed the articles toward her. "We could be friends, you know. You can help in making a greater Poland." He got to his feet and said, "Tell me about the Grünwald painting."

Her silence only increased his impatience. If it had been a man he would have slapped him across the face, but he restrained himself. He knew how to plant fear in her heart that no woman could bear for long.

"These are very, very grave charges," he said slowly. "Accomplice to the murder of two German officers. There are no trials, no inquiries. It's as simple as the axe or the rope. A terrible waste for you, but then, I think you will help us."

They stared each other down. There was still that faint smile of self-assurance on his face. "'Do not fear, we are glad to have found you." His voice was calm and pleasant enough. "What do you know about the Grünwald painting?"

She wondered how much they already knew. Could she be the only one the young SS officer had recognized? No more harm could come to Kordian and Lolek. But what about Victor and the curator and his wife, and now Professor Woda?

He bent over his desk and pushed a button.

"You look tired," he said. "You must be tired, of course. That's understandable after these last few weeks – the war, the journey. But now you are among friends and first you must rest."

The door opened and a uniformed guard walked in smartly. "Yes, sir."

"See this woman to her cell, please." His tone was as pleasant as that of a hotel receptionist advising the porter to see the lady to her chamber.

"Security wing?" the guard asked, his broad face impassive, saluting quickly and repeating his question. "Security wing, sir?"

"Not now. Left wing." Gossberg didn't bother even to look back at the guard but walked toward one of the large windows. He stood looking out onto the courtyard as she was led out.

Ceila was taken to a medium-sized room. It had a comfortable bed, a wooden chair and a chest of drawers. Other such rooms shared a common bath. It was freshly painted, clean and bright. There were no bars over the windows. Here she was a guest – except that the door was locked.

28

Late the next morning she heard the click of boots on the corridor floor. The pace slowed and came to a halt at her door. The sound of the key and the door opened. The uniformed guard was outlined in the doorway. He said, "You will come with me."

The long walk gave her time to think. She would have to fight as best she knew how. How did a woman fight a war? They halted at the door of Gossberg's office.

Ceila stood in the middle of the room. The Gestapo officer stood in front of the same window as the day before. He remained standing there for some time. Then he dismissed the guard and raised his arm in a cold salute.

"Good morning," he said, motioning toward the chair.

"Good morning." She sat down and folded her hands in her

lap.

"Fraulein Rozek–" he began, walking slowly toward her. "Am I correct? Cecilia Rozek?"

"Yes, I am."

"I hold the deepest regard for your safety."

She did not speak, her eyes avoiding his stare. He became annoyed.

When she returned his gaze her face was expressionless as stone. His eyes went to the black and blue mark on her left arm. Her boots, though new, were scuffed, and her skirt ripped on one side.

"They can get very rough sometimes," he said. "Did they hurt you any?"

"Nothing to complain about."

He walked to the desk and, seated on the edge, crossed his legs so that the highly polished boots showed to their best advantage.

"I'm not a difficult man to deal with, and you should realize that I must ask questions. You, naturally, must give the answers. If not now, well, tomorrow or the next day, or next week. I have the time, but my superiors grow impatient."

Gossberg elaborated on the circumstances of her arrest, the murder and a witness. A dossier was presently being drawn up on her, but he already knew that she had been employed at the Warsaw Art Museum and was instrumental in the disappearance of a piece of art in which important persons in Berlin had an interest. He told her that she needn't hold back anything or lie. With her full cooperation she could not only save her own life but receive a passport to leave the country.

"And, being American born," he said in a low voice, "it would be nice to see old friends again, don't you think so? So–" he hesitated for a moment, as if to let it all sink in – "If you please, would you tell me – where is the Grünwald painting?"

She gazed down at her hands clasped in her lap, then looked him straight in the eye. He held his breath, as if her stare troubled him. Here was a real woman whose charm would turn any man's head. But the man in him was one thing, the Gestapo Commissar another.

"Tell me," his voice friendly, "Where is the Grünwald painting?"

"I do not know," she said.

"Were you a member of the art museum staff?"

"That I was."

Her brain fought to be cunning, to tell him just so much and no more, to yield, now that she must, but yield with skill. Her heart began to pound and the palms of her hands felt damp.

The proud look in her eyes angered him. "Now, see here, Fraulein Rozek, you mean to tell me you were on the museum staff and knew nothing?"

She said nothing.

"Did you know that the painting had been removed from the museum?"

"Yes."

"By whom?"

"Some of the employees."

"Where did they take the painting?"

"I do not know."

His face went white. "Fraulein, didn't you leave Warsaw by wagon with the museum staff?"

"Yes, we did."

"Why?" He glared fiercely.

"My mother was killed and my home bombed. I was just another refugee trying to escape from Warsaw." She was earnest.

GRÜNWALD

The color returned to his face and his voice was quiet. "What was in that wagon?" He decided that she wasn't very practiced at lying. He reiterated, "What was in that wagon?"

"Us."

"And who is us? And please – please don't lie to me as I've witnesses to the number of your group."

"The curator and his wife and three friends."

"Where were you going?"

"We hoped to catch up with the foreign diplomatic corps as they proceeded toward the Rumanian frontier."

"How far did you get?"

"Here – Lublin."

"Please go on."

"We split up. The curator and his wife returned to Warsaw when they heard the city surrendered. My two friends and I remained here."

"And–?"

He walked behind the desk and slumped down into the leather chair. They could go on like this for days – a word at a time – a yes or a no.

"And, what you are trying to say is that that's all there is?" He nodded, smiling, brushed back the blond hair neatly over the right ear. He sighed. His fingers drummed atop his desk.

Gossberg sat up straight in his chair. His slim uniformed body swelled as he shouted, "Hessel!" He glanced at her, up, down, and up again. His smile was no longer friendly.

She wondered why he hadn't pushed the buzzer on his desk to summon the guard.

There was the sound of shuffling feet and the door opened. Hessel appeared. It was the same brown-shirted escort. "Yes, sir!"

"Will you please direct this woman back to her cell." He

always used a pleasant manner with his subordinates. He turned his attention once more to Ceila. "I was hoping you'd be more cooperative, but there is always tomorrow. Only the next time we meet, someone else might be listening to your story." He watched her leave the room without even the hint of a smile.

Back in her cell, she realized that the scene presently enacted all over Poland had the essence of Greek tragedy. The very character of the Poles, their historical ties, their fatalism and courage, made their actions inevitable. She understood only too well that there could never be a happy ending; there was no escape and only a little hope.

29

Professor Woda, seated at his desk, heard the urgent voice of the Armenian. "German officers, sir." The staff of Nazi officials and the propaganda chief of Lublin district had arrived for an inspection of the museum.

There were five of them, with stern faces. They looked at the refugees who stared back, wide-eyed like caged animals. From their faces, their gnarled hands, like the black earth, it was impossible to tell their ages, but they were mostly old people. There was something about the stillness, as if they awaited a signal to attack.

"Swine," General SS Gruppenfuhrer Odilo Globocnik snarled. The aide in the Gestapo uniform chuckled. He was a skinny man, with bulging, expressionless eyes. He rocked from one foot to the other.

General Globocnik, pushing fifty, strutted like a huge cock, breathing heavily. His black uniform, decorated with medals and ribbons, was impeccable.

"You Professor Woda?" The general asked in an easy-going Viennese accent. From his headquarters in the old castle, he had organized his own command of butchers named the "Death's Head Brigade." Globocnik was the real boss of Poland, entrusted with the task of "eliminating" all enemies of Germany. He did not wait for the professor to answer. "We've come to inspect your museum, if that is what you insist on calling this pig sty. Will you direct us through this mess?"

Woda nodded. Globocnik had joined the Nazis in the late thirties, when their ambitions had been spurred by the incredible success of Hitler's promises. Globocnik, the Germans discovered, was a real bone crusher who never gave a second thought when it came to breaking heads or burning down a synagogue. The Nazi party appealed to his German-Austrian character. The love of militarism was already there. He became a full-time functionary and soon headed the Gestapo in Austria. Here was his real opportunity to prove what a real Nazi he was by exhibiting a lust for cruelty.

After a casual inspection, Professor Woda was asked to remain outside his office where the officers assembled in conference. When Woda was ushered into the office, he found them calmly inspecting a few paintings. They moved slowly from one to the next. Globocnik took a few deep draws on the black cigarette holder and flipped the ash onto the marble floor. The professor dug his teeth into his lip, his eyes ablaze at the Nazi insolence.

Woda moved toward the group – General Globocnik, Dr. Dagobert Ludwig and the colonels. It was the skinny aide who saw him and spoke quickly to Dr. Ludwig. When Woda stopped at the desk, they all turned with the exception of Globocnik, looked at him and dressed their faces in smiles.

"I've always had a great appreciation for art, Professor Woda," Dr. Ludwig said. There was little in his voice to hint that he was an official Verordnungsblatt of the Governing General – one of the many university professors used as special curators whose task was to direct the confiscation and shipment of collections and properties to Germany.

Woda was happy to be approached by Dr. Ludwig and not Globocnik. Unlike most of his fellow Nazis, this was a sophisticated man with a continental manner and a sparkling wit. A middle-aged man, scholarly in appearance, wearing horn-rimmed glasses and impeccably dressed in a tailored uniform with no medals or decorations.

"That I can imagine," Woda replied.

"Art – ha!" General Globocnik did not bother to turn around. He blew a smoke ring from his pursed lips. He watched it rise and grow larger, then sneered. "Appreciation is as varied as the object or the man."

"Definitely so," said the professor. "Either has its possibilities."

Globocnik still did not turn. He stood with shoulders high, legs apart, his eyes directed at a horse painting by Jozef Chelmonski. He was as if separated from everything and everyone. The others appraised Woda the way a lion looks at his prey.

None of them frightened Woda. He had seen men like them before – Germans, Russians, Austrians, as well as Poles. Dr. Ludwig appeared the least concerned as he approached the desk and introduced himself in a reserved, dignified fashion. He inquired about the professor's position and offered a few random observations about the museum. He looked distinguished behind the heavy brows and piercing eyes. Out of uniform he would look like any other businessman. He willingly chose to be part of Hitler's march of destiny. He could have been a success in any capacity. He had some qualms at first about the Nazis but soon submitted to the fundamentals in the creating of a Greater Germany.

Professor Woda felt at ease in the presence of this man. While Globocnik, in his driving ambition founded on violence, traveled furthest with the Nazis, Ludwig became a fellow traveler because of his vanity and inability to cope on his own outside the Nazi party.

"They tell me," Ludwig said, "you have been a very efficient man, of considerable intellect. A historian, a writer, a teacher, and I'm sure a very understanding man. I don't think I need to remind you that the war is over. There is no reason that we cannot see eye to eye, like two intelligent men. Don't you agree?" He paused as if waiting for a reply, but immediately started in again. "We are a proud and honorable nation and respect the ideals of the people we deal with. It is now time that we work and build together for a better world. There are matters of great importance to be settled here today."

Professor Woda remained silent. He could only wait to see how much they knew. He was pleased that everything was conducted in this rather informal atmosphere.

Then Dr. Ludwig explained that he was specially delegated by Berlin to take charge of all affairs pertaining to art and requested that the professor hand over the keys of the museum.

Ludwig held up a typed report. "I have here the new orders pertaining to all objects in the art museums and private collections. As of tomorrow, we start crating articles selected for shipment to Germany." He calmly watched how this registered on the professor's face. "You will seek suitable quarters elsewhere. Of course, we are not the monsters we are made out to be and will allow you time to move your family and these refugees. Do you understand?"

"But – but – Doctor Ludwig," Woda cried out. "What about your scruples and the national pride and morality you just spoke of? You said the war is over. We'll build a better world. And now this . . ."

Globocnik turned abruptly on his heels and, hands on hips, stared from black eyes at the professor.

"You fool! Fool! Fool! All fools! Thinking you can survive in your dribble of righteousness, pride and honor." He went on screaming, his bloated face flushed. "Where has it gotten you? Germany has taken more in a year than any country has in ten, so don't talk to me about your damned morality and wisdom. Cleverness, my friend –" he extended the palm of his right hand as if seeking rewards. "Not principles and empty sermons, but brute force has accounted for more than all your assumptions of truth and scruples."

He smiled fraudulently. His black eyes remained cold and distant. There was something about the hard manner in which Globocnik stood that made the Professor wonder why he was filled with so much hatred and what the Poles had done to make him so hateful. A uniform, a club, a gun – all that he needed to be a god.

"One thing is sure," Doctor Ludwig said. "The war is over and our countries are at peace."

"A terrible price to have to pay for any peace," Professor Woda said.

"True, but peace nevertheless. No reason that we cannnot work together. Look what cooperation has gotten the Italians and the Slovaks." Ludwig began to pace. He halted suddenly and stared at the Professor. "We need some information, and remember, any assistance you offer shall certainly be amply rewarded.

"Where is the Grünwald painting?" he inquired in a matter-of-fact tone.

"I heard reports that it was taken along by the fleeing government officials." Woda replied with equal calm.

"You lie!" General Globocnik injected. Woda scrutinized the fat face with its rugged jowls and hair as light as wheat plastered flat to the skull. He noticed the clenched fists, huge as boulders, and wondered how many teeth they had knocked out. Woda knew human nature as a hunter knows his forests.

The general said, "We live in a most suspicious age." He croaked hoarsely, "I'm a generous man, professor. Those who belong to our ranks enjoy well-merited privileges, but those who abuse my kindness are gone forever.

"You are in big trouble, and so is your beautiful female accomplice, whom we presently hold in the old castle. Not always a very pleasant place to stay, you know."

The general waited for Woda to unravel after learning about Ceila's arrest. He played it like a puppet master, confident that the professor was sinking closer to that point where he would plead for the life of the woman and pay the price. He stared at the Pole as if his glaring eyes could pry the information from him.

When Woda didn't utter a word, Globocnik picked up a report from the desk and proceeded to reel off a confession Ceila was supposed to have made. Among the names mentioned was the Professor's.

Woda sighed deeply and looked calmly about the room. "I would think," he said, "that they had made contact with the fleeing government and deposited the canvas with them."

"Don't lie to me!" Globocnik shouted, taking a step forward. "Are you trying to be difficult?" His eyebrows rose threateningly.

"I have too much at stake here to try to be difficult,"Woda assured him. He studied the general,who stood with his hands deep in his pockets and his chin stuck out, a tiger that began to show his claws.

"My dear professor." He began to unholster his pistol. "Just how much do you have at stake here?" He drew a deep breath, expelled it slowly, and aimed at Woda's head. With an unwavering hand he deliberately squeezed the trigger. The shot shattered the silence – then the tinkling of splintering glass.

"That, professor," Globocnik said, "is how your life will be spilled if you pursue this foolishness with me." Without so much as glancing at Woda, the German walked to the table where only seconds before had stood a crystal vase of red roses. It was a mess of dripping water, broken glass and dying roses. He put the pistol back into the holster,then ambled back to the desk, swaying from side to side like a bulldog. He sat down on the corner and waited, pouting.

Professor Woda remained silent. The room was very quiet, and after a while, the German started bobbing his head up and down with elaborate sarcasm. "As long as we're all in the same frame of mind, tell me, professor, where is the painting?"

Woda answered promptly, "I can only guess."

Globocnik carefully lit a cigarette. He blew a large but imperfect circle in the professor's direction and watched it lazily disintegrate. "Have you ever been to America, Professor Woda?"

Woda did not answer, afraid that the Nazi was trying to trick him into saying something foolish.

Globocnik guessed his thoughts and smiled. "You needn't be afraid. You can answer truthfully."

"I've never given the matter any consideration."

The German took another draw at the cigarette and this time blew a perfect circle and watched it rise slowly toward the ceiling. "I've been there. New York, Madison Square Garden, Cleveland, Milwaukee – but Milwaukee I didn't like, too windy. It was just the beginning of great things, the great crowds, everything – the beginning of a dream come true."

Woda said nothing.

Globocnik got up, slowly walked around the desk, a faint smile on his fat face. "Who would believe, who would believe that we would go so far so fast? Who knows, it might not be too long before the Fuhrer will be speaking to the American people from the steps of the White House. Wouldn't it be wonderful to know that you could be there and not have to worry anymore? A passport, all the money you will ever need, security and first-class passage for you and your family to America. Good, ha?"

"Yes." The professor's voice rose softly. "Well now, for someone young in years, a most wonderful opportunity. But for one my age, I'm not so sure such a big change would be advisable."

Globocnik paled. He wasn't a police investigator all his life for nothing. He sensed that he had gone too far too fast, but he did not know how to back up. Yes, he had done a stupid thing. Woda was shrewd. He turned and looked at Dr. Ludwig. Those intellectuals could always see those things.

The learned German looked from one to the other slowly, examining each player in the game. "We will discuss this matter more completely in due time. You may leave now, professor."

No sooner did the professor leave than Globocnik started to pace the room, cursing every oath he ever knew before slumping behind the desk, swearing that he would show who was in authority here. "Nothing will be gained," he scowled, "if we fall into softness of feelings. When God introduced justice into this world, he also created hatred, and that is how we have learned to hate the Poles." He spoke more calmly. "Herr Doctor, we have touched upon a very sensitive matter, this Grünwald painting. This Professor Woda openly defied me. These people are far too romantic and not very practical."

"Never mind, Herr Globocnik," Dr. Ludwig smiled. "Let us not give them issue to unify them. After all, we too have a task to perform here, and the elements and time are on our side, right?"

Before they left the museum, Dr. Ludwig sought out the professor personally and counseled him to weigh in his mind the alternatives of treason and resistance. In a matter of days, inspections, investigations and the crating of certain pieces of art work began.

30

The old royal castle was filled with prisoners. There were Gypsies, mental cases, Jehovah Witnesses, drunks and thieves. Many Jews, Ukranians and Poles were arrested on varied charges. The wealthy were arrested to account for the money they had withdrawn from their banks. Following the rich in order of arrest were lawyers, doctors, clergymen, engineers, scientists, teachers, university professors and public officials. Leading citizens began to disappear.

Many were arrested for minor civil and military infractions. Their terms were short and they enjoyed liberties such as sharing a cell, where they played cards, took exercises and walked around the central courtyard. They were always good for smuggling news and letters in and out of prison for a fee. But most of the prisoners lived in perpetual fear.

Ceila was left alone the next two days. The morning of the third day the guard appeared at her cell. Scowling, he jerked his thumb for her to follow him.

They went to the office where Gossberg had made the initial interrogation. Gossberg was standing beside the desk talking to a colonel who now occupied the leather chair behind the desk. A huge German shepherd dog sprawled at his side. The animal sat up as she entered and eyed her steadily. The guard took a position in the corner of the room, where a black-uniformed SS man sat with a notepad on his lap. A truncheon and a long black whip lay on the floor beside him.

"Good morning, Fraulein Rozek." Gestapo Gossberg greeted her politely as she approached the desk. "Sit down."

SS Obersturmfuhrer Anton Dyga pointed at the chair nearest the desk. "No one is going to harm you." He was smiling – more of a sneer. He was a solid, stockily built man with a broad face and small brown eyes set in deep sockets under heavy brows. The dark, glossy hair was greased to his head in the manner of Hitler. His flat face was distinctly Slavic.

Like most Volksdeutsche from Poland's Silesia, who spoke Polish, he had all the complexes of "inferior" Germans. As with most Volksdeutsche he had an un-German, Slavic name and a strong inferiority complex that compelled him to prove himself two-hundred-percent German. This he had done well, with a heavy hand that he handled like a club.

Constantly at his side was the German shepherd, Borys, referred to by the Poles as "Head Doctor" because it was the dog who often decided the fate of a prisoner. The animal was specially trained for prison duty.

Obersturmfuhrer Dyga began. "Your name is Cecilia Rozek?" He addressed her in German, since the report on her revealed that she spoke the language.

"Yes, sir."

"Secretary . . ." At this point Dyga's face flushed red and he pressed his fat lips together venomously. "Secretary?" he repeated, looking up suddenly and staring coldly at her. She felt defiant. She returned his stare.

"You don't look like a secretary." His eyes skimmed over her body. There was contempt in his tone. He rose from behind the desk and walked slowly until he stood over her. He walked around her twice, scrutinizing her, then said, "I am first rate at deciphering any stupid double talk, drivel or lies. I have no patience with individuals who play games. Maybe you haven't had the chance to show us how tough you can be. Well today, maybe you'll have that chance. That should make you feel very important." As he leaned over her, she had the urge to spit in his face.

He turned and walked back to the desk. "You are an American by birth, correct?"

"Yes."

"But at the same time you are a Polish citizen, am I correct?" His tone was quizzical, sarcastic. He pursed his lips. He was leaning over the desk, his eyes closed, waiting. As with most Germans, he had been told at an early age that Poles, through some decree, were his inferiors. Long ago he was told that by nature the Poles were all liars and, by God, he would get the truth because of his own qualifications. A minute passed and she did not answer.

Ceila tried desperately not to show her fears. His eyes passed over her again. His eyes moved about the room and, like trained dogs, the other Nazis smirked and nodded. Much to her surprise, he didn't shout. He sat down on the corner of the desk. He spoke slowly in a resonant voice.

"We only want to be fair with you," he began. "We know

you are an American by birth, even though you prefer to call yourself a Pole. We also know your mother was killed in a bombing over Warsaw. We know that for the past number of years you've been employed at the Warsaw Art Musuem and that, coincidentally, the disappearance of the Grünwald painting took place about the time of the departure of the museum staff. We are not asking you to betray your friends or to turn your back on your country, honor and duty. The war is over. Our countries are at peace. Our only desire is for complete Polish-German collaboration for a greater Europe. You alone can serve for the good of all concerned – you and only you." He flashed a forced smile.

"You Poles are a weird lot . . . just think what the other countries have gained by collaborating. You have everything, everything to your advantage by cooperating. What I ask is neither dishonorable nor a betrayal, and yet to refuse could be treason. You will not only be amply rewarded but we will guarantee your safety."

The voice went on, authoritative and reasonable, with the rhythm of a metronome. He got to his feet and, leading the dog by the leash, turned it over to the SS functionary with the notepad.

Ceila heard the words without listening to them. The emotional plea of Dyga, these last few days in the prison, the oppressive tension and intense heat in the room, all had drawn her mind and body tight. All were startled when she burst out, "You just told me all about myself, what more do you want of me?"

He drew himself straight as he approached her – the haughty confidence of a victor. He glanced at Gossberg, nodded gently for him to watch how a real professional goes about his business.

"We just want the truth. Where is the Grünwald painting, my dear?" he said softly.

"I do not know," she answered in a choked voice. "We all separated when we arrived in Lublin."

Dyga's face flared red. He gestured to the functionary with the pad on his lap. His voice was cold and impersonal. "Did you get the touching story all down, Katzmann? So touching, I'd hate to have missed a word of it."

He turned and slapped both hands hard on the top of the desk. "You persist in this stupid cat-and-mouse game?" He slapped her across the face with the back of his hand, knocking her to the floor. "You fool! You bitch! I'll teach you to play games with me!" He stood over her, as though to kick in her face.

Borys leaped toward her, snarling, fighting at the restraining leash held by the SS functionary. It took all the man had to hold the beast back until Dyga gave the order to "stay."

She lay on the damp stone floor, afraid to move, afraid to open her eyes for fear she might see the oncoming heel of his boot. She felt the throbbing, the salty taste of blood in her mouth.

"Get her to her seat!" Dyga shouted. He waited until she was seated then bent over her. "Come, come now. For goodness' sake now, woman, you have nothing to fear if you tell us the truth." He seized her hair and jerked her head back: "Well then, I hope we've reached an understanding. There is a limit to my patience, you know." He asked calmly, "How would you like to go home to America?"

He continued to hold her head up by the hair. He studied her eyes. "You would like to go home – now wouldn't you?"

"Yes." She fought back the tears.

He let go. "Well, then, my fine friend, tell me where the

223

Grünwald canvas is now."

She stuck to her story. Only this time she admitted that two of her friends had been killed the day they arrived in Lublin.

"You lie!" He tightened up. "I told you it will go hard on you if you insist on lies." He reached for his pistol, removed the shell clip and held it by the barrel. "Put your hands on the desk."

When she did not move he nodded to the guard who shoved her up to the desk and placed her hands, palms down, on the desk. A drumming thud, as the butt of the pistol hammered with a swift stroke against the flesh and bone of her left hand, breaking two of her fingers. She uttered a muted cry.

"You'll talk! You'll talk," Dyga bawled loudly. "Or I'll break your fingers one by one. And when there are no more fingers, I'll break your jaw and your nose and your teeth one by one. You'll talk before I'm done with you!" Slowly, deliberately, he moved toward her and, with a back swing, smashed the butt of the pistol against her cheek. Blood spurted out of the side of her eye.

Dazed, she remained standing, leaning against the desk, holding on while blood started to drip from her lips.

Gestapo Dyga slipped the shell clip back into the pistol, his face a raging red, the purple veins about to burst. He pointed the muzzle of the gun at her heart.

"I'll give you another chance," he said. "Where is the Grünwald painting?"

"I told you I don't know, but you won't believe me," she said through swelling lips.

He smashed his fist into her face. She gave a small cry. The guard lifted her to her seat.

"You're a goddamned liar!" Dyga shouted.

A sharp pain rocketed through her as a rubber truncheon

landed on the back of her neck. Another fist smashed against her mouth. She felt a tooth crack. Blood flowed freely from her chair onto the floor. Dyga's voice continued to drone far above her, excited and growling. "Get her out of here! I'll see her tomorrow after a sun treatment." He raised his voice in delight.

The blows, the fatigue, lack of food, all made her weak and nauseated. She could faintly hear the growling voice, "Get her out of here before she throws up all over the place!"

They dragged her from the room to a dingy washroom. She vomited into a smelly urinal. Her muscles contracted in pain. When she was done they dragged her to a security cell where she collapsed onto the floor.

Dyga, after she had been dragged away, turned to his comrades. "She's a filthy liar like the rest of them. What else can you expect?"

"She's a strong-willed woman. Commendable, in a strange sort of way," Gossberg said.

"Stupid is more the word for it!" Dyga shouted back. "What has she to gain by all this? You could never trust a Pole. You grow so suspicious that in the end you can't do anything with them."

"Disgusting they are, of course," Gossberg said, "but you can't deny that there is a cunning realism about them that is uncanny and somewhat enviable – and certainly enduring."

"I cannot understand why those who are crushed insist on dying gestures of defiance. Martyrs are most difficult." Dyga shook his head and walked toward the door. He turned and made a fist. "Use it! How do you think we got where we are?" Again he lifted his fist. "Use it! It's the only language these people understand. I want that information and I want it now!"

He retraced his steps until he confronted Gossberg. With gloved hand, forefinger waving, he said, "That painting is here in Lublin. We must find it." Then in a voice that was quiet, almost soft, as if he were talking to a child . . . "This could mean a handsome promotion, even a visit home with the family." He laughed and nudged Gossberg on the chest. Still laughing, he walked out of the room.

31

On the third day since Ceila's disappearance, Professor Woda called on Victor, as he had every day.

"You are much thinner than when you first arrived, my American friend," Woda said, walking in with a small sack of provisions. It was already late afternoon. Victor had spent hours near the door, listening to every footstep that passed. His worry about Ceila mounted every hour.

He poured the professor a glass of vodka then waited.

Woda leaned forward in his chair: "It's still early yet; I don't think you should be unduly concerned."

"Concerned! My god, man, how can you sit there and tell me not to be concerned!"

The professor got up and was about to put a consoling hand on Victor's shoulder but held back. "I understand," he said, and sat down again. "The town's a hornet's nest. You never heard such angry buzzing."

"I was hoping you had some word about Ceila. Is there nothing, absolutely nothing we can do?"

"What can anyone do when there has been no word? Until then we can only sit back and wait. We don't know what they know, and I'm sure no one has talked or they would be like wolves at our door. We'll learn eventually. Ceila is not known in this part, so it'll be difficult. They arrest people every day."

They talked of Ceila. "She has always been like one of the family," Woda said. "My impressions have long been that she practically ran the museum herself these last few years. The curator depended on her for everything and her comprehension was nothing short of brilliant."

"A most remarkable woman . . ." Victor paused. "A most remarkable . . ." He choked with rage.

Again Woda warned Victor that he shouldn't leave the apartment under any circumstances – that Woda would continue bringing him food and keep him informed.

Woda sipped his vodka and regarded Victor. "Do you understand? We can't take any chances on your being picked up. It's more than just your own safety that we are concerned with. There is no telling how much they already know."

He got up and was about to pour himself another drink when he noticed the bottle was empty. "Your gloom is quite comprehensible," he said, staring at the empty bottle. "I'll see about some spirits the next time I'm about."

He put his glass down and started toward the door. "There always seems so much to do and so little time to do it in . . . I'll see you about the same time tomorrow."

Victor saw Woda to the door. He watched him disappear down the stairway.

The days that followed were filled with torment. Reminders of Ceila were everywhere. Her face appeared, then blurred. By week's end he professed full blame. How could he ever face life again without the woman he could have saved and in a sense had helped destroy?

Each night was worse than the night before. Victor could not sleep. He rolled off the sofa and lit a cigarette. He wanted above anything else to shave and step out into the fresh air and stretch his legs. He resisted the temptation. The heat of the room made him uncomfortable. All his energy was concentrated on keeping his senses.

He tried to read, but that didn't help. It was almost as if reading contributed to his misery, and he would fling the printed matter across the room.

He should never have let her go out alone. Time and again he awoke with a start in the middle of the night. Each time he looked around hoping to find her there. Hours passed before he fell asleep from fatigue.

32

Six days passed. Professor Woda shook his head. He watched the Nazis plunder the museum. He kept his eyes open, now puffed and red rimmed. Still he kept a vigil over the wanton destruction.

He developed an almost superhuman sensitivity to sound. He could tell they were coming long before they walked up the stairway. He counted the footsteps until they pushed their way through the doors. He was forced to yield in desperation. At times he walked closely behind the pilfering Nazis, hoping to talk them out of items they laid their hands on, saying a particular object wasn't worth the effort. The answer was always, "Orders are orders."

When soldiers pulled down historic banners from their staffs and tore them to pieces, he would place his body protectively between them and the collection, only to be shoved aside and advised at the point of a gun, "Old man, we are not here to play games."

By the end of October the last of the refugees was forced out of the building until only the employees and a few hangers-on remained. Day after day he watched the Nazis fill bags, boxes and suitcases with historic collections, antiques and priceless silver pieces, and haul them off. Each day more and more items disappeared from the walls, shelves and showcases. Slowly the museum was emptied. It was doomed.

Soon after the Germans left, the professor and the employees would search the building for loose stone-work, boards and holes where they might hide paintings and other art objects.

Many objects not removed by the Germans were destroyed. Everything of value was taken – tapestries, sculptures, bronzes and marble, rich collections of porcelains and historic furniture. The library, engravings, drawings and manuscripts were hauled away. Much of this went into furnishing functionary apartments, but most of it was shipped to antique shops in Berlin and to German homes.

Most shameful was that this wanton plundering of a nation's cultural heritage was directed by German specialists and professors. They had come on short visits before the war and had become familiar with the museum collections. From notes they were able to seize the rarest and most valuable items.

After a week of pillaging, the great treasures had dwindled to a few objects – the splinters and tatters that littered the floors. The professor moved about picking them up, hoping something might be saved from this rubble. Much of his calm and deliberate shrewdness vanished. Deeper grew the furrow upon his brow, from worry.

He had lost many friends. He imagined the terrible ordeal

Ceila was suffering. He racked his brain as to what course to follow. He felt so helpless, he didn't even dare to mention her to anyone, or, for that matter, admit that he knew her. That was just what the Germans were waiting for, and even now they might have spies about to test him. How long could she hold out? How long before they beat it out of her, that poor woman.

There were other considerations – the employees, the few remaining refugees and his family – and there was still the museum.

Seated there at the window, he saw a long, black limousine round the corner and start to slow. The chauffeur in a corporal's uniform picked his way carefully around the rubble in the street. The automobile stopped in front of the museum. He saw the woman's smiling face amidst the circle of Gestapo officers helping her out of the car. This was no ordinary woman. Besides General Globocnik, there was the Black uniform of an SS Brigadefuhrer and a thin-faced SS Unterstrumfuhrer whom the professor had not seen before.

The woman lifted her head. Her face was hidden under the wide brim of a black hat. The professor knew it would have to be a pretty face. She wore long black gloves and carried a small black purse. She looked up sharply and walked quickly up the stairs. Globocnik walked beside her.

"I don't know why you insist on calling on this place," he said to her. "After what my men have crated away, it is hardly worth the effort. And we don't want to be late for my garden party." He laughed, exhibiting an exceptionally good mood, bursting with self-importance and pomposity.

Globocnik marched into the conference room as though to a drumming cadence. Unsmiling, he addressed the professor. "My lady companion has some strange desire to visit this pigsty."

"What still remains of it," Woda replied calmly.

The general turned to the others, nodding for them to follow. All were in the best of spirits, as if in anticipation of an orgy. Globocnik dispensed with any form of introduction, but from the conversation that followed the professor learned that one of the men was SS Commander Franz Stangl and the thin-faced, long-nosed SS Untersturmfuhrer was Herr Eickmann.

The woman took a long, deep breath when Globocnik took her by the arm. As they walked, she glanced with a quick eye from side to side, taking it all in. She did not appear to have taken much notice of the professor. She chattered constantly as they moved along. Professor Woda finally excused himself and returned to what still remained of the library.

Woda could see that the woman had the ability to do everything extremely well. In her constant chatter Woda sensed that there was something elusive about her.

She was about thirty, he guessed, her face tanned, the dark eyes enormous. Her red hair under the wide-brimmed hat, long and rich in color, was pulled back and tied at the back of her neck by a short, white ribbon. She carried herself with the charm of a continental enchantress. She spoke only in German. She wore a black party dress with shimmering sequins that highlighted the soft rounded back and bare arms. She hardly appeared helpless, though definitely feminine. Strangely, she was constantly in the professor's view, as though she wanted him to notice her.

He had picked up a book from the floor when he saw her leave the others and walk directly toward him. Her smile friendly, her voice warm, she was trying to be impersonal.

"I understand you speak German."

"As you wish," he replied in German, as if her question was of no importance.

He looked at her with urgent suspicion.

She nodded, then said in a polite voice, "I have news for you, my friend." Her voice was firm and distinct enough to be heard by the officers. "I have friends in Paris who are interested in your problems."

The professor dismissed her with a cautious glance and turned to the bookshelf. He turned and said, "I'm not particularly interested unless it has something to do with the Germans changing their minds."

"Well," she said, walking within reach of him. "Now I understand where your sympathies lie. Don't be afraid," she whispered in excellent Polish. "I'm here to help you."

The professor remained cautiously silent. He watched her with a decisive, if nervous, cordiality that made it obvious that by his silence he risked nothing.

The smile was gone from her face. "You're still not interested and you have your reasons to doubt me. I understand. I have a message for you. Your government in exile is very much interested in the Grünwald painting."

Woda bowed and said, "Of that I'm sure. So is everyone else. Tell me more, please." By asking questions he could listen and not take chances. "And who are your friends in Paris?"

"Excellent, Professor. But don't be a cynic when I tell you that I'm here to help you."

He remained convincingly unconcerned, as if he were only a custodian.

She asked, "You are Professor Woda, am I correct?"

"That I am. What is it that you really want?"

"I'll be truthful with you, professor. It concerns the Grünwald painting. I see that I fail to convince you of the authenticity of my visit. Your secret, as far as I am concerned, is closed, and I will report it as so."

Her voice seemed to come from far away.

"When I leave, I want you to consider deeply what I've been trying to tell you. It is difficult to talk to you, and that I can understand. A BBC radio commentary will let you know when to make your move. When, I can't say, but soon, please believe me."

"I still do not understand what it is you want of me," he said.

"Not much more than what my German friends want of you." Again she began to speak in a voice loud enough for the Germans to hear. "I understand your predicament and only want to cooperate." She moved to the far side of the library and pointed to a large gray square on the wall where a canvas had hung. She did not turn but asked in Polish, "What happened to the Tade Styka painting of the old professor that used to hang here?"

Woda was aghast. How did she know about this particular painting? He asked her, "Are you sure you aren't mistaken?"

She walked up to him and put her hand on his arm. "I am your friend. The world has heard about you and sympathizes with you. I will help you."

He blurted out, "I don't know you. Why do you insist, whoever you are? I don't know what you want of me, but if it will ease your mind any, the Grünwald painting left with the exiled Polish government. Now, I hope you are satisfied."

"Do you know Warsaw? Tell me, have you ever heard of a Count Skarbeck?" she asked.

"The newspaper publisher, naturally. Who hasn't? Next you'll be telling me you are his mother, wife, sister or something like that."

"I could be, you know." She smiled.

Woda's face grew serious. "You don't make jests of a man as great as the count."

She glanced over her shoulder. "You do think of him as a great man, don't you?"

"I'd stake my life on that, and–" he stopped. Could she be setting him up?

But she would not let him stop there. "You must have known him well. I'm positive of that. A personal friend, maybe?"

Her voice was polite; he could not resist answering. "Not exactly. I met him a number of times. I remember him first from his reports on how the rape of Spain was the testing ground for the Germans. And how he tried to alert the world to worthless pacts which sold out one country after another. He alerted Poland to the fact that she couldn't trust anyone any more than she could trust Hitler."

Her body stiffened. Her eyes looked hard when she spoke. "Please don't be bitter. I will help you." Again she seemed to reach out for some formula to convince him. "The code for you to make your move will be 'London BBC – Grünwald – ready.' "

The professor shook his head and was about to say something when a heavy step and a large shadow approached them. It was General Globocnik with the piece from a marble sculpture in his hand. Woda's face flushed as he watched the German smile triumphantly as his glance swept across the empty shelves and bare walls. "We've shipped the best art work to Germany, where it can be more fully appreciated. We will soon make Berlin another Rome, with the treasures of the world."

He walked up to the woman and held out the marble piece. "Here, my dear, a little token of my deepest admiration." As she reached for the gift he continued, "My dear Christine, I didn't know that Professor Woda was an acquaintance of yours. Are you thinking of the possibilities of gaining still another agent?"

She placed the gift on the desk as if it might be hot. "Thank you."

Globocnik took her hand, pressed the fingers to his lips, then said, "The professor has some superb qualities, but I'm positive he would hardly make a good agent. He's too set in his ways and life has been rather kind to him, I would say."

"Why, Herr Globocnik, how suspicious you are indeed." She smiled.

"My darling, I never overrate your abilities. But really, don't you think the professor here could help us? It's imperative that we find the Grünwald canvas."

"Have you asked him?"

"That we have, but our efforts have proven quite futile. But it won't be long now." He reiterated, "It won't be long now." Globocnik walked around the room, glancing at the titles of books remaining on the half-empty shelves.

"Anything soon?"

"Christine, my dear, sometimes I wonder whose side you're on."

"Nothing to lose any sleep over." She laughed, locked arms with the German and directed him toward the door. She held out her other hand to the professor. "Goodbye, and keep listening." She turned back to Globocnik. "Do tell me, do you know where the Grünwald painting is?"

"Only that it is here in Lublin. We're no fools, you know. We feel they hadn't the time to get the painting out of the country. It's here all right, somewhere, right under our noses. We're no fools, you know." He stamped along the great conference hall amidst the debris scattered about the floor.

"And who knows, it might be in Paris." She looked at him. "Or even this very instant on its way to London. One never knows."

"Christine, you never cease to astound me. We are no fools.

238

We aren't blind." He bent over and whispered, "The Gestapo has moved in and tomorrow or the next day, watch the feathers fly."

She took the remark calmly. "Let me know what you've learned, then I will tell you what I know." She was still smiling when they walked out of the building.

Professor Woda was perplexed. She said something about helping and to listen, but what was he to listen for? She never did quite explain. Something about London, BBC, and the Grünwald. Spy? Agent? What next would they try?

33

It was a dull, gray day. Professor Woda hunched over his desk. His thin, long fingers massaged the gray hairline of his temples. His thoughts were dark. With the Polish government in exile, the Germans were looking for a political stooge among the Polish leaders, but no one would accept.

With the French and English in the war, the professor hoped the Nazis would ease some of the pressure. But now, with the Russians on the move, could this be the end? Would history repeat itself and again remove Poland from the map of the world?

His thoughts returned to the Grünwald painting. Secreting the canvas in the basement seemed to be the only choice, but once the museum was completely in the hands of the Germans they would conduct a thorough examination of the building. He had watched them tap the stone and tile floors and walls with metal rods and hammers. If anything was hidden, the Germans wouldn't rest until they found it.

Someone was approaching. There was a short knock.

"Who is it?"

The door opened and young Edmund Koscik stepped inside.

"Oh, it's you."

Edmund closed the door behind him. "I have a report for you." He took a comb out of his back pocket and walking toward the desk combed back his light-brown hair.

Professor Woda waited. "Well?"

The student was wearing a dark blue sweater over the baggy tan corduroy trousers. Still too young for the army but old enough to go chasing skirts. "There was a report on BBC radio. Something about the Grünwald painting having arrived safely in London. Now, that's what I call a real dandy trick when all along the Nazis have been trying to get their paws on it." He sat down on the corner of the desk. "There was something about it being moved to a secret place outside of town for the duration. Now what in the devil could all that jabbering mean?"

Professor Woda listened. "Tell me, tell me all that you heard."

"The report went on to advise the Ukranians to beware of German promises of establishing a country of their own – that the Nazis were prepared to promise the moon to anyone who would side with them."

"No – no – no! About the Grünwald painting!" He leaped to his feet and grasped the young man by his shoulders. "About the painting! What did they have to say about the Grünwald painting? Tell me boy, tell me !"

"There was something–" the youth hesitated – "something of interest to all the friends of the Grünwald painting, whoever they might be. That for their information the famous canvas had been flown from Paris to London and that it will soon be ready to be secreted for the duration, whatever that means."

Woda began to pace the room. He thought about the visit of the strange woman the previous week. Could this be the help she spoke of? If the report was from London, this could not possibly be just another Nazi trick. She did say something about helping – but how could this possibly be of any help? Unless it would relieve the pressure. Such a report, which surely was monitored by the Germans, could alleviate some of the pressures. What about the comment on moving the canvas to a secret hiding place? How did London know, when there it was, under his feet? He was convinced the BBC report was for his benefit, but how?

Professor Woda stopped and looked at Edmund. "How in the name of God was she able to get word back there so fast?"

"Who got where, what?"

Woda grunted and resumed pacing the floor, rubbing the palms of his hands together in the gesture of a man about to start on a job.

"Could this be the break we've been waiting for?" He reached for Edmund's arm. "You are sure, boy, you are positive of what you heard?"

"I speak only what I heard. My friends heard the same report, and we decided you should know about it."

"Fine fine, my boy. You've done a man's job. Thank you, thank you." Woda hurried to the door and shouted. "Walter! Bolek!" He turned to Edmund. "Run down to the carpenter shop and have the Armenian come up. Hurry, hurry!"

When they'd all grouped around him, Professor Woda closed the door. He cleared his throat then started to speak as he might to a class. There was to be no misunderstanding.

GRÜNWALD

"My good friends, young Edmund here has just related to me a most fascinating radio report from BBC London. I have every reason to believe that the message was intended for us. It might startle you to know that the Grünwald painting is here in this very building. We must start preparations immediately."

They stared at him.

The Armenian carpenter was the first on his feet. "What are you trying to tell us?"

"My fine friends, you look at me as if I've gone mad. Far, far from it." Woda smiled and continued. "Matejko's Grünwald painting is here, in this very building. You've been walking on it for weeks."

The man called Walter hunched over the desk. "How could this be possible?"

"Amazing but true. It's time we make ready. The Germans will soon take over this building and unless we start our move it could be too late, and possibly the end of us, too. It is now our total battle for survival."

They all started talking at once. Woda slipped into one of the chairs. The Armenian walked up and hovered over him. "What do you propose we do? How do we move such a large canvas from under the noses of those bastards? There's always at least five guards on duty all the time."

"That's why I called you all here," Woda said – "to decide what is to be done. Our only course is to get it out of the building and out of the city."

They considered where the painting could be hidden once it had been removed from the museum. There was even the suggestion of cutting the canvas into four parts, each section to be hidden in a different place.

The professor was able to deal with a number of individuals with different ideas. Strange things happened to people under pressure. Most would submit to anything to survive but a few found sources of endless strength. Those were the ones with whom he surrounded himself.

There was tall, thin Edmund, just a schoolboy, hardly eighteen, but the strongest of the group. For the last two years, he'd been a part-time employee, an apprentice. There were Walter and the Armenian, who worked in the carpenter shop and helped renovate old pieces of art work. Since it was finally decided that the canvas be buried in an underground vault outside the city, it would be up to them to design the concrete receptacle and condition it against decay or mildew. Then there was old Bolek, forty-odd years with the museum, a mason who made repairs of the museum building.

While moving Professor Woda's personal belongings, the canvas would be secreted among some old rugs and loaded onto the lorry. A site along one of the least-traveled roads was selected. It was close to the road but well out of sight in heavy brush. Once the lorry was loaded, Bolek and the Armenian would ride with the professor. The other two would proceed on foot by different routes. The lorry would not stop. The canvas would be unloaded on the move, placed into a well-lined and protected box, lowered into the vault and covered with earth. The hour selected was at dusk, when there was still light enough to work by but dark enough to give partial concealment. Each would then proceed in different directions, each sworn to secrecy, with only the professor and old Bolek with the coded cards. Should anything happen to any one of them, there would always be one around to see that the proper authorities would learn the whereabouts of the canvas.

"When do we make our move?" young Edmund asked.

"That, my boy," smiled Woda, "depends on the Germans. My orders to move must first come from them." He stood up and reached for his hat. "We'll make our move then, but we start now. Edmund, you come with me. You three, see what you can assemble as a suitable watertight container, large enough for the painting, that can be assembled on location."

Woda started for the door, waving young Edmund to follow. He took another glance at the others: "We're going in search of suitable ground and won't be back until we find the place." The two disappeared behind the doors. The other three started for the carpentry shop in the basement.

34

Ceila lost all sense of time. Each day was a nightmare. Every time she heard approaching footsteps and the key at the door she went into shock. For hours she'd lie awake in pain, one eye partly open. She could only sleep when exhaustion overcame pain.

The cell contained nothing but a straw pallet and a slop bucket. There was a small barred window on the far wall. The window was too high to enable her to see down into the old castle courtyard, but all hours of the day she could hear the torture sessions. Each morning and sometimes late in the afternoon, firing squads eliminated prisoners.

Most of the cells had no toilets. The place stunk of excrement. Inmates rushed at newcomers begging for water and bread. Everywhere people were sick, with more and more typhus cases reported daily.

Every Gestapo and SS man was law unto himself – judge and executioner. Every guard and minor official knew that he could plunder, torture and kill, no questions asked.

Ceila's courage and defiance of the Nazis in the face of their brutality had its effect on the Ukranian guard. When they first brought her to the security section he looked at her with no emotion and urged her forward with a slight shove. Now he began to show signs of compassion when he learned that she was American born.

Besides his duties as guard and keeper of the keys, he brought the slop they called food and water. He had been converted to the new order by the Nazi promises of establishing an independent Ukraine. About forty, he was a short, heavy-set man of little schooling, with an expressionless flat, broad face. His black hair blended with bushy eyebrows over slit eyes. He had seen much cruelty but managed at times to show a simple heart with a mixture of sympathy.

The vanguard of the invading German armies consisted of units of such pro-German Ukranians. When the Nazis were unable to distinguish Jews from Poles, Ukranians were used to point them out. The native Ukranian population cooperated actively with the Gestapo, and Ukranian auxiliary policemen were even more brutal than SS men.

In Ceila he saw such beauty as he had never seen before. What a pity, what a waste, that she would never again bathe in the waters of the roses, nor dance again like some wild flower swaying in the warm breeze. The Ukranian stood watching Ceila until it was too much. He locked the door and slowly walked away.

Ceila knew the sound of every cell door and the heavy-booted stride of every guard. Each time they came for her she cried out. Their powerful hands would grip her and drag her for still another session with the Gestapo.

This day the iron doors clanged behind her. The two SS guards led her to the chair nearest the desk. When they let her go, she staggered into the chair and almost fell to the floor. Her face was black and blue and distorted. One eye was closed as if nothing were there. Her lips were caked with blood and swollen. They resembled raw meat. Her left hand was mashed to a blackened pulp. From the one fairly good eye, smarting with tears, she still managed to stare disdainfully at the uniform before her.

The questioning went on for at least an hour. To a woman beaten into semi-consciousness it seemed a lifetime. The gray room, the stone slab floor, the uniformed men floated in a constant swirl. In this swirl she could barely distinguish the shouting voices: "Swine!" "Idiot!" "Liar!" Powerful hands gripped her and held her up. The rubber truncheons struck across her neck. She fell face down to the floor. This could only be the end. It passed when they put her in a tub of cold water and finally dragged her to her cell where she collapsed in an insensible heap.

After the Gestapo guard departed the Ukranian guard took charge. As a man would help a hurt dog, he pulled her onto the straw pallet where he left her. Later, when she had difficulty eating the slop, he encouraged her to eat. He brought an extra ration of water. She began to regain strength until she could sit up against the wall. She stammered out, "Thank you."

"Don't thank me," he said. "I hear you are American. I have cousin in America, in Pittsburgh."

All she could do was mumble. He left.

The unexpected friendship of the guard strengthened her morale. She realized if there was any hope left she would have to play up to him. On his next visit she made small talk, inquiring about his family.

"But I am not married," he said.

"What a pity," she mumbled. She overwhelmed his ego with pleasantries, repeating how well suited he was to the responsible and privileged position he held.

Later, she lay in her cell, realizing without any sense of triumph that she had again survived a Nazi beating. Through the one good eye she could barely discern the blue sky and the drifting clouds. She lay listening to her heartbeat. The terrifying thought was that this was not the end. They would be back. If not tomorrow, then the day after.

Suddenly, it wasn't the idea of dying that filled her with fear but the possibility that while semi-conscious she might betray her friends. If she must die, the sooner the better. Only a few days ago she had plans to leave the country. How swiftly all that had changed.

Her mind began to drift. Here at the Lublin castle she would be crushed like an insignificant fly, an anonymous death. No relatives, no friends, no one would ever know what happened nor even where her body lay. There was no struggle, no fight left. Death beckoned as if life had never existed. The important thing was not to succumb at the last moment to some animalistic instinct to cling to life.

She thought about her family, her childhood, her many friends. Especially Victor – Victor. If only he were safe and free to leave. She couldn't do any more for him. She would have to leave him in grief. She would do anything, even die, to protect him. He had remained because of her.

That night she stared into the shadows, recalling scenes and faces she would never see again. At least her mother was dead, and Kordian and Lolek.

Then the faces were all the same – only pain and suffering. She felt no idealistic or patriotic thoughts – only the hate that covered the world. She had no regrets for anything she had done. It was a small part of living

Once she had decided to take her own life the actions came naturally. Her mind was free of fear and despair. A second or two and it's over. She would wait until after the hour when the guard had made his last round for the night.

But there was a letter to write. It would not be difficult to get it smuggled out of the prison.

Next time the Ukranian guard made his rounds, she asked for water. He complied, and as he waited for her to drink, she asked, "Could you bring me some paper and a pencil?"

"This is impossible." He reared back. "It's against the rules."

"I understand." She touched him on the arm. "It is only a harmless letter I wish to write to an old friend. In no way could this hurt you, and you will be amply rewarded. You will be paid."

"But how can you reward me? You will never leave this place . . ." There was a faint smirk. She knew he was interested.

"I, myself, have no way to pay you, but the man to whom you would deliver the letter will reward you well. Please, don't be afraid."

He took the cup from her. "I'll see if I can help you."

"Thank you. Thank you."

"Don't thank me. Only note that your friend rewards me as promised." He walked out of the cell toward his regular station.

Later that night he brought paper and pencil and listened to her instructions.

"You are to deliver this to a Profesor Woda at the art museum. Do you understand? Professor Woda and no one else.

He will pay."

She took the paper and pencil. "I will have this ready for you in the morning when you make your last round. Do you understand?"

"Yes – as you say."

In order not to incriminate anyone should the letter find its way into the wrong hands, she addressed it, "Dear Friends." She knew that they would understand. It hurt her not to be able to address it to "Dearest Victor." To have the letter sent to him could lead to his capture. Should the letter get into German hands, they would learn where he was. Professor Woda, she believed, would know how to handle the situation.

35

Professor Woda had completed another routine check of the museum building. He staggered to the chair behind his desk. It was shortly before noon. The sun had receded behind the clouds and stayed. A chilly early November breeze whipped up the dust in the streets. The dull gray overcast left its imprint upon the professor's face.

Dr. Ludwig stood in the office doorway. Three uniformed aides from the Gestapo were with him.

"I hope you will not mind our intrusion," Ludwig said. He still had the stamp of a cultured European with none of the arrogant hostility of the three at his side.

"Come in, come in."

"I'll come right to the point," Ludwig said. "We're here on a matter of grave importance."

"All our meetings are of some grave importance." A hundred and one thoughts crossed Woda's mind. What did they want this time? What did they really know? Had they forced it out of Ceila?

The aide handed Dr. Ludwig some official looking papers. "Sit down, Professor."

It was the first time Woda had been allowed to be seated in the presence of Germans. "Thank you."

"I have acted in a very realistic manner up to now, but I have here a decree from the Fuhrer himself." Dr. Ludwig presented the papers. "I'm sure you understand that I only follow orders."

The professor said nothing. Another decree wasn't going to make that much diffeence.

"This decree–" Ludwig leaned over the desk – "concerns the confiscation of this building. It requires that all properties and all works of art, movable and immovable, together with all accessories, be sequestered for their protection." He hesitated. "I must advise you that under Section Two, this building is on the list of properties to be regarded as artistic property."

"But – but – this pillage and plunder!" There was a note of irritation in Woda's voice. "It is in violation of The Hague Convention of 1907. The war is over. What is the reason for such a decree?"

Ludwig leaned forward. "We are not common plunderers. Under this decree, the Fuhrer and Chancellor of the German Reich have 'legalized' this order for the proper administration and protection of all such properties. The measures may seem rather harsh to you, but you must remember that there is still a price to be paid for our war losses and the cost of occupying armies."

"But we did not start this war," Professor Woda cried. "We did not want this war!" He knew he was acting badly, but he found renewed confidence when he realized that nothing was mentioned so far about the Grünwald painting.

"That is strictly another matter," Ludwig said, bringing the paper closer to his eyes. "I would like to inform you further that Section Three concerns all who are under obligation to supply, on request, all information and data. Under Section Four, what are and what are not artistic or cultural assets shall be decided by me. And Section Five should be of particular interest to you since it concerns those who are liable to imprisonment. All those who conceal, alienate, remove works of art, as well as those who refuse to impart correctly information obligatory under this decree." Ludwig inhaled deeply before concluding. "I hope I have made myself clear in this matter, Professor Woda."

Woda held his tongue. He knew the Nazis cared nothing about protecting artistic works. They cared only for the prices they could bring on the Berlin market and their own personal use. He had long expected just such a move. The decree had one compensating value: it was his excuse for getting the Grünwald canvas out of the museum.

"Just one more thing before we leave," Dr. Ludwig remarked. "We'll be taking over this building tomorrow morning. I want you out of here by then – out!"

Woda nodded and followed them out of his office.

Ludwig and his aides stopped to view the conference chamber. One of the aides said, "Look at that. A pigsty." There were still refugees around, and these cold nights the place was opened for the many drifters still criss-crossing the country. The mess was still there – the papers, rags and sacks. "These Poles are sure a lazy, shiftless lot, aren't they?"

The professor wanted to reply, "Everything was right and proper until you came."

Dr. Ludwig stopped long enough to inform the guard that the professor would be moving out. He then got into the staff car with the others and drove off.

Woda stood at the window. People in the street hurried along with their faces turned upward. The sky was dark with gray clouds. There was the faint scent of rain in the breeze. The brisk air had a refreshing effect. When he turned and re-entered the building it was with a happy gait.

This was it at last. The Nazis had played their hand. It was his turn to make a move.

One by one Woda summoned those he held in confidence. Only young Edmund was nowhere about. He told them about his meeting with Ludwig. "They intend to move in tomorrow. We must make our move today. They are beginning to squirm and, as you might have noticed, since the BBC report they have eased up security around here by removing two of their regular guards, which leaves us with only one pig to worry about."

"Whatever you say, Professor," Bolek said. "I only hope it doesn't start raining before we get moved."

"As much as we've prayed for rain these last few months, never did I think I'd have to pray that it would hold off. Then he asked, "How is the hole? The cement is dry by now, I hope."

"It should be. We finished yesterday at noon. All's ready."

"You can't imagine how long I've waited for this."

"It's still risky," Walter said.

"I know, but so is living. We'll work according to our plan. It shouldn't take more than half an hour after I bring up the wagon. We'll fold the painting in two then roll it into some old canvas and rugs. After we're through loading, Bolek and Stefan will ride with me. Walter and Edmund will walk by another route to the place. That way, if any of us is stopped, there will be someone there to bury the canvas."

"What if they stop the wagon?" Stefan the Armenian asked.
"We can't think of that now," Woda replied. "I want you all
here at five. Go about your chores as usual. The changing of the
guard is at six. The one still on duty will be tired and careless."

He was about to dismiss them when the Ukranian prison
guard appeared at the door and asked for Professor Woda.

"I am Professor Woda." He walked up to the man. "What do
you want?"

"I must speak with you."

"Speak up, then."

"I must speak to you in private," said the Ukranian,
nervously scanning the faces of the others.

"Just a minute." Woda turned to his men. "You may go
now." He turned to the guard. "You come with me."

They walked across the main hall to the library where Woda
ushered the man in first. "What is so important that you have to
see me in private?"

"A lady friend of yours has sent me."

"What lady friend?"

"Ceila was her name – Ceila."

Woda stepped back quickly, as he would withdraw from a
fire. He stood transfixed. Could this be another German trick?

"Who are you? I do not know any Ceila."

"I'm guard at the old castle where she was imprisoned," the
Ukranian said slowly, not sure of himself because of the
professor's actions. "This lady sent me with a letter for you."

"What letter?" Woda was growing tired of pretending. He
was very much concerned with Ceila's welfare. "How is the
lady?"

"She is dead." The guard began to fumble at the buttons of
his uniform. He pulled out a piece of paper. "She gave me this to
deliver to you before she took her life. She said you would

reward me well. I've had it for four days before deciding to come to you. One can't be too careful these days, you know."

Woda stood waiting. The guard did not hand him the letter. "How did she die? Why did she give you that letter?"

The Ukranian spoke haltingly of Ceila's bravery in withstanding the tortures. "At last," he said, "she had to be dragged back to her cell where I was in charge. Later, when she was feeling a little better, she asked me for paper and pencil to write a letter. When I read it I saw that there was nothing that could hurt anyone. She then told me where to find you and that you would reward me."

Tears burned Woda's eyes. He turned away. Ceila was dead! Her image came to him so alive that he felt he could reach out and touch her. It disappeared. She was lost forever. He felt empty.

"Oh God, why?" he said aloud. He snatched the letter from the guard's hands. They stood staring at each other. "You did well." The professor swallowed as he fought back tears. "I will pay you for your troubles. Thank you from the bottom of my heart. You have earned my gratitude for bringing this letter."

He looked hard at the uniformed figure and saw nothing to fear from this simple man. He fumbled in his pants pockets and pulled out a number of tightly-crunched bills. He started to withdraw a few. He changed his mind and handed the entire roll to the guard. The Poles had bribed hundreds like him before and later were blackmailed by them by holding over their heads the threat of exposure to the Nazis.

"Now tell me what happened? How did she die?"

The Ukranian turned away. "They left her alone for a few days, and one morning they found her hanging from one of the bars over the window of her cell. She had used her skirtwaist for a rope."

Woda took the man by the arm and led him out of the building. He thanked him again before returning to lock himself with the letter in the silence of his office.

The first soft knock on the office door startled the professor. It was Bolek and the Armenian. Walter later appeared and said, "I ran into young Edmund and told him to report at five. He said he would."

They all noticed that the professor was greatly changed. The spirit and energy of two hours before was spent. He sat with glazed, sad eyes.

Stefan asked, "Are you all right, Professor?"

He nodded but continued to sit silent.

Stefan leaned over the desk and stared into Woda's eyes. "Are you sick? Can I get you something . . . or–?"

Woda sat, inhaled deeply and said, "No . . . no . . ." He waved his friend aside. "I'll be all right in a minute. Soon – soon all this will be over for all of us." He heard Edmund's footsteps.

"Well now, young man." Woda stood up: "We were beginning to wonder if we'd be seeing you again."

He walked around the desk, patting the youth on the back as he headed for the door. "Come now, young man, there is work to be done before it gets any darker. Come along, now."

The professor turned to the others. "You men start packing my stuff." Then he turned toward the exit. "But wait to roll up the canvas until I return with the wagon. It will take me but ten minutes."

He walked out of the building, down the stairs and up the street. There was very little activity. A few raindrops had fallen previously but had hardly settled the dust. Was he making a mistake? These Germans were making him do many foolish things. He pulled up the collar of his suitcoat to hold out the chill.

It was almost fifteen minutes before he arrived with the wagon, got out and approached the soldier posted near the door. "We are ready to start moving, but it would be much simpler to go out the back door. Can I have your permission to open it?"

"Hardly," the guard replied. "The door is locked and I have no key."

"Yes, the keys to the rooms have been handed over to Doctor Ludwig, but I might have an extra one to the back door." Woda had more than one duplicate key – one to all the doors.

"In that case you could try. But I will have to check before you leave."

"I'll go and see."

Woda was back in a minute. "Yes, I found one. I'll pull up in the back."

The men were waiting for him. In no time they had the first part of the load on – the huge Grünwald canvas folded in half and rolled amongst some old canvasses and rugs to make it appear to be a large carpet. It took Bolek and Stefan to lift the whole thing onto Walter's and Edmund's shoulders.

They had started out when the German soldier walked up to them and asked, "What have you got there?"

"Just an old rug," the professor answered quickly, pushing Walter from behind so they would not falter.

The soldier blocked the way. "Let me see." He braced himself in front of Edmund. The youth's face turned pale. The soldier eyed the roll, fingered the frayed edge of old carpeting, then stepped aside. "Good," he said. "About time you got some of the lice and bedbugs out of this shit house."

When they were finished loading, Woda sent Edmund after the soldier. He gave them a cursory inspection, then asked for the key from the professor and waved them on.

Walter and Edmund had already started off on foot in one direction. The professor, Stefan at his side, urged the team down another street. Bolek sat in back, seeing to it that nothing fell off.

They started rolling at a slow pace, as if in no particular hurry. Woda knew the town well and sought out all the back streets. He kept looking over his shoulder. But with the exception of a ghostly figure now and then the streets were empty. The Germans were pulling people in by the hundreds for the forced-labor camps. Thousands had been rounded up and shipped to Germany as factory and farmhands.

Woda looked around and felt at ease only when traffic was so sparse that he could drive the team down the centers of the alleys. Near some bombed-out houses they passed an old man, bald and hatless, emaciated as the two dogs at his heels. With blinking eyes he stared after them for some time before he and his animals ambled lifelessly away.

The streets were sticky with dirt. The odors of garbage filled their nostrils.

The wagon rolled on. It would be dark within the hour, just light enough to serve their purpose. Woda urged the team forward. The streets of Lublin faded behind.

They approached a heavy clump of brush, and Woda pulled on the reins. The horses slowed to a walk. Before Bolek could jump from the wagon, Walter and Edmund had already leaped out of hiding and were pulling at the old carpets with the Grünwald canvas. They moved quickly and slipped the thing off while the wagon continued to roll.

They wrapped it all in waterproof material and placed it in a wooden crate of oak, also watertight. In minutes the whole thing was placed in a concrete vault with the lid cemented into place.

GRÜNWALD

It was buried under five feet of earth. The ground was arranged to leave as little evidence of disturbance as possible. When the three were done they departed in separate directions. Everything had gone off as if it had been rehearsed a thousand times.

The professor and Stefan continued on with the wagon without as much as a look over their shoulders. They rolled on to a little house in the country that the professor and his family were to occupy for some time to come.

That night it started to rain. It rained far into the night. Soon the whole countryside looked as if nothing had been touched for the last century. Five feet underground, the Grünwald painting waited out the Second World War.

36

No one could recall when it had last rained so heavily. Not even an animal would venture out into the downpour.

Victor heard the heavy footsteps and knew something terrible had happened. He ran to the door and flung it open. He watched Professor Woda climb up the stairs with the heavy step of the blind, soaked to the skin. Victor reached out for his arm and assisted him to the stove.

"Hurry. Get out of those wet clothes. I'll get you a blanket. You'll die of pneumonia even before those goddamned Nazis get to you."

"I'll be all right. I'll be all right." Woda huddled over the stove. He needed something warm inside. "Do you have a little vodka?"

"Sure, just as soon as you get out of this wet coat." He

wrapped a blanket over Woda's stooped shoulders. He got the bottle and poured. "Here, this should help."

"Ha-a—, that should do a man a lot of good." The professor wiped his lips with the back of his hand. He removed his wide-brimmed hat that kept dripping over the stove with a hissing sound. Woda wasn't as wet as had appeared at first – only the pantlegs and boots. The sheepskin poncho wrap had kept the professor dry. Victor shook the heavy skin and draped it over a chair. "Sit down and take those wet boots off."

The professor took his time. Victor refilled their glasses and sat down on the couch. He could only wait. He felt that Woda's visit had to be important for him to be out on a night such as this.

They sat listening to the rain beating down on the rooftop and splashing against the windows. Victor asked, "Can I make you some tea?"

"Yes, yes, please do." The professor did have something to say. He looked at Victor. "You can't imagine how happy I feel to inform you that the Grünwald canvas is safely put away. Yes, we finally managed to dispose of it, and properly at that." He took another hard swallow. "All this worry, and it went off without a hitch. I'm so glad, so glad that it's all over. We can breathe much easier."

"That is good news. I'm sorry I couldn't have been of any help."

Here was a man, whose courage would never allow him to drift. He'd always be at the helm.

"Didn't need any." Woda waved at Victor, putting his mind at ease. "Good to see the rain again." He watched Victor place the pot on the stove. "God only knows how we prayed for this rain two months ago, and just look at it now – almost as if to drown out all the guilt and hate."

Woda got to his feet and started to pace the room. He looked old, blinking his eyes and sniffling: "I've got news that should cheer you regardless of everything else. You'll be leaving tonight."

"Tonight?" Victor wanted to embrace the professor. "Tonight? Christ, I was beginning to think the time would never come. It's the best news I've heard in weeks. When? How soon do we start?"

"Yes. Some friends will help you out of the country. I expect the man here any moment now. This storm should provide excellent cover from the patrols. If it had only come a few weeks earlier, yes, if only . . ."

Victor asked, "And Ceila. What about Ceila?"

Tears choked Woda's words. "I had a visitor today. One of the guards from the castle. I – I just don't know how to tell you. Ceila – our Ceila is dead."

Victor stood there in shock.

Ceila is dead, dead, dead! Why didn't they leave when he'd first asked her? Why? He swallowed hard.

Finally he was able to ask, "How – how could it happen? We had planned to leave together."

"Yes, we had all wished she'd leave with you." Woda patted Victor on the back then sat down at the table. The only sound was the drum of rain on the windowpane. With trembling hands he lifted the teacup to his lips.

Victor threw himself into the chair beside the professor. "But how, how in God's name could it all happen so quickly? Why? Why didn't anyone do anything? I – I just sat in this goddamned forsaken place and waited and waited, when – when – all this time she . . ." He choked up and cried like he had never cried before in his entire life.

Woda shook his head. "No one knew where she was. We waited and hoped, but no word until it was too late. I can only imagine that she did it to protect us all. They have ways of forcing people to talk, and this she must have sensed." He went on to tell about the visit from the guard and what had happened to Ceila.

All of Ceila's warnings, all of her reasons for implicit caution passed through Victor's mind. He was a fool, a deluded, gutless fool!

Woda braced himself and pulled out her letter.

"Here." Woda held it out. "It's her letter. I'm sure she protected us all to the last. In order not to incriminate anyone, it's simply addressed 'Dear Friends.' I'm sure . . ."

Victor reached out as if to grasp the letter but restrained himself. "Is it for me?"

"I'm sure it is. She belonged more to you than to any of us. I'm sure she had you in mind when she wrote it. She took no chances that it might get into the wrong hands. The Germans would not only know who you are but where if she had asked the guard to bring it directly to you."

With the letter trembling in his hand, Woda said, "This has been the tragic existence for our women, for they, above all other women of the world, have had a more difficult life – sweet but gallant, subservient but bold. Warm of heart, the most gentle of mothers, and yet lionesses prepared to lay down their lives when the family sanctum was endangered. Our Ceila was such a woman. This is all so cruel and unfair."

Victor took the letter. Ceila was everywhere. Such love, such happiness as he had never known – now sorrow and pain. Things began to blur. He wanted much to read the letter, but the tears blinded him. He had to get away, be alone, anywhere. He turned to the professor. "When do I leave this place?"

"Tonight. Tonight. It must be tonight. Tomorrow could be too late." Woda got to his feet and walked to the window, watching the rain splash the glass. A bright flash of lightning and the nearby crash of thunder sent him reeling. He poured himself more tea, sat down when Victor began to talk. He passed judgment unmercifully upon himself.

"Victor." Woda took advantage of a pause. "Please, my dear friend, don't be so hard on yourself. There was nothing anyone could do without endangering the entire scheme."

They were conscious of the moment's accusing silence. Woda, in a consoling voice, said, "She must have loved you very much, even to the very end."

Victor held the letter as if it were sacred. He had known much of death these past two months. Most of the people he knew here were now in the grave. Kordian. Lolek. Now Ceila. Three who deserved to live. These last few days he suffered a torment he had never realized possible. He had drunk heavily. He had paced the room. He had had no desire to eat and couldn't sleep. He had tried to read. Like a caged animal he had lain down only when drugged with exhaustion. But each time he closed his eyes, his mind had clouded with haunting thoughts of Ceila, driving him into renewed anguish. For hours he had sat at the window or stood in the doorway looking out over the ancient blackened rooftops. He had known love here. Now he hated it.

Professor Woda got up, reached for the vodka bottle and poured some into his cup. Holding up the bottle he said, "Have some. It'll do you good."

Woda had to change the topic. "I can't understand the delay. I left specific instructions for the man to come directly here as soon as he showed up. They're planning the big push for the border now that the rain has started. They'll get you out of the country, don't you worry."

"When?" Anything was better than sitting in this apartment. "Stop treating me like a child. I understand there is a risk involved, but I've got to get out of here. I'll start off on my own if I must."

Woda tried to explain. "Perpetual optimistic lunatic that I am, I'm sure that some good will have to come of all this barbarity. Oh, God. If it could only come soon. I only wish that I were your age and could leave with the others. A hundred thousand men are ready to leave the country. From the first days of the war the formation of a Polish army in France was started."

"But how soon? When? When?"

Woda sighed. "I've been in your shoes, I understand how you feel, and all those thousands of anxious young men heading for the border. All wanting to escape, to fight again no matter what the cost."

The rain had eased somewhat. "I think I better go see what delayed our man. He should have been here by now."

Victor helped the professor with the heavy poncho. Just before Woda bowed himself out, he said, "Get some sleep, my friend. You'll be starting soon enough."

Victor drew the bolt on the door and leaned against it. He listened to the professor's footsteps until the sound faded in the beat of falling rain.

Suddenly he felt an overwhelming anger at the loss. Why? Why? It was all so senseless – couldn't the war have passed her by? It was over, all he wanted was for Ceila to live.

Slowly, with leaden feet, he moved toward the table and pulled up a chair. He remembered the letter in his hand. He stared at it. This had no scent of flowered water. This was cheap notepaper with yellowed, frayed edges and tear stained where the professor had read it time and again.

Ceila was everywhere. Her sad eyes laughed up at him, lips parted. He could hear her voice. There was still a ghostly scent of her perfume from the sweater she had left behind.

He suddenly had the strong urge to fling open the door and run, but where? The rain splashed the window. Where?

He started to read the letter.

"How difficult it is for me to write you this letter, but the humble, like the great, must face death too. But I am not happy knowing that I have to die, even though I realize that everybody has to die sometime.

"I die free, yes, free! Life in prison has certainly taught me to get rid of all kinds of pettiness to which people normally succumb. The human soul cannot be held captive any more than one's country kept in chains."

Victor found it difficult to breathe. He cried silently then buried his face in the folds of his arms on the table.

Outside the rain grew more intense. The sky thundered with angry rumblings and the earth trembled.

Victor resumed reading.

"The human soul cannot be held captive, provided a person does not of his own will close himself up in the few walls of narrow concepts and prejudices.

"I do not have it in me to ask them to spare my life in return for the terrible betrayal of my many friends and the country that I love so much. In comparison to all that I hold so dear, my life is of such minor value in this universe. For what reason should I have more right to life than those thousands that have already perished in this war? If only all this suffering and sorrow would end with me.

"What will be afterwards, I am unable and don't even try to imagine. I trust that what was good and noble in us will not be lost, that it will help us to come closer to some great purpose, to some perfection. It would be a pleasure to believe that on the other side one will find again all those one has loved, because how could it be that such powerful feelings, such love and understanding, should just be lost forever? I owe the only happy hours of my life to Victor and my poor, poor friends. Tears dry up quickly. One forgets one's worries. But the memories of beautiful friendships remain forever and brighten one's life in this darkest of hours. Kordian's and Lolek's images never leave me and have kept me company on many difficult nights. It is much easier for me to think about death because they have traveled the road before me. And my poor, wonderful mother – why must it always be the finest who go first?

"I shall remain calm to the very end. My last duty to my country and my many friends is to die bravely. Be brave! Farewell.

Yours, Ceila."

Victor sat staring at the paper in his hand. It was some time before he rose from the table and walked to the couch. The rain was slackening. Misery began to lessen. Exhausted, he fell asleep.

37

A few minutes of sleep. Victor awoke to the sound of footsteps and a knock on the door.

He hurried to open it. Professor Woda and a man entered; the man, shaking the rain from his clothes, removed his black leather coat and cap. He put a small bag down on the floor. Victor helped the professor shed his wet coat.

"I was beginning to worry you would never come," Victor said.

"I was worried about you myself." Professor Woda moved to the stove, rubbing the circulation back into his cold fingers. He watched Victor pour them a drink, hands shaking. "Look at you, you look like a man who's been at war with himself."

Victor attempted to smile.

"I want you to meet my friend." Woda completed the

introductions.

Victor looked at the man he was to know as Zalewski. The man's appearance was not at all as he had pictured, but he felt comfortable immediately with the strapping, extremely handsome man, a pilot in the Polish air force. His pale blue eyes were penetrating.

Zalewski's lean body appeared spindly in the oversized dark-blue sweater. Long-legged, he had the solid conformation of a gymnast. His face was square and soft, more like a poet's than a soldier's. His hair fell in golden ringlets across the back of his neck.

The young Pole looked puzzled at Victor's appearance. "Are you sure you can make it?"

The professor answered for him. "Our friend here has just been through a horrible experience. I'm sure he'll be all right once he gets started."

Zalewski handed Victor an envelope. "These are your papers in case we're stopped. The Germans are looking for soldiers in civilian clothes. This identification card was taken from a dead streetcar conductor."

"We still don't know," the professor said, "how much the Germans know about the Grünwald canvas. You can't be too careful. Many such identification cards have been removed from dead civilians, enabling those like yourself to change identity."

"This is all you will carry on you," Zalewski instructed. He made a few suggestions as to what Victor should wear. "With the exception of this ID card, you carry nothing – only the clothes on your back, you understand?"

He pointed at the small bag. "There's enough sausage and cheese to last us four days. We've secured a sheepskin coat for you. It should keep you dry and warm once we hit the

Carpathian Mountains."

Zalewski glanced at his wristwatch. It was ten-thirty. He looked at the professor with a half-smile before he caught Victor's eye. "Come – we have so little time. We'll have to make the most of it while it's still raining. We'll be traveling only at night, except when we reach the forests."

"Yes, yes," Professor Woda agreed. "Time to go. Good luck." He shook Zalewski's hand then turned to Victor. The two faced each other, their hands clasped tightly, as though neither wanted to be the first to let go.

Victor felt the hand grip tighter as Woda's words sank deep. "I know she would want you to be happy. Go now, and don't be too harsh on yourself. Time is the greatest healer of all. Life is not always gentle, but in the end it all passes, like a bad dream."

Tears glistened in Woda's eyes. He seized Victor in a bear hug. Victor felt foolish.

Victor felt that the professor was pleased to see him go. He had changed considerably these last two months as his gaunt figure and spotted complexion indicated. But the warmth and beauty of age were there.

"What about you, Professor?" Victor asked. "Can't you go along?"

"My place is here," the Pole replied in a soft tone. "With my family, with my people and my country."

"But you no longer have a country."

"You are wrong, young man, to think that Poland is finished." There was a note of indignation in his voice. He ran his fingers through the sparse gray hair and leaned forward. "Victor, my fine American friend, not all Poles have resigned themselves to fate. By the time you leave this country, you will have the opportunity to see thousands like this man, courageous and thinking only of the day when they are free to fight again.

"What do you take us for? We are not sheep waiting to be led to slaughter. We'll not sit back as if we were already dead." There was urgency in his voice. "Just you wait. When this first horror has abated and the people learn that the Nazi is no superman, that he lives, breathes and dies just as any other man, what then? The Poles will never submit to them. Once this is all behind us, we'll rise on all fronts until we drive these bloodsuckers from our land. Yes, it will be painful and much blood will be spilled, but we will do as we must."

Professor Woda inhaled deeply, then smiled: "Keep your feet dry, and the best of luck to you both, and God bless you."

Victor finished putting on the heavy black coat and broadbrimmed hat they had gotten for him. He looked into Woda's friendly eyes.

"Thank you," he said. "Thank you ever so much."

"Don't thank me. Just remember us."

"Always. I'll always remember you."

Zalewski lifted the bag and placed it on the the table. He buttoned his leather coat and slung the sack over his shoulder. He nodded to Victor. They started toward the door. The professor said, "Now don't get lost."

They laughed. Zalewski opened the door. They went down the step and into the dark street. There was no sound but that of the rain. The smell of dampness mingled with the friendly odor of chimney smoke.

Victor lowered his head. Inside was a yearning to be home in America. There was excitement at the thought of getting out of Poland, but some part of him was being left behind. He fought back a sudden impulse to run and pulled his neck deeper into the collar of his coat. He hastened to keep up with his new friend.

Together they moved down the street. Here and there a few yellow lights filtered through drawn shades. The only sound was that of their footsteps splashing as they stamped through puddles.

Twenty minutes later they were in the suburbs. They moved off the cobbled street and swung into a narrow alley that led to a path through an apple orchard. The forests were not very far. Their pace had been rapid. Victor wondered how long it would be before his legs gave out.

They had been in the forest at least an hour before Zalewski decided to stop and rest. Victor slumped to the wet ground and braced himself against the trunk of a large pine. He was soaked through and it was cold. It would be ironic to escape the clutches of the Nazis only to die of pneumonia.

After a short rest they moved on. Zalewski told Victor the woods were full of escapees like themselves. Time and again they drew up and were joined by a growing number of men on foot all moving with that same aching eagerness. The forest thickened with them, almost a man for every tree, an army on the move. Far into the night they walked with uncanny instinct. Their feet found their way around trees and through dense underbrush.

Day after day came the heavy rains which the Poles had prayed for in September. The country roads became muddy tracks, and the Germans preferred not to wander off the main highways. Many guerillas were in the woods and remote villages. Large numbers of German patrols never returned. The Nazi pilots, hampered by poor visibility, could not spot the great exodus across the Carpathian Mountains. The Poles came out on the other side of the frontier, in Rumania and Hungary.

The wind finally blew the rains away. The sky hung low with gray clouds. They walked in tall timber. The whole world was walled in by trees. The journey had not been as dangerous as it was strenuous. The worst of it was trying to keep warm and trying to sleep in rain and icy wind.

When Victor grew despondent, he looked around him at the men of war. Few were dejected. They moved on to fight again. Their last battle had not been fought.

Victor watched them discard their smart uniforms and put on peasant shirts and pants and rags of all sizes. They moved on in twos and threes. They were no longer soldiers; only a mass of men stained with mud.

Their strength drained. They slept during the day and marched at night. They stole fruit and vegetables from the fields. They cursed and they laughed. What they could not buy they stole from the peasants at night – dry, warm clothing and heavy sheepskin coats.

Word reached them that most of the frontier guards were poor shots, intentionally or otherwise. Most of the people of the Danubian nations were in sympathy with the exiles and helped them with food and clothing. They hid them in their homes.

Four days had gone by. Dense forest yielded to open countryside. It was a glorious afternoon, the first day that it hadn't rained. The fields and peaceful hills and valleys were inviting. Soon they would cross the Rumanian border.

Victor wished he could leave the dampness of the forest to dry himself in the sun. He hadn't changed clothes for a week. He felt better when someone pushed a bottle of vodka in front of him.

He sought out a small clearing into which a few shafts of sunlight filtered. It was a matter of hours now to the frontier – to the nearest American embassy. He was sick for America and home.

He sat listening to the shrill sounds of birds and the sighing of the pines. He had a mental picture of Ceila. Slowly he reached into the folds of his clothes and took out the letter.

He read to the part where she recalled him by name. He heard her voice: "I owe the only happy hours of my life to Victor and my poor, poor friends. Tears dry up quickly, one forgets one's worries, but the memories of beautiful friendships remain forever and brighten one's life in this darkest of hours. Kordian's and Lolek's images never leave me and have kept me company on many difficult nights. It is much easier for me to think about death because they have traveled the road before me. And my poor, wonderful mother – why must it always be the finest who go first?

"I shall remain calm to the very end. My last duty to my country and my many dear friends is to die bravely! Be brave! Farewell."

Victor turned once more to the sunny fields. Was this all there is to life? Just another sand pebble to be moved by the tempest of passions and emotions, eventually to be cast aside into oblivion?

Zalewski hovered over Victor. He saw a teardrop stain the letter.

The Pole waited until Victor looked up. He said, "We'll be moving out just as soon as dark sets in. Keep close and keep an eye open, okay?"

Victor nodded – a sand pebble about to move with the tide.